Abby Morton Diaz

William Henry and His Friends

Abby Morton Diaz

William Henry and His Friends

ISBN/EAN: 9783337423872

Printed in Europe, USA, Canada, Australia, Japan

Cover: Foto ©Andreas Hilbeck / pixelio.de

More available books at **www.hansebooks.com**

BY

MRS. A. M. DIAZ,

AUTHOR OF "THE WILLIAM HENRY LETTERS."

WITH ILLUSTRATIONS.

BOSTON:

JAMES R. OSGOOD AND COMPANY,

(LATE TICKNOR & FIELDS, AND FIELDS, OSGOOD, & CO.)

1872.

WILLIAM HENRY AND HIS FRIENDS.

PEOPLE, both small and large, are continually coming
to me with, "Mr. Fry, can't you tell us something more
about William Henry?" or, "Do, Mr. Fry, give us a few
more particulars about the folks at Summer-sweeting
Place!" or, "Mr. Fry, how are they all at the Farm?"

Such requests seem to take the ease out of my mind; for
though just as willing to tell as my friends are to hear,
and more too, yet I know perfectly well that some
others in my place could make a much better thing of it.
Indeed, as has already been intimated, the publishers,
when they spoke to me about editing "The William-
Henry Letters," as good as told me that I was the last
person they should have pitched upon, but for my having had the advantage of an intimate acquaintance with
the two families.

Now, I don't feel the least bit *touched* by such intima-
tions, any more than — any more than a slice of bread
would at being told it wasn't the whole loaf. Every
thing is well in its place; and, for some purposes, a slice
may be better than a whole loaf, — to set before a person
of delicate stomach, for instance, or to give a child between meals. Thus I, Silas Y. Fry, being, as it were,

1

but a slice of bread, compared with your great standard
writer, which is to say, the whole loaf, might think it
worth while to set down many pleasant little trifles entertaining enough to the common run, such as he, in his
greatness, would hardly take the trouble to speak of.

My idea is just to give a plain, simple account of the
goings-on at the Farm during my stay there: no big
talk, no flourishes. "Mr. Fry," the gentlemanly publishers remarked when conversing with me on this subject,
"there are times and seasons for all things. There is a
time for fine writing; but this is not the time. All we
expect, all we wish, of you, is to tell the young people, in
language such as any one with only a common-school
education might use, some of the sayings and doings at
Summer-sweeting Place."

I am willing enough to comply with this request: for
never did business, pleasure, or duty, take me among a
set of people that so just exactly suited me. They believe
in two things which I believe in: namely, laughing and
hard work. Even the older ones don't think it any
shame to "carry on," as Mrs. Paulina terms it. In fact,
it appears, sometimes, as if they were all about of an age.
Now, there are Uncle and Aunt Phebe, — Billy calls them
so sometimes. — I've seen these two when you wouldn't
judge, by their actions, they were over ten years old.
Mrs. Paulina says she thinks 'tis silly for grown-up folks
to act so silly: but they don't seem to care whether they
act silly or not.

For my part, I like to be among people that are easy
to laugh; and I like to have the laugh right underneath, close to the top, so that any little hit breaks
through the crust, and lets it bubble up. It doesn't make

so very much difference then what you do say. No matter if you're not quite so bright, or can't make wise remarks, or don't know every thing that's in the geography. I shouldn't be ashamed to own up, out there, to not knowing what a boomerang was, or to not being sure which one cried,—Xerxes, or Alexander,—or what the matter was with him; though some of them are great readers, and are pretty well informed about those old fellows. Still, if I should say, "Oh! I'm not quite certain sure, but at any rate he had an X somewhere about him," she'd very likely have something to say about X standing for the unknown quantity; and Billy would say he should like to have an X somewhere about him; and Matilda would tell him his X would soon turn to a V if he had one; and Uncle Jacob would advise him, if he xpected to have X's, to xcel in his business. And so they would keep it going till something else came to the front.

I have an invalid sister (little Silas's mother) residing in a lonely village; and it has been my habit for some years past, wherever I might be living or travelling, to write her a long letter every week, crammed full of my little experiences, for the purpose of cheering her up. "How would it do," I asked one of those beseeching friends mentioned at the beginning, "to make use of the letters which were written during my stay at the Farm that summer?"

"By all means do so," he answered. "They are just what we want."

I said, that as they were written off-hand, and just to cheer up Juliana, why, in went every thing,—no matter how trifling or how foolish; and had I not better take out some of the folly, so as to make them appear better in print, and give them a more sensible air?

"By no means do so!" he cried. "Who cares how they look in print? We have books enough with more sensible airs now. Don't trim. They'll seem more natural than well-written letters: besides, you probably do better at nonsense than you could in the sensible line."

I was doubtful whether or no to call these last remarks complimentary: still, as the advice was easy to follow, I decided to take it, and, as you may say, edit my own letters. Rather out of the common course, to be sure; but, then, why should everybody follow in everybody's footsteps? It never quite suited me to do that. I remember of insisting, when a boy, upon spelling Silas with a "y," because in that way the name looked more shipshape in my writing-book, — thus, *Sylas Y. Fry.* Three loops.

I took a long vacation, and spent it at the Farm. There is no reason why the reasons for my doing so should be given; but, for the satisfaction of those who must know every thing (this to the curious only), I will state that my bodily health was some distance below par, and that, in fact, I had been under the doctor's charge and charges ever after serving in the Army of the Potomac.

"Entire rest, wholesome diet, pure air, and cheerful company, are what you need, Mr. Fry, in order that your system may recuperate." I think that was the word: but, whatever it was, my system did it during those few months at Summer-sweeting Place; for there the doctor's four conditions were fulfilled.

A whole summer at the Farm! Never was doctor's advice more joyfully followed. I had seen, for a year or two, very little of my friends there, because a change of base, that is to say, business, had taken me from the town of M., where I formerly lived, and where I first saw Uncle Jacob, to the more distant town of D.; so that my opportunities of meeting them had been much less frequent.

I went out to the Farm to stay on the first day of July. We were having a pretty warm spell of weather about that time; and I remember that it seemed a wonderfully blessed thing to escape from the dusty town, and tread on grass, and breathe woods air. This was the second year after Billy's leaving Crooked-pond School.

————

The following letter, speaking of my arrival out, would seem to come in well here. I skip the beginning, as it only contains directions for altering the neck-bindings of half a dozen shirts: though I'm not sure but they might be entertaining, looked upon in the light of an enigma; for my sister said it would puzzle a sphinx to go by them.

. . . I arrived out a little after six. Stopped at grandmother's. The doors were wide open, windows too, with the curtains flapping. I marched through the house, rattled the chairs, and hallooed up the stairway, "Anybody here?" But nobody appeared. "Ah! gone into Phebe's," said I, then stepped round through the orchard.

How delightful a cool shady orchard is a poor townman can tell, if anybody can, — especially a lazy old orchard like grandmother's, that never had any sort of bringing up. The trees they sprawl their great limbs about, and twist and bend and lean over; and some of them divide at the bottom, — one half going up, and the other half running along the grass, making a long seat to sit on. Saxifaxes, greenings, horseblocks, and lady-fingers, — none of these think of doing a very great summer's work. Peck and bushel measures are no concern of theirs. They calculate to keep grandmother in sauce and pies, and a few strings of dried apples to hang up in the garret; and that's about all.

Gus, the little barnman, was in the orchard, untying Starry Banner, and leading him off for the night. Starry Banner is the bossy, tell little Mary. I was present at its naming, which took place about a month ago, — the day I came out here to make my arrangements, bossy being then one day old.

"What shall we name it?" cried Uncle Jacob. We all stood round the pen, looking over.

"Name it Dicky Dilver!" Tommy shouted.

Matilda proposed Bounding Gazelle. William Henry said he'd be bound 'twould bound. Its mother was a regular deer of a cow: a five-railer wasn't a circumstance. I suggested, then, Highflyer. Georgiana wanted it Leopard, because it was spotted. Aunt Phebe thought Milkfoam both suitable and modest. Gus said Scott's Pride would be a good name. (Gus served under Scott in the Mexican war: he was probably straighter then.) At last, William Henry proposed that we name it Starry Banner, and thus honor the flag of our country. This idea was probably suggested by seeing Tommy perched on my head, nailing a pair of little flags which I had brought him *crisscross* over the barn-door.

After some discussion, this patriotic name was agreed upon. Then Billy took out his jack-knife, and carved upon a new shingle these words: "Starry Banner, born June 4." He carved the edges beautifully; and Aunt Phebe carried it in, and put it on the mantle-piece.

This Gus is a little round-shouldered old man Uncle Jacob picked up somewhere to help about the barn, but more to keep him out of the poor-house. He's a lively. chatty old fellow, not ill-looking in the face, and was a gallant soldier once, according to his own story. Such a rig as he gets up! They have given him better-looking hats; but he will wear his own little slim one, that was a tall hat once, with a narrow rim, and every bit of the nap off. I think of hiring him to go to Hansonville, just to march past your window half a dozen times a day. Wherever he got that neck-stock. and that little tight, faded-out, bottle-green frock-coat, nobody knows. There's always a slit in the back; and no wonder. But his overalls are big enough, and new enough, and blue enough. His voice is rather high-pitched.

"How do, Mr. Fry?" he sang out as I passed through the orchard.

"How do, Gus? Where are the folks? Where's Billy?"

"All in home. Billy jes' hopped over that fence. Go right 'long, Mr. Fry."

I went "right 'long," hoping to catch Billy, and have a little talk with him. You remember my telling you the last time I was at Hansonville about Billy's plan: "wish" would perhaps be the more exact word, as it has hardly developed into a plan yet. I have encouraged him; for I'm glad to find a boy really aiming at something.

Aunt Phebe's family were still at the tea-table. Billy bounced in at the end-door just as I walked through the front-entry; and we met in the eating-room. Grandmother was sitting there in the rocking-chair with her knitting-work. She'd had an early tea and got all cleared away, and run in to see Phebe. Mr. Carver sat at the window, reading his paper. Mr. Carver is a shorter man than Uncle Jacob, and darker complexioned.

After the "How d'ye do's?" were over, they made room for me at the table; and William Henry, with only half or two-thirds of an invitation, moved his chair up. 'Tis a very common thing for him to slide off of grandmother's meals on to Aunt Phebe's, getting there just as the best things are being passed round. "Doing an inclined plane" he calls it. The girls tell him 'tis plain he inclines to pie.

The family, with the exception of Tommy, had nearly finished eating, and were talking as fast as they could talk, when we went in, about the Fourth; and the subject was kept up through and after the clearing-away. Should we celebrate? How should we celebrate? One proposed one thing, and another another. I said 'twould be independence enough for me if I only sat on a rail and breathed air.

"If everybody celebrated your way," said Aunt Phebe, "there wouldn't seem to be much animation."

"I know it," said Lucy Maria; "and what would foreigners say about our manners and customs?"

"Oh! it's no use," said Uncle Jacob: "we've got to celebrate."

Billy declared he'd celebrate if all he did was to roll down hill all day, and walk up again.

"Mr. Fry, Mr. Fry!" shouted Tommy, "I've got four bunches. Frankie Snow an' me's goin' to stay up out-doors all night."

"Why, Tommy Carver!" cried Georgiana. Georgie is Billy's sister, — about the age of your little Mary, or paper-dolly age.

"Tommy," said Matilda, "put away that pop-gun till you've done eating, — if such a thing ever comes to pass!"

Tommy had just accomplished the feat, by bobbing his head down, of gnawing off some of his gingerbread without the use of hands, neither of which could be spared from the pop-gun.

"There!" cried Billy, "he's popped down Starry Banner's birthday!"

"'Twas joggly some 'fore!" cried Tommy.

Georgie picked up the ornamental shingle with the scalloped edge, and handed it to me.

"June 4?" I said. "Then we ought to have a double celebration."

"That's so!" says Billy. "We ought to have a procession."

"And a dinner," says Uncle Jacob: "I always like dinners."

"Then there must be an oration," said Mr. Carver. "People always have to take the oration before getting the dinner."

"Certainly," said I; "and a poem besides."

"Ma, what's a poem?" Tommy asked, "and that other thing?"

"A poem, my innocent child," said Lucy Maria, "is a long strip of writing that has its lines even. Of

course, 'twill have to keep step, and go two by two, like
the procession. Call it a 'procession of words' if you
want to."

"And the one that makes it up is a poet," said Matilda. "I don't see who'll be the poet, without Mr. Fry
does."

I said, "Oh, no! I never had any thing but a common-school education."

"Won't we have to give bossy something, if 'tis its
birthday?" asked Georgie.

"Hoo, hoo, hoo!— give a calf something!" shouted
Tommy.

"Give it a halter," said one.

"A bell to hang round its neck," said another

"A pair of gilt balls to keep till its horns grow," cried
another.

"Same as you give ear-rings to girls," added William
Henry: "only these are put up where they show more.
Pity girls didn't have" —

"Billy!" cried Lucy Maria.

"I was only going to say, 'Somewhere where they
could wear gilt balls,'" replied Billy. "I wasn't going
to say" —

"There, that'll do," said Lucy Maria.

"Boys would wear ear-rings if 'twas the fashion for
boys to," said Matilda.

"I'll tell you what you might give," said Mr. Carver:
"you might give Starry Banner the freedom of Long
Pasture. That's the way they do in Europe. When a
man is thought a good deal of, sometimes they present
him with the freedom of a town or city. It is written
on handsome material, and put in a nice box, and presented with a speech."

"What does it amount to?" asked Aunt Phebe.

"It is a mark of honor."

"Good!" shouted Billy. "Starry Banner deserves a mark of honor. We'll do it."

"But who'll make the speech?" asked two or three at a time.

"Billy," said Lucy Maria, "that's for you to do: you named him."

"Speeches have to have heads to 'em, don't they?" asked Billy. "I shouldn't know how to part any thing off into heads; but if Mr. Fry's a mind to help"—

I said I shouldn't mind taking the heads on my shoulders, if he would agree to carry out the body of it.

"Before we get too deep in this matter," observed Mr. Carver, "it is well to consider how big fools we are willing to make of ourselves."

"Big as we can!" cried Uncle Jacob.

L. M. (as they often call Lucy Maria) said foolishness always did seem to come natural to her.

Billy said he was willing to do the foolishest thing there was in the world.

Then came a very amusing discussion as to what was the foolishest thing in the world. You must see, at a glance, what a wide subject this opens. We came to the conclusion that there is no absolute standard for folly. What is foolish for a Yankee might be not at all so for a Japanese. You'd say Billy would look very foolish eating his boots; but, were he starving to death in a howling wilderness, that would be the wisest thing he could do.

"I think," said Aunt Phebe, "that folks ought to act just as foolish as they feel, and not be thinking about what other folks are thinking about them."

"That's so!" said William Henry; "and, if anybody felt like acting foolish, 'twould be foolish for him to act wise."

"Don't the age of a person make any difference?" Mr. Carver asked in a semi-serious tone.

"No!" cried Uncle Jacob: "I mean to be foolish, by spells, long as I live; and if I live to be a hundred, and go on crutches, I'll diddle my crutches to make the children laugh."

"Plimmy piece cake," Tommy called out here; which, being interpreted, signifies, "Please give me a piece of cake." I'd give something for that fellow's appetite.

"Well," said William Henry, "then we'll decide to have a procession, and march."

"Shoog-cake, not lassy-cake," expostulated Tommy.

"Don't take such big bites!" cried Matilda.

"Who'll be head marshal?" asked Uncle Jacob.

"You!" cried several voices.

"And who'll be the band?"

"Tommy's most choking!" cried Billy.

"Tommy," said his mother, "don't try to talk with any thing in your mouth."

"I've got a drum; *I'll* be the band!" shouted Tommy, with tears in his eyes. And away he ran to get it, almost knocking down the little barnman, who stood in the entry, milk-pail in hand, listening eagerly to the talk about bands and drums and marching.

"Tommy, come back!" cried Matilda, "and don't be jumping up so till you've done." The rest of us had left the table.

Aunt Phebe remarked, that manners came hard to Tommy; but she couldn't help hoping he'd grow to them.

"Who'll bear the flag?" asked Uncle Jacob.

"I'll bear the flag!" cried the little barnman: "I beared the flag in the army." And the poor fellow straightened himself as well as he could, and held up his fists to show how he bore the flag in the army.

"I'll get up a nice dinner," said Aunt Phebe, "and we'll have it out in the old orchard."

"I'll trim the table with flowers," said Georgie.

"I'll cut the cake up," said Billy, removing some very large-sized crumbs from a plate to his mouth as he helped clear away.

"Eat it up, you mean," said Matilda.

I remarked that Starry Banner would have every reason to feel slighted, unless a poem were written for the occasion; and, after some talk, Lucy Maria said she didn't know but she would try to tack a few lines together, and let Georgie stand up and speak them with a flag twined about her. Billy began to sing, "Go where the Woodbine twineth;" and Matilda laughed at him for not getting the tune right.

Aunt Phebe told Matilda she might invite Susie Snow if she wanted to, and Georgiana a couple of her little girls: a few more wouldn't make much difference.

"I don't know as I shall be in it," said Matilda. "Susie Snow and me don't know but we shall go somewhere."

"Oh! we shall have the best time," said Uncle Jacob. "Some— But never mind: you don't— I've got a secret!"

"What is it?"

"Sha'n't tell."

"Who told you?"

"Sha'n't tell. Guess some folks can have secrets well as other folks."

"What kind of a secret is it?"

"What kind? what kind?—well, a kind of a short kind."

"Oh! we know that," said L. M. "Father can't keep a secret long: 'twill soon be out."

"No!" said Uncle Jacob: "hope to die; black and blue; lay me down, and cut me in two!"

"Where did you get it?" asked Matilda. "Come, tell so much."

"If you do, they'll guess," remarked Aunt Phebe.

"There," said L. M.; "mother knows: I don't think that's fair."

"I had to tell her," said Uncle Jacob, "else I couldn't"—

"Well," interrupted Aunt Phebe, "you are great on secrets, I must declare!"

"Oh! they can't guess," said Uncle Jacob. "They'd never think of such a thing!"

"Plimmy pie?" Tommy put in here.

"No, Tommy," said his mother. "You've had bread and molasses (which was sufficiently obvious), and cake, and sauce, and doughnuts; and that's enough."

Mr. Carver remarked, that it seemed a pity to send the child to bed hungry!

Georgiana wanted to know if Starry Banner's mother wouldn't have to be invited to her bossy's party. This opened a new question: for Starry Banner had several relatives in the neighborhood; and, when you once begin, you don't know where to leave off. There was an uncle ox, who would look finely in the procession; but then, if you had him, you'd have to have some very ordinary cows that were just as near kin.   It was decided not to go any farther than the mother.

"But we'd better invite a few boys and girls to join," said Aunt Phebe.

"Won't they have to bring their own things?" asked Georgie.

"Oh! of course," said L. M.: "all bring their own things."

"Better ask Storcy Thompson," some one remarked.

"Yes," said L. M.: "ask him and his gloves."

"And his patent-leathers," said Billy: "we want one dressed-up one."

"I don't know what you all make so much fun of him for," said Matilda.   "For my part, I like to see folks go looking decent."

"What you looking at me for?" cried Billy.   "That's nothing but a rip."

"A rip right into the cloth!" cried Matilda.   "You can't tell a rip from a tear."

"'Tisn't for want of not seeing them often enough," Lucy Maria remarked.

"Can, too, when the stuff isn't shoddy!" cried Billy.

"Don't get disputing with Matilda," said grandmother. "If you're going to write a discourse, you'd better be setting about it."

Billy said he would spread out a sheet of paper in the barn, or somewhere, and, if any thoughts came, let 'em drop down on it.

"Spread it on a barrel-head!" cried somebody: "then you'll have one head to begin on!"

"Mr. Fry," asked Billy, "which is the way, — to get

the speech all done, and then cut it up into heads ? or take your heads, and fasten 'em together with the speech ? "

I said, that was a secret belonging chiefly to ministers.

" I'm glad I've got a secret!" cried Uncle Jacob in a jubilant tone.

" Poor father!" said Lucy Maria. " He does want to tell it so! Can't we help him? Say, now, how did you come by it ? "

" It came — I had it sent to me."

" Take care ! " cried Aunt Phebe.

" Box, bag, basket, bandbox, bundle, or done up in a paper ? "

" Done up in a paper."

" Take care ! " said Aunt Phebe again.

" What kind of a paper ? "

" Oh ! very good kind of paper."

" What shape was the bundle ? "

" It wasn't a bundle."

" Package, then."

" It wasn't a package."

" Well, what shape was whatever it was ? "

" Oh ! rather longish."

" About how longish ? "

" Well, about — about a third of a foot."

" Irregular, or round, or oval, or — now, what is that four-cornered word ? " asked Matilda.

" Rectangular ! " cried Billy.

" Oh, yes ! or rectangular ? "

" Just about," said Uncle Jacob.

" About what ? "

" Oh ! I haven't told what 'twas about yet."

"But was the — thing four-cornered, or not?"

"Better take care," said Aunt Phebe.

"Oh! they can't guess it," said Uncle Jacob. "'Twas four-cornered."

"But you don't consider how bright they are!" cried Aunt Phebe.

"How thick through was it?" asked some one.

"'Twasn't thick at all: 'twas thin."

"I guess I know," said Lucy Maria. "Who brought it?"

"It came in the cars."

"Express?"

"No. I sha'n't tell any more."

"You don't need to," said Aunt Phebe.

"He — sha'n't — tell — any — more," repeated Matilda very slowly. "I know, I know, I do!"

Then followed some very mysterious whisperings, which resulted in Georgiana's running out, and bringing in some fragments of a white envelope, which Lucy Maria began to put together.

"Poor father!" said she: "we must try to help him out with it."

"I told you 'twould be so!" cried Aunt Phebe.

"Oh!" said he, "they can't find out much by that."

"Bobby Short's handwriting!" shouted William Henry.

"I told you 'twould be the way," said Aunt Phebe. "No use holding on to the bag, now the cat's jumped out. Might as well show the letter now."

"Well, I guess 'twould be a good plan," said Uncle Jacob. "Here, Billy, you read it loud."

2

Bobby Short's Letter.

DEAR FRIEND, UNCLE JACOB, —

I want to write to you about something that I want
to do. I wanted to come and see Billy, and stay some.
I didn't want to stay a week: can't have no fun in a
week. But my mother won't let me, because she thinks
it isn't the way to do, — to make long visits, without the
folks are your uncle or your aunt, or something like that;
and she can't afford to pay board vacations too. So I
wish you would let me do this way: I wish you would
let me work for my board. I would if you would let
me, earnest. I think Billy and me could work very fast
when we two get together. I will work all the time you
say. I like gardens. I know how to dig, and a good
many other things; and Billy could help me, and I could
help him. I guess my mother would let me. I sha'n't
make any trouble. I'm twelve years old, and going on
thirteen.

From Billy's friend,

Very respectfully,

ROBERT SHOREY ("Bobby Short").

I thought, Juliana, you'd like to see Bobby Short's
letter. He's grown from a *bubby* to a *Bobby;* but I
don't believe he'll grow to his real name very soon, —
among us, at any rate.

"Have you answered it?" Billy asked after the reading was finished.

"Mother," Uncle Jacob asked in a very meek tone,
"hadn't we better tell the rest of it?"

"Don't know where the *we* **comes** from," said Aunt

Phebe. "I don't belong to any *we* that's told any thing."

"The idea," said Lucy Maria, "of his asking if he'd *better* tell, when he can't help it!"

"Well, then," said Uncle Jacob, "your mother thought we'd better let Bobby Short come; and he's coming."

"Good! When?" shouted Billy.

"Oh! most any day."

"Good! Bully for him!"

"You two've got to work," said Matilda.

"Oh, yes!" said Uncle Jacob. "I sha'n't think of doing any thing myself, with two such steady hands in the field."

"Dorry might come and spend Independence, if he wanted to," said Aunt Phebe. "One more wouldn't make much difference."

"Dorry can't come till college vacation," answered Billy. "He said so. When we camp out in August, he's coming then."

"Hannah Jane must be sent for right away," said Aunt Phebe.

"Yes," said grandmother. "You'll need her. Your oldest girl is all the girl you've got that always carries her mind with her about her work."

Juliana, if you feel too poorly to go anywhere yourself the Fourth, you can sit still and think about all the things we're up to here. I shall write after it is over, and tell the particulars.

From your loving brother,

S. Y. FRY.

P. S. — I said half an inch longer; but perhaps a third would be sufficient. On the whole, I think it would.

One of them needs to be let open behind, and a small triangle set into the yoke. Do you think the trouble is owing to a shrinkage of the cloth, or to — an opposite proceeding on my part?   S. Y. F.

We had pretty stirring times at the Farm for a few days. Stirring, indeed! Hannah Jane stirred up about every kind of cake in the receipt-book. The birthday-cake itself, I remember, was baked in a four-quart iron basin (the brownbread iron basin), and was frosted and adorned by Matilda. There wasn't room for his whole name; but she wrote "S. Banner" on top with red sugar-mites.

Stirring? Yes. The idea that we were going to be just as foolish as we pleased put new life into us. The poet and orator assumed airs of importance, and were constantly holding counsel together, or calling for white paper. Aunt Phebe said she'd no idea it took so much white paper to write a poem, or so long. I remarked, in reply, that a person who would be likely to know told me that poems had to be elaborated a great deal.

"That means worked upon, don't it?" some one asked.

"Yes," said I, — "worked upon, worked over, worked up. Hannah Jane, there, stirs up her good things, and sifts and flavors, and beats to a froth, and puts in her spices; and by and by, if it gets the right heat, it comes out a good cake. Just so, they tell me, a poet stirs up his good things, and sifts and spices and flavors, and beats to a froth; and by and by, if it gets the right heat, there comes out a poem. But 'tis apt to be heavy."

"Just think," said grandmother, "of all that's going on inside anybody's head!"

Second Letter

DEAR SISTER, —

Now get ready to smile all over your face; for its what you'll have to do, and you may as well be prepared.

Every thing went off well, and better than well. The day, Lucy Maria said, seemed to know of itself that everybody was taking notice of it, and put on its very best looks. 'Twas just warm enough, just cool enough, just sunny enough, just shady enough, just breezy enough, and just right. Mammy Sarah — the washerwoman —

came to help, bringing her daughter Rebecca's baby. Rebecca had gone to the picnic.

Bobby Short arrived early in the morning. *Arrived* is hardly the word, though. When you think of a person arriving, you think of a riding up to the front-door, and a stepping out, and paying the driver, and having the trunk brought in. But Bobby Short tumbled in at

grandmother's back-door while we were eating breakfast. There had been a delay in the matter of his starting, as considerable letter-writing was required before
his mother would let him come "*earnest.*" Billy wrote
him 'twas going to begin early; and he came by some

pre-early train, then cut across the fields, then through
the orchard, then in at our back-door, shouting out,
"Has it begun? has it begun?"

"Poor child! I know you are hungry," said grandmother. "Sit right up."

The boy could hardly get his breath. "Where's Billy? I've got some fireworks!"

"Billy's gone across," said I.

He made for the door; but a polite thought took him, and back he came to off hat and shake hands. Then away he went again.

And away I went too; for I had smelt powder that morning. Tommy and a tribe of little shavers began with their crackers by daybreak. Fourth-of-July powder always does make me feel uncommonly lively. I should cut up a good many didos if other men of my age (over thirty) would cut up too. I wonder if we are all waiting for each other.

I found Bobby Short and Billy preparing to join the Antiques and Horribles. Billy had borrowed the little barnman's bottle-green frock-coat, hat, and stiff neckstock. Bobby Short went as his wife, with a calico gown on, a shawl, an enormous "waterfall" two feet across, trimmed with beads, artificial flowers, and enclosed in a fish-net, and a jaunty hat with a wreath of flowers and plumes set over his smiling round face, and an *antique* parasol. They rode away in an old rickety chaise, tipped back (which vehicle has been about the premises these years and years), and were drawn by Pete Bruel's *antique* scalawag of a horse. Pete Bruel and Old Pete Bruel, and also Quorm and Bunkum, with several of their "little injuns," came up bright and early from Corry's Pond, and left their horses in our barn. The chaise was fastened together in places by ropes, and bits of board. Old Pete's tackling matched without alterations.

Tommy cried to go: so I harnessed Old Whitey into

the riding-wagon, and took him and Georgie, and started on behind at a respectful distance.

We saw the procession from several points of view. It was chased by a laughing, staring crowd, among whom were the Corry-pond delegation and others, *similar*, who looked as if they belonged *in* the ranks.

What odd-looking, countrified, ridiculous figures do seem to swarm on the Fourth! Everybody gets thawed out then. Well, I suppose Uncle Sam likes to have all his children about him on his birthday.

After the procession and the "horrible band" broke up, — oh that din! — we waited to see the picnic set off. Three car-loads. They had music (six pieces), and seemed right jolly for so early in the day.

Upon our arrival home, which was between eight and nine o'clock, we found things going on lively. To please Tommy and myself, I put a lot of fire-crackers in an old firkin, set 'em agoing, and rolled it along the piazza right under the windows to make the girls scream. They were all busy enough inside, packing baskets and canny-pails to carry to the orchard. Lucy Maria called out every few minutes, when William Henry was within hearing, "Boy wanted immediately, — a smart, reliable boy. Apply soon. Must be honest, stout, temperate, and industrious. Auburn hair preferred."

"Man the wheelbarrows!" shouted Uncle Jacob; and the boys wheeled off two great loads.

"Come back for more!" Hannah Jane called out after them.

"My bombazine coat!" cried Uncle Jacob. "Where's my best black thin bombazine coat? I'm going to dress up Independent Day."

"Bless me, girls!" cried Aunt Phebe, "your father's going to dress up! His thin coat hasn't been brought down this summer. 'Tis in the red chest away under the eaves, up garret."

"I'll go!" cried L. M. "I'd go to the ridgepole for the sake of father's dressing up! He's got to have his hair parted, too, Independent Day. Matilda, you must see to that. Here, take this knitting-needle. Don't let him go brush his hair at the *closet-door!*"

To understand this, you must know that Uncle Jacob's *dressing up* usually consists in putting on a starched gingham neckerchief, and brushing his hair at the *door* of the closet where his toilet apparatus is kept, in preference to a looking-glass.

"I can't reach up," said Matilda.

"Here, I'll hold you up," said her father.

I believe Uncle Jacob would like to hold Matilda, or even trot her on his knee, if she would let him.

"I wish I could be tall!" said Matilda. "Here I am fifteen years old, and not tall any. Lucy Maria's most two heads ahead of me. O father! you acting man! Mother, make him put me down!"

"You're going to grow in wisdom first, and stature afterwards," said L. M.; "and that will take a good while. — Here, father, don't you want to sit down and let your little girl make you look like a beauty?"

"You needn't laugh," said Matilda: "he's a real handsome man sometimes."

"Guess we all know that," said L. M.

"If your father wears his best thin black bombazine coat," said Aunt Phebe, "what shall I wear? I want to look as well as he does."

"Your flowered red-and-green mantle will just about match that old swallow-tail," said L. M.; "and I'll fetch it down."

"Where's my checkered neck-handkerchief?" cried Uncle Jacob. "I shall want that."

"'Tis all starched and ironed," said Aunt Phebe, "and hangs up inside the closet-door."

"Here comes Storey Thompson!" Lucy Maria called down from the upper entry, "and his gloves!"

"And a new hat," said Georgie, looking out.

"Panama!" said Hannah Jane. "Poor folks too! He's stiff as a poker."

"Both of his hands hang backside front," remarked Georgie.

"I wouldn't all stare at him," said Aunt Phebe, peeping out. "I declare! He is a dandy chap; isn't he? Now, when I see a dandy chap like that, I feel just like taking my duster and brushing him off. But don't all stare. 'Tisn't impossible but that he's got feelings, after all."

"There he goes into the orchard," said Georgie, "and Dicky Willis."

"I wonder if he does saw wood with gloves on," said Aunt Phebe, "or if somebody made that up."

"Wilson saw him the other day," said Hannah Jane with a faint blush.

Wilson Bryant is Hannah Jane's beau. I'm so glad there's a beau belonging to Summer-sweeting Place! 'tis just what it needed. A beau imparts a romantic air. To be sure, ours lives some way off, and doesn't come very often: but then that only heightens the interest; for we know he's longing to. Sincere affection on both sides; and in sober earnest, Juliana, I do think it a good thing to be sure of a certain amount of true love so near by.

"Found it?" Uncle Jacob called up the stairway.

"Yes. Found it. Sponging the gray off!" L. M. shouted back.

When Uncle Jacob was arrayed in his best black thin bombazine coat, he made me think a little of the pictures of Mr. Lincoln; being so high-shouldered and large-featured, I suppose, and perhaps, too, on account of his good nature and liveliness.

"Oh, dear, what an old fashioned thing!" said Matilda.

"Now, I think," said Hannah Jane, "that father looks better than common."

"Do have your dicky unanimous to-day, father; do!" said Lucy Maria. "Not one corner up, and one down. Suppose those great handkerchief-ends are meant for sails. Hope 'twill be fair wind."

"Here's William Henry come for more things," said Hannah Jane.

"Oh, do see Tommy!" cried Georgie. "He's burnt a great hole in his trousers! See him going hopping! Burst one of his toes, I guess. He's crying. There, now he's laughing 'cause Uncle Jacob's trying to go like him."

"Mother Delight says, that, when children cry, she knows they are alive," remarked Aunt Phebe. "What ails Matilda? O Susie Snow!"

Susie Snow came running with both arms spread out, and Matilda ran with both her arms spread out; and they collided under full headway, with an explosion of kisses that made all ring again.

Next thing, Tommy came on to the piazza with a small regiment just like him, all looking as if they'd seen service. Their fire-crackers were gone, their torpedoes fired off, their powder was *flashed ;* and they had a listless, woe-begone air, as if their lives would run to waste for want of something to do.

"Ma, can't all these come to it, if they'll bring something," cried Tommy, "and be in the band?"

"Yes; I guess so," said Aunt Phebe: "a few more won't make much difference. But they must tidy up a little."

"Put on white trousers!" Lucy Maria called out after them, for they went off like a flash; "or light-colored as you've got!" she added.

"And red, white, and blue in your button-holes!" shouted Georgiana.

"Billy, mayn't I wear your trainer-clothes, up garret?" Tommy asked.

"Yes; I don't care," said Billy.

"There's Jacky looking through the fence!" cried Matilda, — "Jacky and old Tim! Pray, don't let's have them!"

Jacky is the little black-eyed fellow I told you about, — the one Billy and Mother Delight *discovered* at the time *that ride* was broken short off in such a funny way. That old man — the one who had the privacy with Billy's *lady passenger:* you remember? — moved here after Jacky got a place, and lives in a little tumbledown house back of the hills. Jacky does chores for Mrs. Paulina, and does mischief on his own account. Everybody is down on him; and I don't wonder. But Tommy had rather play with him than with any other boy. Nothing would have pleased Tommy better, in his secret heart, than Jacky's coming to our "Fourth of July:" still he hadn't the courage to speak of it, knowing very well how the little black-eyed was regarded.

"Jacky here?" cried Hannah Jane. "I'm sorry he's found it out. Wonder what great boy's old linen suit he's jumped into!"

Aunt Phebe looked out of the window. "What a kind of *outside* look they do seem to have!" said she.

"They are outside," said Georgie.

"I don't mean outside the fence, but outside our concerns," said Aunt Phebe. "I've a great mind to let them come, — Jack and Tim both."

Tim is the old man. Seems to be a simple, harmless, good-for-nothing old fellow enough.

"Oh, I wouldn't!" said Matilda. "We don't want such kind of folks!"

"I can't bear to see them have that outside kind of look," said Aunt Phebe. "How earnest Jacky stares!"

"Oh! let 'em come," said Lucy Maria, — "only two of them. I'm sure we're all created free and equal Independent Day, if no other time."

"I should really like to see Tim eating a good dinner," said Aunt Phebe.

"And we are none of us going to behave very well to-day," I suggested.

"There!" said Matilda, "father's invited 'em! I believe father would invite all creation!"

Tim and Jacky came inside the gate, and sat down on a log; Jacky almost holding his breath at the thought of having been invited, when he was so used to being driven off.

Next came some of Georgie's girls; and away went Georgie like another steam-engine, and then away they all went to the orchard with their baskets. I took a canny-pail of something on my head, and marched off after them. Found the table spread under a saxifax-tree. The girls were making bouquets at a fearful rate. The boys were putting up swings, and doing every thing the girls asked them to. Bobby Short, however, had gone down by the Boiling Spring, where Georgie's bird was buried (*vide* Wm. H. Letters), to study the *poem;* for, as Georgie felt too bashful to "speak a piece" out-doors, he had been elected *poet.*

At eleven o'clock, Uncle Jacob blew the horn, and called aloud for all hands to "Form on!"

Tommy's boys had brought their musical instru-ments, consisting of fifes, trumpets, whistles, bird-calls, and an harmonicon. Those who had none went through the motions of tromboning, drumming, &c. Mr. Snow's little contraband came with his trumpet, and, being a wonderful blower, was taken into the band.

"For we are all of a color Independent Day," says Lucy Maria.

I never saw anybody fit into a place better than that little chap fitted into the band. He seemed made on purpose to march and to blow. His eyes flashed, and his cheeks puffed out like bladders, and every bone in his body kept time. He was dressed in white clothes, and had on a little round cap without any forepiece, with his curls frizzing out all round.

The girls were mostly in white, and the boys in white trousers, or "light-colored as they could," with red-white-and-blue bows. All that went in the procession had little flags on their hats, or their bonnets, or their *horns*. Uncle Jacob's hat was a black Leghorn one with a broad brim, and the brim turned up behind.

As Lucy Maria had been busy about other matters, the box that contained the "freedom of Long Pasture" was handsomely adorned by Matilda with emblematical paintings, — much better than could have been expected. The centre-piece on the cover was a wreath of buttercups and daisies, natural as life. In one corner she painted a milk-pail foaming over with milk. as a hint to Starry Banner of what would be expected some future day; in another corner was a milkmaid, churning; in the third a cheese, with a mouse nibbling it, to make it look more like a cheese; and in the fourth a pair of calfskin boots. Around the sides ran a wreath of clover-blossoms; done so well, Billy said you could almost smell of them.

When every thing was ready, we began to come into line; and this was the order of

THE PROCESSION.

First. The Band; six pieces.

Second. The Hero * of the Day, wearing a large wreath, and supported by two patriotic boys.

Third. Mother of the Hero of the Day, having a small flag tied to each horn.

Fourth. Orator and Poet, arm in arm, bearing boughs of *laurel*. [We'll make sure of them beforehand, says Billy.]

Fifth. Color-Bearer. And, as his back would not uncrook, he straightened his neck, and marched with his chin in the air, holding up with both hands the flag of his country.

Sixth. Uncle Jacob and the Boarder (S. Y. F.), carrying each a beanpole, with *the box* slung between.

---

* It is my impression that *a calf* is usually represented by a masculine pronoun.

Seventh.   The Girls, two by two.
Eighth.   The Boys ditto.
Ninth.   Mr. Carver and Grandmother.
Tenth.   Tim and Susie Snow's Father.
Eleventh.   Aunt Phebe and Mammy Sarah, dragging Rebecca's baby
in a roller-cart.
Two small dogs acted as marshals; and old Towzer, with a stately air,
brought up the rear.

The procession moved at a given signal, halted to give
three cheers at the *birthplace of our hero,* and then
passed on in *perfect order* to Long Pasture.

The great red gate had been taken off its hinges, and
the gateway arched over with boughs.   At the moment
of entering, each boy set off a cannon-cracker, the band
gave a flourish, and the drummer beat a roll on his drum.

"Hurrah, hurrah, hurrah!"

But, while the two patriotic boys were cheering, they
forgot to support Starry Banner; and, in the midst of
the racket, he sprang through on a tight gallop, heels
in the air.

"High-flyer indeed!" said one.

"He's taken it!" cried another.

"Taken what?"

"The freedom of Long Pasture."

"After him, boys!" shouted Uncle Jacob.   "Quick!
The bars are down!   He'll get in the bog!"

The procession now broke rank, and took chase, led on
by the two marshals; and a pretty race we had over hills
and hollows, through bushes and briers!

"Here he is!"

"No, there he goes!"

"Catch him, Rover!"

"At him, Spry!"

"Bow, wow, wow!"

"Wow, wow, wow!"

"Now he's in a corner!"

"No : he's slipped through!"

"Look out there!"

"Grab his ears!"

"Tommy's kicked over!"

"Never mind!"

"Bow, wow!"

"Here comes the cow!"

"Look out for the cow!   The cow!"

"Head her off!"

"Oh, dear!"

"Jump up and take another!"

"I've got his tail!"

"Hold on!"

"I can't!"

"There he goes!"

"Head him off there!"

"Jacky's got him by the leg!"

"Keep hold, Jacky!"

Jacky kept hold; trust him for that! And thus, after a tight scrabble, and proceedings not laid down in the programme, Starry Banner was brought up to the stake; for a strong stake had been driven into the ground in order that he might be chained to the spot during the speaking. Finding escape impossible, he lay quietly down; and the mother, with looks of pride and a gentle "Moo!" took her place by his side.

Old and young then seated themselves upon the fragrant hay; and the poet, "*twined in a flag,*" mounted a high rock, accompanied by your brother, who, in pre-

3

senting him to the audience, made these few emphatic
remarks : —

"We are aware, my friends, that the poem usually
follows the oration. Should it be asked *why* we deviate
from the common custom, we answer, that this is *not* a
common occasion. [Cries of ' *True, true !* ' from the
audience.] And I would state further, in behalf of the
orator and poet, that, as our great country is being praised
and glorified this day by eloquent lips all over the land,
they will, in addressing you, confine themselves to the
other branch of this celebration. I will merely remark,
lest these Fourth-of-July proceedings should not otherwise be legal, that said country extends from the At-
lantic to the Pacific, and that the American eagle is a
very large bird.

"I have the honor of introducing to you Robert
Short, Esq., the great future agriculturist."

Bobby Short came forward with a smiling face; made
his best bow; and although the lines were exceedingly
mild and simple, having been composed for a little girl
to speak, he shouted them out in the most sturdy manner, and with unceasing action of the arms. In fact,
his delivery was more than good.

ADDRESS TO A CALF ON HIS BEING PRESENTED WITH THE FREEDOM OF LONG PASTURE.

Happy Bossy, creature bright;
Frisky one, with heels so light;
Bossy with the beaming eye,
Capering right joyfully, —
Take, we pray you, from our hands, —
Take these sunny pasture-lands.
This is your home;
Here you may roam;

Race, if you will, from hill to hill,
Or tumble over in the clover;
No living to earn, no taxes to pay:
So toss up your heels, and caper away;
For here are treasures rare for you,
Grass and flowers so fair for you, —
The sweetest flowers you ever knew,
The tenderest grass that ever grew, —
Golden buttercups so bright,
Honey-clover red and white.
Wander where the waters flow,
Where the willow-trees hang low,
Or bounding over the hillocks go.

Oh, what a beautiful, beautiful home!
The birds sing here, and the butterflies come,
And the grasshoppers hop, and the honey-bees hum.
Just look about you, we implore you,
On the beauties spread before you.
Why, the *starry banner* itself, my dear,
Is not more fair than our pasture here.
Suppose we play *'tis* a banner now,
Spread out in some way, we don't know how:
The little flowers the stars shall be;
And then the stripes —just let me see —
Why, the lights and shadows that fall on the land,
Sure they very well for the stripes may stand.
But I fear, dear Bossy, you don't understand.
So frolic and play
And be gay while you may:
For the beautiful summer is passing away;
And winter must come, and then you'll see
What a terrible snowing and blowing there'll be!
Thus summers will come, and summers will go;
For you can't be always a calf, you know:
So, pray, think sometimes, while you're capering now,
" Oh! what shall I do when I grow up a cow?"
Make a firm resolution, that *never* shall fail,
That you'll *never* chase children, nor hook down a rail,
Nor get in the corn, nor kick over a pail.
Be a cow of sweet temper, a clever old *Mool;*
Be a cow of ambition, and give the pail *full.*

The poem ended amid immense cheering, clapping of
hands. shouts. and waving of flags. during which the
poet, after acknowledging the applause by many low
bows, modestly seated himself among the audience to
hear the oration.   Then came "Yankee Doodle" by the
band, followed by "Tramp, tramp."   Aunt Phebe improved this opportunity by taking the orator aside, where
she touched up his hair a little. turned down his trousers-legs, blew off the dust, straightened his bow, and, by
some dexterous sleight-o'-hand. shook him out even.   He
was then conducted to the stand by your brother (it
seems more modest to speak of myself in the third person), who introduced him as follows : —

"My friends, your choice of an orator is certainly a
happy one and a fitting one.   With great exertions has
the young man risen oft at early dawn to drive the cows
to pasture ; and hasted at eventide. before the falling of
the dew. to 'call the cattle home,' dealing no cruel blows.
but cheering them, instead, with kindly words.   I have
listened, you all have listened, to his cheery 'Kermool.
kermool. kermool !' or the softer 'Cush, cush. cush !' and
to their gentle low in reply.   And if, straying afar, they
lost their way, he it was who followed them — untiring.
shall I say ? — through bush and brier.

"But I will not. my friends. by any feeble words of
mine. detain you from the rich treat now awaiting you.
It gives me great pleasure to introduce William Henry.
Esq.. formerly of Crooked-pond School."

William Henry stepped forward. manuscript in hand.
and was received with the most uproarious greetings.
He bowed to Starry Banner. then to the remainder of
the audience, moistened his lips with a glass of water

that had been placed *convenient* on the milking-stool, took out a large white cambric pocket-handkerchief, with which he wiped the moisture from his brow, cleared his throat, ran his fingers through his hair, stood erect, left arm thrown behind, and made ready to begin. I must state, however, that, in pulling out the white cambric pocket-handkerchief, he pulled out with it a shower of little strips of printed paper, which flew about like a small snow-storm. [Loud laughter from the audience, and several exclamations of "*Boy wanted!*"]

The orator smiled benignantly upon the crowd; then, recovering his composure, he placed his black-covered manuscript carefully upon the milking-stool, the legs of which had been extended to meet the occasion, and with an air of the utmost solemnity began

THE ORATION.

STARRY BANNER, FRIENDS, NEIGHBORS, COUNTRY-MEN, AND FELLOW-CITIZENS, —

I feel that a worthier person than myself might have been chosen to address you on this occasion. [Cries of "Oh, no!" "Oh, no!" "Impossible!" from the audience.] I need not inform you that my time has been short and precarious; for, in the words of a not very-well-known poet, — if you will permit me to quote poetry so early in my address [cries of "Oh, yes!" "Oh, yes!" "Poetry forever!"], — in the words of the poet, then, we've had

> " Turnips to sow,
> Grass to mow, ,
> Hay to stow,
> Weeds to hoe,
> Errands to go,
> And endless running to and fro."

[Cries from the audience of "That's so!" and "That's so!"]

My friends, this is the proudest moment of my life. ["Doubted."] Still I have accepted with humility the greatness thrust upon me; and the sense of my weakness is very strong. The faults in what I have to offer you will excuse: they are my own. If there be any thing to admire, those who have so kindly assisted me, male and female, should receive the praise.

My address is made up mostly of advice, and is therefore mainly addressed to the hero of the day; as the older among you have no need of advice, and the younger can get it anywhere. Excuse me for not making greater preparation. [Cries of "Go on!" "Go ahead!" "Let's have what you've got!" "We don't expect much!" "Hurrah for Billy!" &c.] Thus encouraged, the speaker proceeded: —

Upon this day, the birthday of our country, and, Starry Banner, of you, with the blue sky above us, and the green grass below us, and the waving trees about us, I present to you, my young friend, the freedom of Long Pasture. [Here the box was lowered by its bearers, with a flourish by the band, and was committed to the charge of the two patriotic boys. The orator went on.] Here roam at your own sweet will, eat the feed, drink the water, and lie down in the shade.

But remember, my young friend, that life is not always summer. ["Hear, hear!"] A time shall come when this green grass shall wither, these pretty flowers droop their heads and die. The little brook shall cease to flow, and the trees hang with icicles. [Sensation.] So conduct, that, when the dark barn shall be your only home, the days of this summer-life shall be pleasant to remember.

Our poet, to whose beautiful lines we have just listened, has asked you a very important question, — a question that should be taken out of poetry, and put into prose: "Oh! what shall I do when I grow up a cow?" What shall you do? and what shall you be? for every cow has a character.

Now, cows are of two kinds, — good and bad. The bad I shall divide into four heads.

First, The ugly or vicious cow.
Second, The stray cow, or runaway.
Third, The hooking cow.
Fourth, The jumping cow.

First, The ugly or vicious cow. This animal has a fierce eye and a quick motion of the head. She has sometimes to be led by a rope. She is a pest in a neighborhood. At milking-time, she either refuses to give down, or puts her foot in the pail, or kicks it over. Her owner is always willing to sell. I am glad to have it in my power to say that the ugly or vicious cow is not very common. What few there are should be sent to those countries where cows are made to work in the fields. [Applause.]

Second, The stray cow, or runaway, or I might call her the never-satisfied. The next pasture always seems better than her own. "How tender that grass! how sweet that clover! If I were only over there! Oh! what excellent milk could be made of such feed as that!" She never sees any thing good in her own grass; for her eyes are always over the fence. And if the gate should be left open a crack, or a gap made in the stone wall, — why, away she goes! and by the time the sun sets in the western sky, and darkness covers the face of the earth, she may be away beyond the huckleberry-hills. [Sensation.] Try, then, to be satisfied. The grass over the fence appears greener, probably, because it *is* over the fence. There may be brambles hid beneath it, after all. A contented disposition is a good thing. Get what good there is your own side the fence, and make the best milk you can of the feed that's given you. [Immense cheering.]

Third, The hooking cow. Hooking cows frighten children. They also hook down rails. The evils of hooking down rails may be seen with half an eye. [Cries of "True, true!"] When the rails are down. it is all up with the farmer. Just suppose, for a moment, that all cows were hooking cows, and all rails could be hooked down. Where, then. would be our corn, our cabbages. our turnips? Where, I ask, would be our winter's hay? ["Nowhere!" from the audience.] Foolish creatures and blind, not to see that fences are put up for their own good, to keep their own selves from starving in winter! In the charming volume I hold in my hand [taking small book from pocket] will be found the following lines: —

> " Little boy blue, come blow up your horn:
> The sheep's in the meadow, the cow's in the corn."

We have reason to believe that the second animal mentioned in the last line was a hooker and a stray cow also. It was, no doubt. all her fault that the sheep were in the meadow. The amount of damage done is not known.

In some cases, however, hooking may be a very proper action. The cow with the crumpled horn didn't do a bad thing in hooking that dog. She took the part of the weak; and this. if you are going to take any part, is the part to take. Then, O Bossy! if ever, is the time to show your *pluck*. Why did that dog worry that cat? She had merely done her duty. The rat ate the corn. and he needed catching. [Sensation and cheers.] No doubt it was because that great dog felt big and proud : wanted to show what great things he could do. It is to be hoped his fall knocked the conceit out of him! [Sensation and cheers.]

Therefore, my young friend, when your horns grow, don't be poking them into everything and everybody. Above all, don't frighten little children; for they're afraid of hooking cows. Suppose they do wear red shawls : the poor things can't help it; they don't make their shawls! How can cows do so? Don't they see how frightened the children are? — how they creep along by the fence, looking for a hole to get through? Oh! when you grow up, be gentle to little children. If you meet them going to school. look the other way : they'd a great deal rather you would. And, if they come to pick a few huckleberries in your pasture, play that you are very busy with your nose in the grass, and can't stop to look up; or be lying down. and too lazy to move. If you run to welcome them, as would be the politest way, they won't understand it : they'll scream and run. [·· True, true !·"]

The speaker, after wetting his lips, and wiping the moisture from his brow, went on to, —

Fourthly and lastly, The jumping cow. Some cows

are always making a mistake, and thinking they are deer. I've seen a cow try to jump over a wheelbarrow. Now, the cow was never made for jumping. She is of heavy build, and should be satisfied with walking, — content to lead a quiet life, and do good in a quiet way. Suppose it is a quiet way, so long as she does do good. And the good done by the cow can never be reckoned. Can you reckon the milkpails that foam at morn and eve throughout our land? Can you reckon all the little children waiting for their bread and milk? Can you reckon all the churns in motion? Can you reckon all the quarts in all the cans in all the carts that milkmen drive? Think of the bread, which, but for cows, would go unbuttered! the strawberries unmoistened by cream! And from whence should we derive our boots and shoes? [Sensation.]

Cows, then, can do good, but never distinguish themselves by jumping. True, there is, or was, one exception, — "the cow that jumped over the moon." Why she did so can only be conjectured, as only the naked historical fact has been handed down. Thought the man in the moon was calling her, perhaps; or thought the moon itself was shaking its horns at her, and so got mad, and flew at the moon; or perhaps she was trying to get into the milky-way! What became of her afterwards, or whether she ever came down again, is not known. She must have come down again, I should think. Or is she up there still? — chasing a comet maybe, or dodging the shooting-stars! Gone to try it over Jupiter's moons, perhaps!

But time is passing, the audience fasting; ["True, true!"] and I will close this address. And, in conclud-

ing, I will say, young friend, that you have this day received an honor never before paid to Bossy; but be not
therefore proud, or *set up* like that golden calf we read
about, but ever bear this and all other honors with meek-
ness. [Tremendous applause.]

The oration and poem were both ordered to be
printed. How do you like them, Juliana? I was going
to tell you all about the dinner and toasts, but am
obliged to break off here. May speak of them in my
next. As regards little Silas's new clothes, it will be
cheaper to buy the cloth, and have them made in the
house. No matter if he isn't so well satisfied. If you
accustom him to being satisfied, he will expect to be satisfied through life. Might have a tailor cut them. I
enclose patterns of *tricot*. Forgot to send them in my
last. Inquired for *tweed* and *satinet*, as you asked me,
but couldn't find any. The little counter-jumper said
they'd *gone up*. Might have meant in price; but I
thought, from his looks, he meant *in toto*. That little
pair of checkered pants fitted Jacky quite well. Send
other clothes, do, when you have them. I can't help
feeling interested in that child, rogue as he is. Your
box is all ready to go back. I put in, among other
things, a pair of light-colored cassimere trousers for
little Silas. The cloth cost six dollars a yard. With a
little alteration, I should think he might jump right into
them. Be sure and tell him the cloth cost six dollars a
yard! Oh, how early pride shows! don't it? Lucky for
you I'm small of my age; isn't it? — lucky, I mean, as
respects my clothes being handed down. Aunt Phebe
insisted on putting some of the goodies into your box

we had left from the dinner. Only for being in such a
hurry, I would tell you every thing we had spread before us on that table under the saxifax. Just take a
slate-pencil, little Mary, and write down all the good
things you can think of, and you may be sure we had
them; and needn't be afraid of putting down ice-
creams (we made those), or floating-island, or strawberry-
short-cake. And of course, on Independent Day, we
had *Washington-pie!* Mrs. Snow sent two kinds of
cake herself, besides lemons and nuts; and Etta Calloon,
a little city child who stays in the country summers,
brought a large supply of cocoanut-cakes. The table
was a sight to behold! In the centre was a large dish
of stars and stripes (cakes you know) frosted and gilded.
But the funniest thing was a platter of little bossies,
fried as doughnuts, and standing on their legs quite
well. Billy handed these round, asking everybody to
take a *fatted calf!* That young gentleman showed
such an alarming appetite, even for him, that many felt
it their duty to warn him against taking up public
speaking as a profession. We noticed a heap of the
best of the goodies walled around his plate; and, when
this barricade was inquired into, he said those were
what he was keeping to eat when he'd done! After
this, everybody kept passing things that way for Billy to
eat when he'd done.

I don't think anybody enjoyed the dinner more than
Mammy Sarah and Tim. Jacky wasn't detected in any
misconduct, except getting ice out of the ice-tub on the
sly. Somebody proposed catching that young scamp,
and putting him up in ice, to keep him out of mischief.
He stoned Matilda's Leghorn hen the other day: and

whatever he did to it nobody knows; but the hen has gone with a one-sided look ever since, as if she were trying to hide her tail under her wing.

Our day ended gloriously. Bobby Short's fireworks went off like a book. Then we sat on the piazza, and sang patriotic songs. "John Brown's Body," of course, for Billy; though, on account of the day, he was allowed to join, *pianissimo*, in all the patriotic songs. John Brown is never denied him. Lucy Maria says 'tis cruel to keep him from singing out that *Hallelujah Chorus*, even if he don't get the tune; and, as others are for the most part forbidden, he usually does this one with a great deal of *ad libitum*.

In haste, as ever your brother,

SILAS Y. FRY.

Extract from Another Letter.

. . . That was as jolly a day as you'd wish to see. The children had a good time. The old folks made themselves like little children: so they had a good time. I don't see why folks should be so afraid of becoming like little children, when that is just what we are commanded to do. Mrs. Paulina's remarks amused me considerably. Lucy Maria had said all along, that our proceedings, and "spendin' so much time," would astonish Mrs. Paulina beyond the power of even asking a question. I went over there, next day, to carry back her lemon-squeezer (we employed four lemon-squeezers), and heard her squeezing the particulars out of Storey Thompson. It comes natural to say squeezing; for that fellow is just about as soft as — well, putty's the word, though (putty's one of Billy's words). His face has just about as much expression; and yet, as L. M. says, it is made of pretty stuff, — fair complexion, large cheeks, wavy hair, blue eyes, features regular, a good face enough if somebody could only set a candle behind it.

Mrs. Paulina knows just what people ought to do and ought not to do.

"How many kinds of cake? Ice-creams? Tea and coffee both? Carry her silver spoons out doors? All hands march? Grandmother didn't! Now, I am struck up! Child's play, child's play!"

"I didn't go in the procession," said Storey: "I thought it seemed foolish." I had stopped outside to speak with Jacky, who was crying with a *stone-bruise* on the ball of his foot. I had a stone-bruise once myself. Boys that go barefoot often have them. You must remember a very bad one of mine, and how I suffered; for you did your best, you dear soul, to amuse me. But the day before it broke I cried all day long, and actually rolled over and over on the floor in my agony; and though a great boy, almost as big as mother, she took me in her arms, and rocked me just like a baby. So, you see, I knew what Jacky would have to pass through.

I wish you could see the little fellow! — a very little fellow, and so spry! — spry all over, every joint and muscle, and head too, I might say; for it goes this way and that, like a bird's. Such snapping black eyes! and they look blacker for his face being so pale. 'Tis rather a long face for a child, and just as smooth as marble. He must pay his way, or Mrs. Paulina wouldn't keep such a rogue.

"Now, while they were 'carrying on,'" said Mrs. Paulina, "I accomplished a sight, — scoured up my floor, skimmed eight pans, darned my stockings, and most made a sheet, besides ripping an old dress to pieces. So much clear gain, I call it. All done while most everybody was a-spendin' their time."

How differently different people look at things! Now, I think ours was "clear gain." All that fun, and good humor, and good air! . . .

Do keep me informed of the state of your health, and thus keep some anxious thoughts from the mind of
Your loving brother,   SILAS.

This Jacky was a little fellow, who at that time did chores for Mrs. Paulina. Our families took some interest in him, because they were the means, or rather William Henry was the means, of Tim and Jacky coming into the neighborhood. Instead of explaining this myself, it will be better to introduce here a letter I received from Billy the latter part of April, describing a wonderful ride he had, which ended in a very sudden and rather ridiculous manner. It is one of the most entertaining letters I ever read.

William Henry's Letter to Mr. Fry.

MY DEAR FRIEND, —

I think just the same as I did then about that that we were talking about (you know), and I hope I shall do it some time or other; and I think a feller most fifteen years old ought to be doing something pretty soon. Father laughs, and says, "Oh! wait till the Corry-pond Lot is sold." That's what they all say when any of us want a pile of money; but you see that won't sell, because 'tis such a bad place to get wood from, and so far to draw it, that it don't pay. So our great, great, very great Uncle Wallace didn't do us such a great, great, very great kindness, after all. Father's offered it low. He's paid high taxes enough on it. You see it comes wrong to have prices low and the taxes high.

You wanted to know about my ride, and how it came out. We didn't come out so much as we went in! Write a "talkee, talkee" letter, you say, like that you sent us once from Washington (alluding to a letter of mine telling about the contrabands), and make it long, so as to improve my handwriting (and I am willing to do any thing for the sake of improving that; for it will have to be improved some way or other): so I have taken a sheet of foolscap-paper, red and blue rulings. I want to begin to get used to that kind of paper; for 'twill seem like making a beginning of — you know!

I suppose you remember, that, when you left here that morning, we seemed to be about ready; but we were a long time getting started after that. There were so many things to hinder us! — first the thills broke; and then Mother Delight she —

(I will interrupt the letter here in order to make an explanation. This ride was undertaken wholly on Gus's account. For some days, the poor old fellow had been suffering from ague in the face. One cheek was swollen up even with his nose, and the eye on that side had *gone out*. He insisted upon it, that Quorm, an Indian who lived in the woods about five miles off, would cure him if he could only get down to his hut; and, to satisfy him, Uncle Jacob told William Henry he'd better harness up Old Longlegs (Old Pokey the girls called him), and take the old man down there.

The other hinderance, just on the point of being mentioned by Billy, was a delightful, joyous old woman then spending a

few days at the Farm. Her real name was Keziah. Tommy
called her " Mother Delike " once ; and the girls changed it to
" Mother Delight," because the name suited her so well. This
was when Aunt Phebe was sick. Tommy wanted something
of his mother, and they told him to go to Mother Keziah.
She was taking care of Aunt Phebe then. Tommy had just
begun to talk, and he pronounced it Muzzer Delike. She was
one of your rosy, chubby old ladies, with bright black eyes, and
black-and-gray curls shaking about her temples. — S. Y. F.)

— wanted to go too, and that hindered : but we made
out to start some time or other. Gus had his chops
tied up in a muffled handkerchief, and looked funny, as you might guess. His hat couldn't but just keep
on. I never did see a fellow stick to any thing as he
sticks to that hat! Uncle Jacob says he believes there's
money hid in the lining. Wish I had it!

We were just going to harness up when we found out
that one of the thills was split slanting, and had most
come apart. We expect some of Tommy's little fellers
jumped on it, ransacking round, chasing cats. So I went
over to see what Mr. Slade could do for us. Didn't expect
to get his best one, or even to get any, unless he thought
of something we could do for him. That's always his
way. He'll never do a favor for anybody without making 'em feel 'tis a great put out to him, or else getting
them to do something to make up. If I hadn't been in
a hurry, I'd have gone a mile before taking up with that
old jolting rackertybang!

He said he'd lend me his green one if I would carry
a couple of Shanghai fowls to a man that lived about
two-thirds of the way along, that was going to swap off
a goose for them ; and I agreed to. I suppose I hopped

4

round spryer than common, being in a hurry ; for he said
he wished I was his boy.   You see he's got the rheumatism, and that makes other folks seem spry.   I'd thought
to myself, I'd about done being anybody's boy ; but, if I
had to stay there with him and Mrs. Paulina, I'd run
away.

I dragged the old thing home, and was going ahead
with harnessing up, when Aunt Phebe called me into the
buttery, and gave me a great piece of company-cake.   I
expect she did it to make me clever, and do something
she wanted me to ; and it did.   Says she, " Billy, Mother
Delight has found out where you are going, and she
wants to go too, to get some roots and twigs that grow
down Corry Pond way, and to see Angeline."   You see
that's her daughter that she calls " my darter Angeline,"
that lives about half a mile from Quorm's.   Angeline's
husband is Pete Bruel, son of old Pete Bruel.   Puts up
his horse in our barn sometimes for nothing.   Guess
you've seen that old scalawag of a horse ; looks like the
old Sancho, with so much neck to him !

Aunt Phebe said she wanted to carry down some
things to her daughter's children down there, that she'd
picked up going her rounds ; and said she'd given her
some encouragement that I'd take her.   " Of course, she'll
be a bother," says Aunt Phebe ; " but what of that if you
make up your mind to that beforehand ?   Everybody in
this world has to be bothered, and has to be a bother,
some time.   I don't know how I should have held out
when you had the measles, if she hadn't taken hold ; and
we're liable to be sick any time."

You might guess I'd rather not do it : and that isn't
putting the way I felt half so strong as it was ; for who

wants to ride by houses with two such ones? But I
couldn't say "No" top o' that cake and top o' the
measles, you know. And when I came to think it over,
"Who cares?" says I. "Guess I can ride by with anybody I want to; and whoever don't like the looks needn't
look." So I said "Yes;" and then I had to run over to
Mr. Snow's, where she'd left her bundle of things for her
darter Angeline's children, and that *cloak and umbrella.*
Lucy Maria had them once to dress up for a tableau in, —
a floppy silk umbrella faded out almost white. She says
'twas pea-green "forty-eight year ago." 'Tis kept shut
by a wide brass ring; and the handle of it sticks up
half a yard longer than the sticks, and is ended off with
a great ivory head with a grinning face on one side. The
cloak is puckered round her neck, and hangs straight all
the way down, with two side-holes to run her arms
through.

When Uncle Jacob found she was going, he put some
hay in the bottom behind, and our wagon-cushion for
Gus to sit in there, and put the rocking-chair-cushion
on the bench for her. She was going to wear her
squash-hood; but Lucy Maria made her borrow grandmother's bonnet, and all of 'em said she looked tiptop in
it. I guess you'd laughed if you'd seen us starting off.
First thing we did was to get her in. I wanted to stow
her bundle under the seat: but she was afraid 'twould
jolt out; and something did jolt out, — but wait till I
come to that, — and so she hung it on her off-arm.
Both her arms came through those side-holes; and, when
she got seated down, what does she do but grab hold of
that umbrella-handle, that's long enough for a fishpole,
with both hands, and hold it right up in front to steady

her! for she said the road was considerable jolty down
that way (and that's so) every time. When I took my
seat, my end of it didn't go down so low as hers did: so
you see we didn't start quite even. There isn't much
height to her, but considerable circumference and weight,
especially with all she carried and wore. I sat on a bunch
of hay. They all stood round the door, making their
parting remarks. Uncle Jacob told me to drive *slow*,
and hold him in if I possibly could! My grandmother,
to drive slow, and get back quick as I could: said she
shouldn't have one easy minute. "Be back by supper-
time!" says L. M.: "there'll be a *boy wanted* about that
time!" Matilda stuck a bunch of flowers back of his
ear, and he started off at quite a jog for him. That was
about half-past nine. And, now I've got started, I'll go
on at quite a jog myself, and write as fast as I can.
You know you said I should need to learn to write rapidly.

We drove ahead pretty fair, considering: but I say,
now, that I'd a good deal rather have a woman take care
of me when I have the measles than be taking hold of
my elbow when I'm trying to drive; and so would anybody. "Mustn't run him down hill!" "Look out!
there's something coming!" "*Now* whip up, dear!"
"*Now* hold him in, dear!" Enough to make a fellow
mad. I wished she hadn't come. I never like to ride
with a woman that goes "Cluck, cluck!" with her tongue
to make him go. What does he care for her "Cluck,
clucks"? And catching hold the reins in bad places just
where she better be letting 'em alone! I got mad, but
made out to keep in, — not in the wagon, but in myself.

We were much as two hours going on account of hav-

ing to walk him slow in the hubbiest places; for Gus's
face was too tender to bear much of a jolt. Then we
lost some time on the fowls. Had to go out of our way,
and the man wasn't at home; but the woman said she'd

tell him to catch it, — goose, — and have it ready when
we came along back.

We got to Quorm's all hunki-dori, right side up with
care! Quorm was good as a kitten (sometimes he's

awful cross), and looked grand as you please. Somebody
has given him an old soldier's coat with brass buttons.
Didn't match his trousers very well (old things), nor his
bare feet.   Poor Gus! he shook hands with him, and
tried to smile and say something; but 'twas no go.   Poor
fellow! he was pretty bad off; and his smile turned to a
groan.   They two were chums in the poor-house last
winter, when Quorm was sick and had to go there.

Quorm made Gus sit down, and looked at his face
inside and out; then off he went down to the pond
and back again, with a cloth in his hand, and something
in it with only its head sticking out.   This was a
leech.   He stooped down, and told Gus to open his
mouth (didn't let him see what was in the cloth), and
made the leech take hold of the gum where the ague-
spot was, and suck!   And in a short time Gus felt
better, and could talk some; and Quorm let him drink
out of a bottle.

Pretty soon my lady-passenger came in with the
things she'd been after in the swamp, — roots and things;
and the old fellow invited us to stay to dinner.   He
had something stewing in a little three-legged black
kettle that hung down low over the fire, — something
that smelt nice; but who knew but what 'twas wood-
chuck or muskrat?   And she said afterwards, that she
wouldn't have eaten a meal's victuals in that hovel if
she'd been starving; and Gus couldn't chew.   We
didn't know, then, we'd lost our lunch.   Hannah Jane
gave us some pie and doughnuts in a tin pail, and made
me take a roll of string, as it might come handy in case
of accident.   It did come handy, but not in any way
that she expected.

We left Quorm's about one o'clock. Angeline lived half a mile farther on. We thought we'd save our lunch till we got there, then maybe get some milk to go with it. But, when we got there, every window and door was fastened, and nobody at home but a good-sized yellow dog, — a slim, high-going dog. 'Twas a little mite of a house, standing all alone by itself in a lonesome field, and not so much as a barn in sight. She got out, and Gus got out, and we tried all the shutters (outside shutters they were), and both doors, and the cellar-door. By this time, the dog had got stirred up. She didn't know how to get her bundles inside, and I couldn't tell her. Gus said we'd better drop 'em "down chimbly." This made me think of the scuttle; and I told her, if she'd keep off the dog, I'd climb up by the water-hogshead and water-spout: so she kept him off with her umbrella, and I went up like a kite. But the scuttle was fastened inside. We didn't dare to leave them on the doorstep, for fear of some old squaw, or other old straggler, stealing them; and, if we hid them under the woodpile, how would Angeline know? I took a strip of birch-bark I found, and wrote on it with a piece of black coal out of the ashes-barrel, "Two bundles under the wood," and was going to shove it under the crack of the door; but she said, "Lor', Angeline wouldn't take any notice of a chip!" So I took my coal, and made a string of little boys taking hold hands round the writing, so as to catch the children's eyes. Something like this. No, I won't make it here: I'll put it on a piece of paper separate.

Going from our house to Quorm's, we had good luck to help us along all the way; but, going back, bad luck seemed to try to bother us all the way, and tried so hard, it broke its back. You'll see when I come to that.

No milk: so we concluded to do without. But now, what do you think? That old wagon — we thought, to be sure, they were all right under the hay somewhere: but a board had got loose and worked up, and the doughnut thing tipped over; and all we could find was one doughnut (all the rest went through); and that I gave to the lady-passenger, of course. But she divided.

I guess, if I'd let the newspaper alone, we should have

gone on very well, — all but being hungry. In a newspaper she did up her roots in I saw some advertisements, and asked her to let me cut them out with my jackknife, when we were going along level; and I expect that was when we took the wrong road. I haven't told Lucy Maria that. she makes so much fun; all the time calling out when she wants errands done, "Boy wanted!" Let her!

I was going to turn round; but Gus. said he guessed 'twould come out into the main road. for he'd been that way carting wood. Well, we rode and rode, and kept riding; tried half a dozen different roads, — some of 'em blind roads, that didn't go anywhere, and made us back out. Met several ox-teams, and inquired; but they told us so many roads we mustn't take, and we three couldn't remember alike, — one thought this, and another thought that. These woods-roads are very puzzling and confusing when you get going wrong!

At last, we came to a cleared place where there was a little small house and a whitewashed barn. The girl I brought to ride said she must have some nourishment, and wanted me to knock at the door, and ask for something either for love or for money, if nothing but a cracker; and I did.

You better guess that was a curious kind of woman. I knocked at her front-door; then went round to the back, and knocked there. Pretty soon she opened it part way, looked as if she was scared, and spoke so too: of us, I s'pose. L. M. says she should if she'd been there alone and seen us coming.

A tall, slim, sickly-looking woman she was, holding her shawl over her for fear she'd catch cold, and kept sort of behind the door.

After I'd questioned her some about the roads, I told her we'd lost our way and got hungry; and couldn't we buy something to eat, — a pie or some gingerbread?

She said she hadn't been baking much lately.

"Couldn't you let us have a loaf of bread?"

"Well, no; not very well," says she. "I don't think we've got any more on hand than our folks want for supper."

Then couldn't we have some milk? She said her pans were all set, and she didn't feel willing to break them up.   Then I thought of crackers.   "Haven't you got some crackers?"—"Wal, no; none to part with. We have to be savin' of our crackers."   Never saw such a woman!   "Wal," says I pretty spunky, "have you got any water?"

"I just emptied the pail into the teakettle," said she; "but you can draw some.   There's the well."

I guess she was beginning to get acquainted; for, when she poked the pail out, says she, "If you'd jest as lives, you can bring it back with some in it: 'tis rather a hard well for a woman."

I was a good mind to empty it out; but just for curiosity, to see if she wouldn't look a little mite ashamed, I carried it back rather over half full.

"Didn't fetch it over'n above full, did yer?" says she.

Oh, if my red hair didn't feel mad!   I laid on the whip.   "Get up!" says I; "let's be out o' this!"   A feller get's mad easier when he's hungry.   I was so hungry, that seems as if I could smell Quorm's stew just as it smelt when we were down there.

We did come out into the main road after a while; but 'twas way ahead of the gooseman's house: so we had to turn back.   They were just eating supper.   The man said he concluded we'd gone along: so he let her go again; and I'd have to help catch her.   So I told the girl I carried to ride she'd better get out and come in, and Gus too; and they did.   The woman asked us to take some supper; not earnest, but that kind of a way women ask when they know you are going to say, "No, I thank you!"   But I tell you, when that woman found out we hadn't eaten any dinner, she stepped round

lively, and brought out about every thing she had in
the house!—great big platter of cold meat and cab-
bage, turnip, and other things; then hot tea for my
pasengers. "Bully for you!" says I (to myself). I was
ashamed to eat more'n a quarter of what I wanted.
First time I ever ate turnip, cooked ones; but I ate most
a whole one, and loved it. Gus could chew some; and I
guess she thought we had good appetites. Gracious! I
should no more dared to take all I wanted to—why,
there wouldn't have been any thing left!

We had a scrabbling time, but grabbed the old goose
at last, and hurried her into the wagon: for 'twas getting
late and chilly, and I wanted to get home; for I knew
grandmother had begun by that time.

Now, what do you think? That goose got loose, and
made trouble. I'll tell you how it was. 'Twas when we
were going through the last piece of woods. Gus had
the care of her in behind; and my girl got to telling me
a story about her father killing a bear (you see we felt
pretty talkative after we'd had our tea), and I hadn't
looked behind for some time. Gus, I expect, got asleep
(he'd been kept awake a good deal nights); and, going
over a hummock or a rock, it jolted out, and the same
jolt started up Gus just time enough to see her light on
the ground. He squalled out, "Billy! hoash, hoash!"
But Longshanks he'd got going down, and couldn't make
his old legs whoa right short off; and the goose being
tied up in such a hurry, or else the string wasn't stout
enough, she worked herself clear in half a jiffy.

I hopped out, and walked along towards her softly, so
she needn't think anybody wanted any thing of her. But
she wasn't any such a goose! She stepped off fast as I

stepped toward. I almost had her once, though ; and should, if it hadn't been for Mrs. Benjamin coming along with her span. Mrs. Benjamin put out her long face, and wanted to know what those people were stopping up the way for. I said I was catching my goose ; and, if she'd wait a minute, I'd have her. The driver said, if we were shorthanded, he'd jump off and help ; but she shook her light-colored curls, and said she couldn't be hindered by no goose, and we must turn out. So I had to discharge my crew, and back up a very sideling place. She had to scrape her carriage getting by ; and I didn't care so very much, she acted so uppish !

(A lady who usually spent her summers in the vicinity of Summer-sweeting Place. She was formerly a poor girl living in the neighborhood, but married well, as people called it ; that is, she married a rich man, a man in the city, — Mr. Benjamin Calloon, a trader from " down East," who had scraped a fortune together in various ways, but who had little education or refinement, and not a jot of principle. His wife was commonly called Mrs. Benjamin, she being particular to emphasize the name in that way. Mrs. Benjamin liked to astonish her old neighbors. — S. Y. F.)

Made us good deal of trouble, though ; for goosey got farther in among the trees while we were fooling round. Gus helped some, and my lady-friend stood and flapped her apron : but 'twas a dodgy place there, and they were neither of them any thing extra for spry ; and I was glad enough when a little chap hopped out from behind the bushes. He was spry as a squirrel, and beat every thing dodging.

"Got any corn ? " says the little shaver.

"No," says I. But it came natural to put my hand

in my pocket; and there were a few kernels of corn left
of some I didn't parch the night before. I threw these
down; and, while she was pecking at them, we grabbed
her. and tied her by the ankles so tight, she couldn't but
just breathe, with that string Hannah Jane gave me.
While we were in among the trees, the horse started : I
might have known that, being headed for home. He
went a pretty good jog, and got along *quite some*, as our
Jersey feller used to say. We took chase; and little Spry
beat me running, and wasn't a bit afraid to stand right
in the middle of the road, and catch him by his bits.
Then we went back after the passengers. We came
across that chap again afterwards. And now comes the
very worst thing that happened to us: I guess you'll
laugh when you get to it.

By the time we started again, it was most dark, and
getting chilly. After we'd rode along a while, the road
went down a hill, — a long, quite steep, winding hill. This
was between two and three miles from our house. There
were woods both sides at the top, but not all the way
down; and, towards the bottom, there was a very old-look-
ing house, that stood a little back from the road on the
left-hand side. I held him in : and we were a-jogging
along all right, when he shied out at a bunch of hay in
the road (he shies out easy between daylight and dark);
and that old woman she grabbed the reins sudden,
and that turned him short off, and somehow he hit his
heels. and that set him off on a run. Oh, how he did
go! I couldn't hold him in one mite! She hollered
and jammed my arm so, she jammed the strength all
out of it!

Just before we got to the bottom, I happened to think

of a bright thought. I happened to think of steering
him up against the side of that house, so he'd have to
stop, and couldn't help himself; because I knew there
was a sudden corner to turn in the road not a great ways
ahead, where he'd pitch out the whole of us. So I
steered him off that way towards the house, well as I
could, with all my strength; and he steered off. He
isn't such a dreadful hard-bitted horse as he is apt to
shy off. Well, what do you think happened to us next
thing? Now, I guess you'll believe what I told you at
the beginning, — that we went in more than we came out!
'Twas all over in a quarter of a jiffy. From the top of the
hill to where we came to a full stop, it wasn't more'n a
minute, if 'twas that. He turned off, going lickertycut,
we holding our breaths; and, just as we got most close to
the house, that horse took a lurch to the left, and away
he went with the thills. But the wagon didn't go. The
wagon kept straight on, and went straight through the
picket-fence about a yard from where the fence joins the
house, and stopped close to the front-window with every
thing standing, — no, not quite standing; for me and my
girl we pitched forwards. I went the farthest, being easy
to go. Gus only keeled over a little, his heels sticking
up; and there he staid till I told him he was alive.

There was an old man standing at the window.
Guess he thought the wagon was bewitched, or something; for he said afterwards that he didn't see any thing
of us till we rolled by without any horse. My arms,
when I came to my feelings, were just as weak as water:
I couldn't hold on to any thing.

Course we got out, for 'twas no use sitting there; and
I went to find the horse, and they two went in. There

was a little piece of woods back of the house ; and there
I hunted and hunted. There wasn't much daylight left
then. Guess I hunted much as a quarter of an hour or
more, and then went in without him. They two were
sitting up at the fire (she'd complained of feeling
chilly), warming themselves, with that old man, — quite
a smiling, reddish, ragged old man, small sized. There
didn't seem to be anybody but himself that belonged
there. He was tending the bread. The bread stood baking before the fire, between the andirons, in a sort of tin
contrivance something like a square-cornered chaise-top.

Just after I went in, that little spry chap, the one
that helped us, came in. The old man asked him where
he'd been to, and sent him to chop some wood. Then he
asked my female assistant if she knew of anybody that
wanted a boy ; for that boy ought to have somebody to
take care of him.

" Your grandchild, I 'spose ? " says she.

" No ; no kin to me."

" How old is he ? "

" In his 'leventh year."

" Orphan ? "

" Wal — not exactly : mother's dead ; got a father."

" Good boy ? "

" Wal — smart. Tricky, though."

" Why don't his father take care of him ? "

" Wal, wal " — Then he said something to her
low, that I couldn't hear half so well as if he'd spoken
louder.

" You don't say ? "

" Yes," said the old man. " And I'm getting pretty
much past labor ; and he'll have to earn his living."

Then they had some more privacy. Says I to myself, — not out loud, — "No fair for her to be having privacy with another feller when I'm carrying her to ride!" She told him she went round considerable, and would speak about it. I told her Mr. Slade wanted a boy. Then it came into my head about his old wagon; and then I thought, "Suppose the horse had gone home, how scared they would all be!"

"I'm afraid he's gone home!" said I.

"They'll be scared e'ena'most to death!" said she.

"I'm going!" said I.

Gus said he could walk well enough; and she said there was a house part way along where she could stay all night. So he helped her carry her budgets, and took the goose in his other hand: and I put like a streak for home; for I knew grandmother had been begun ever since sunset. Running along in a place where the road slanted down towards the gutter, I saw something shining in the moonlight from under the grass, and went to look; and 'twas the pint pail that had our sausage-meat in it. Didn't see any doughnuts shining up.

Well, I kept on with my running till I got most to the house; and you'd better guess I was clear out o' breath. Thought there was considerable stir in Aunt Phebe's yard; and, when I came nearer, found the whole family dodging about there quite excited, — Uncle Jacob with a lantern, Aunt Phebe, her three girls, and Tommy. "Halloo!" says I: "who's turned you all out doors this time o' night."

"Billy, Billy! *are* you alive? — say quick!" L. M. called out.

"Live as anybody!" says I.

"Come in to your grandmother!" says Aunt Phebe.

So they dragged me in; and there stood my grandmother just as pale, and Georgiana crying out loud.

"Here he is!" they all cried out simultaneous that went in with me. You see, grandmother was expecting to have me brought home damaged on a barn-door, or something, after she knew the horse had come home in such a fix.

"Oh! how did you get home? how did you?" she cried out.

"Running, mostly," says I. I was so out of breath, I could but just speak; and some out o' breath, I tell you, by that time.

"Where's Gus?" cried one.

"And where's Mother Delight?" says another.

"And where's the *wagon?*" cried Uncle Jacob.

"The wagon?" says I; "the wagon — the wag" — And then it tickled me so, thinking where it was, that I *squelched* right out laughing; and the funny of it kept coming over me every time I set out to tell; and I couldn't stop myself, after a while, being weak, you see. First I'd begin and get a little ways, and then way I'd go again.

"Hysterics!" says grandmother: "'tis what he's been through."

"Yes, yes!" I screamed out. "'Tis! 'tis! 'tis what I went through! 'tis what all of us went through! That's it. Oh, dear! oh, dear!" And I bent myself up double, laughing; for I couldn't stand it.

"I'm afraid there's something out of joint," says she.

"Yes, yes!" says I; "so there is, — there's a picket-

5

fence out of joint!" And away I went again. Aunt
Phebe said to me, " William Henry, stop! Your grandmother'll be sick abed." That cross way got me sober;
and I went ahead, and told.

I don't expect ever to hear the last of it. They are
all the time joking me about not stopping for trifles;
and putting things through ; and taking girls out to ride,
and making 'em walk home, — Lucy Maria most of any.
But I mean to find some way to plague her. But Lucy
Maria is hard to plague, because she'd just as lives
laugh at herself as anybody. There's a great deal more
to tell. I've skipped ever so many things! but no matter. If you hear of any thing *wanted* in my line, — you
know, — send a feller word. My folks think I shall have
to go into some retail store, where they give considerable pay to begin with : but I'd a good deal rather get
into one of those great wholesale places as we talked
about, and do with less, and work my way up; and then
I shall be somewhere. But father's hard up for cash
just now, — the fire in the woods, you know, — and he
never did have very much. But that great fire in the
woods — that hurt him. 'Twas pretty tough seeing all
that corded wood go! Please write soon.

From your friend,

WILLIAM HENRY CARVER.

Both Mr. Carver and Uncle Jacob had met with losses —
severe losses for them — from a great fire, which not only over-
ran acres of standing-wood, but burnt up a large quantity of
cut and corded. They were not men who would allow themselves to be made unhappy by money-losses : still, as Uncle
Jacob said, it was no use denying he wished the fire had gone

out before it reached their lots, they needed the wood-money so much to pay debts with, and to lay out in various ways.

Grandmother lamented that it should have happened just when Billy wanted a few hundred dollars to start him in the world. Uncle Jacob said fires generally did happen at the wrong time. Mr. Carver said he did not regret it very much on that account, and quoted a saying of old Squire Somebody, that five hundred dollars was better to give a young fellow than five thousand, and five dollars than five hundred, and five cents than five dollars.

The question of what should be done with William Henry was pretty thoroughly discussed about that time by both families; or rather, I should say, the question of what William Henry should do with himself. It seemed to be the general opinion that he should follow his own inclinations, after being sure in his own mind what those inclinations were. Mr. Carver had been at great pains to teach his boy to think. If William Henry expressed an opinion, " Show your reason," Mr. Carver would say : " let us know why you think so." In talking with me one day, he said, " Mr. Fry, I want the boy to learn to judge for himself, to decide for himself, and, above all, to respect himself; " not meaning that Billy ought to set up for a wiseacre, — wise in his own conceit, — but only that, before making up his mind on any subject, he should study into that subject, and not depend on others doing it for him.

I think my Summer-sweeting friends had some very sensible ideas about bringing up children. Mr. Carver seemed to have thought a good deal on the subject, as indeed he had on many other subjects. " Teach a boy," he observed to me one day, " to be afraid, not of what the world will think of him, but of what he will think of himself. If he can look inside of himself all alone at night, and say that he approves of himself, it is pretty certain he has done right: else what is the use of a conscience?" In the other family it was just the same. Aunt Phebe told me, that, when her girls were little, she used to say to them sometimes at night, — suppose, for instance, it was Lucy Maria, — she would say, "There's a little girl in this house named Lucy Maria: you know more about her than anybody. Now, think back, and see how you like Lucy Maria."

A Letter from Mr. Fry to his Sister.

MY DEAR SISTER, —

Sorry you don't feel equal to joining us at "Coot Pint;" but of course our life there will not have much regularity, and could hardly, with propriety, be recommended to an invalid. Some time next month, when Dorry comes, we shall adjourn there. The shanty is engaged for a week. It is at that place I wrote you about once, — that high cliff, where the trees come down so near the edge, that, if you had a pole and line adequate to the occasion, you might sit in the woods, and catch cunners. How it does make my mouth water thinking of those cunners that we are going to have ! — brown, crisp, hard, fried right out of the sea.

We've just been sitting on the piazza, discussing our plans, and also discussing the main subject; namely, Billy and his business, — quite an entertaining conversation, which was suddenly put a stop to by a *duel*, as will be seen when you get so far. As little (?) Silas is as yet undecided what business to choose, or, as he says in his letter. is "looking about to see which way to jump," I'll be kind enough to put down some of the talk without any extra charge.

"Before making up your mind." said Mr. Carver, speaking of choosing an occupation, " it is well to first look on the dark side, to think over all the disadvantages, all the unpleasant things, about the business you have in view. For instance, if you incline to be a doctor, don't let your mind dwell on driving up to the door in a nice gig, stepping in with your little trunk to stay fifteen minutes, and get two dollars for it! Dr. Sweetser told me this once about himself: It had been a very sickly season. Most of his patients lived miles away, and in different directions; and he had been hard at work for weeks, with scarcely a night's sleep; was all worn out; couldn't sleep even when he had the chance, for the dangerous cases kept him awake, thinking and worrying, and consulting his books. One hot afternoon, he was riding home from a little village, or bunch of houses, ten miles off; and, in going up a piece of rising ground. he leaned back in his chaise. and let the reins drop, just because he felt too much exhausted to sit up straight and hold on to them. There happened to be an old man setting fence alongside the road; and this old man looked up to him as he rode past, and said to him in a drawling way, 'Leetle too easy life, doctor; leetle too easy.'"

"The old man looked on the bright side," I remarked.

"'Tis easy enough to look on other folks's bright side," said Aunt Phebe.

"Billy couldn't be a doctor if he wanted to," said Hannah Jane.

"That's so!" said Billy; "without I find a money-bush growing up in the pastures."

"As to that," said Mr. Carver, "a person, as a general rule, — there may be exceptions, — can be any thing he wants to, if he *wants to hard enough*, and is willing to work hard enough. But let's stick to the main point;

which is, that every employment has its unfavorable side,
—a lawyer, for instance. Just think of a lawyer, who
has, perhaps, a man's whole fortune, perhaps a man's
life, depending on his exertions, his skill, his brain-
power! — what anxious days and nights he must have!"

"And they'd just as lives be on the wrong side as the
right!" said Aunt Phebe. "They have to go according
to where the pay comes from!"

"Ministers have the easiest time," said Matilda:
"they only work one day in the week."

"When do you think they write their sermons?"
asked L. M.

"Oh! that doesn't take but little while."

"But they have to get their ideas from somewhere," I
suggested.

"They have those all in their heads; don't they?"
asked Matilda.

"I've heard 'twas pretty hard work to think out a sermon," said I.

"And there's a whole meeting-house full of folks to
preach to, you know," said Mr. Carver, — "learned folks,
stupid folks, bright folks, foolish folks, fault-finding folks;
and one sermon has to suit all of them. Now, I think
ministers have a hard time. Then there is teaching:
that seems an easy life to people who sit in the windows, and see the schoolmaster go back and forth with
his good clothes on. 'Only five or six hours a day, and
all that pay!' they say; not thinking of all the time and
money it took to fit the man to be a teacher.

"Or the worriments he has!" cried Aunt Phebe.
"From what I've had to manage of my own, I know
what it must be to manage forty or fifty, no two alike."

"Take the trades," said Mr. Carver: "the carpenter and the blacksmith hammer and pound their lives away; painters breathe poisoned air; farmers are liable to droughts, floods, frosts, and dull markets. Remember, we are looking, now, on the dark side. I don't talk in this way to discourage our young man. I wouldn't run away from difficulties: I would fight them. But you have to see them, or else you can't. I want Billy to think of the bad things before making up his mind, but *never afterwards.*"

"He must be thinking," said Aunt Phebe, "which of all these bad things he can get along with the best."

"And, whatever he decides upon," said Lucy Maria, "stick to it.

"Yes, that's it!" said Mr. Carver. "Young men ought to know sure, at the beginning, just what they're aiming at, — whether to paint pictures, or be poets, or great generals, or learned scholars, or merchants, or machinists, or any thing else. Set up their mark, and keep aiming at it."

"Now, let's see which Billy wants to be!" cried L. M. "Do you want to be a poet?"

No: Billy thought he didn't care to be a poet.

"Do you want to be a learned man, — one of the kind, that when they're on the track of an idea, or of some unknown creature, will give up dinner and supper for the sake of it?"

"Not by a long chalk!" cried Billy.

"I know!" said Matilda, "he wants to be rich, and live in that grand house he wrote about once when he was a little boy, — with gilt books, and blue easy-chairs, and silver dishes!"

"So I do!" cried Billy. "I want a good large house, and full of every thing nice, and money in the bank just when I'm a mind to send for it!"

"Sure of this, are you?" asked his father. "Sure?"

"Yes," said Billy, "sure!"

"Have you looked on the dark side?"

"Isn't any dark side to being rich!"

"A rich man told me once," I remarked here, "that he used to lie awake night after night, fretting about his losses; worrying for fear banks would fail, or stocks would fall. And, moreover, he said he was found fault with everlastingly. Everybody expected him to give. His poor relations thought he ought to support them; and the more favors he did, the more curses he got. At last, he gave away the biggest part of his money to be rid of the care of it; bought a little place and sat down, with a snug library about him, and a fiddle, to take comfort."

Then Lucy Maria told about a lady her cousin Myra knew, who inherited a large quantity of silver-ware, — solid silver. The house was twice broken into; and, after a good many nights of lying awake, she hired a watchman. Then she lay awake to watch the watchman; and at last packed up the silver, and sent it to the bank; and there it staid the rest of her life.

"Well, Billy," asked Mr. Carver, "are you willing to run the risk of having to take care of a hundred thousand dollars?"

"That's just about what I am willing to do!" said Billy, "and more too!"

"Then one thing is settled: you know what you want. Next question is, How will you get it? in what business? That question is settled too, I suppose?"

"Oh, yes!" said Billy. "Mr. Fry and I have talked it all over; and I'm going to be a clerk in some great wholesale firm. Begin low, and keep going up."

We then proceeded to discuss the trials and liabilities of business-men; but, in the midst of our conversation, Tommy came running in all out of breath (this may as well go in alongside of our important discussion, since trifles, and matters of consequence, do come alongside each other in life). — Tommy came running, panting, and in the very last stages of excitement, to say that "Benny Joyce's new rooster's fighting with Billy's rooster; and Billy's rooster's down; and Benny Joyce's new rooster's on top of Billy's rooster, and a-tearing Billy's rooster all to pieces!"

"Don't believe it!" cried Billy; and away he ran to see, and we after him; for it was a very interesting case. Billy's old Yellow-Legs has long been the champion fighter of the neighborhood. A handsome creature too; very tall, and of immense strength; and, according to Georgiana and Tommy, he can say "Cock-a-doodle-doo" plainer than any fowl about here.

We all ran to see, and found Tommy's story painfully true. Yellow-Legs was down! Benny Joyce's new rooster mauled him, as he himself had often mauled others; then flew to the fence-post, and there crowed as aggravating a crow as could possibly be crowed! Yellow-Legs has crawled under the currant-bushes, whence no amount of coaxing can start him.

Two days later. — I know you will be anxious to hear from our *fallen hero*. Fallen indeed! Dead and gone; perished from "pure, pure grief." This morning he was still alive, and able to stand; but nothing we could do or say would draw him from his hiding-place. The interest became intense. We gathered about him; we threw down corn; we called "Cup, cup, cup!" in the most beseeching and tender accents. We even brought one of his old enemies before him. But all in vain. He would walk now and then a little way behind the bushes; but he never showed his head outside again. Though often supplied with food, he would take but a kernel; grew weaker each hour; and so pined away. To-day, at noon, he stretched himself upon the ground, taking no notice of any one but Billy, and of him only by a feeble motion of the wing; and, in the course of the afternoon, breathed his last breath. The coroner's jury decided that mortification had taken place. Lucy Maria wrote an epitaph, which I would send if I had a copy. Uncle Jacob said he could recall the names of some public men, politicians, for whose tombstones, substituting "man" for "fowl," the same lines might do. Mentioned one in particular, who was known to have pined away and died after being beaten by the rival candidate.

This event gives us a text for conversation, as many an event has done before.

"An awful warning against jealousy!" L. M. remarked to Billy. "Now, when you're a clerk, if some other clerk keeps going up faster than you do, don't crawl under your office-stool and refuse to eat."

"Guess no danger!" said Billy.

Billy continues to cut the "Wants" out of the advertising columns, though knowing it can amount to nothing at present. Those columns have a fascination for him. The girls declare, that, whenever they take a newspaper to put over a loaf of any thing in the oven, the heat goes right through the slits. His pockets are full of these little printed slips; and grandmother says she even finds them in his boots, just as she used to "chrysalises" once. Says 'twas always so with Billy, — when he went in, he went in all over. If 'twere turtles, the backyard was full of turtles, and she had to keep a broom in the entry to sweep them back; if 'twere rats, he'd sit hours by a rat-hole with his bow and arrow; if 'twere picking up old iron, he would tip over all the ash-barrels to look for nails; and, in kite-time, there'd be paste on every door-latch all over the house. Aunt Phebe said she remembered kite-time, and how she had to hide her newspapers to get the reading of them.

"A letter from Dorry!" Billy is shouting; and I will close at once.   Always your brother,

S. Y. FRY.

Mr. Fry to his Sister.

. . . Billy and Bobby Short are making great preparations. Dorry writes that he wants to bring his sister Maggie; says she is just crazy to come and go with us. Our *good time coming* is not very far distant now; and our talk is divided between plans for that, and Billy's plans about beginning at the bottom, and keeping going up. Did you ever hear of *illustrated* conversations? We have them here sometimes, *illustrated* on the spot by our resident female artiste, Lucy Maria. I'll give you one that was partially illustrated.

"It is one thing to begin at the bottom," said Mr. Carver, "and another thing to *keep going up:* isn't that so, Mr. Fry?"

"As far as my observation goes, it is," I answered. "Even in the small establishment in D——, where I am book-keeper, we have quite an experience in boys; and it is suprising how quickly the character of each is found out. I've heard the partners talking about *the new boy* many's the time."

"'How's the new boy?' Various answers are given. 'New boy? — *shirky*, decidedly *shirky;*' or, 'Talks too much;' or, 'Lazy;' or, 'Sly.' 'Not to be depended upon.' 'Too scared of a little extra work.' 'Always behind-hand.' 'Unfaithful.' 'Deceitful.' Of course, the answers sometimes run the other way. Our best hand, when he first came there, was about as ungainly a chap as you commonly see; but it wasn't long before I heard one partner say to the other, 'We must hold on to that fellow: he's one of the kind you can depend on.' It is really astonishing in how little while a boy's air and manner will reveal his character without his having the least idea of it. 'Ten minutes' talk, and a good long look, is enough to tell by,' I heard a great merchant say once. There are, of course, exceptions to this rule."

"I suppose," said Mr. Carver, "that Billy still means to take his chance."

"Yes," said Billy very decidedly, "I do. I mean to take my chance:" then added in a lower voice to me, "And I know myself just what I mean to do when I get there; but no use telling everybody."

"Well," said his father, "if your mind is made up, I shall only say this, that, when the unpleasant things begin to show themselves, it won't do to be thinking that some other business might be easier, or might bring in money sooner."

"Like that *cow* you mentioned," said Lucy Maria; "always looking over the fence."

"No," said Uncle Jacob: "you've got to keep your own side the fence, and make the best milk you can with the feed that's given you."

"It's a wonder," I remarked, "that, among other things, we've never thought of William Henry being president! There's that place open, so juvenile books say, to every boy in the nation. I hardly ever heard a speaker address a lot of boys that he didn't tell them there was a chance for any one of them to be president."

"When I'm president," said Billy, "guess I shall feel like my other cow, — jumping over the moon."

Mr. Carver remarked, that, in political life, some poor feeble men seemed to be always trying to jump over the moon.

"But how in the world is Billy going to pay his way in the city?" asked Hannah Jane, who had been pondering, meantime, on the main question.

"As I have said before," replied Mr. Carver, "a person can do whatever he wants to if he wants to *enough*. If a boy hasn't it in him to get over difficulties, he hasn't it in him to make a business-man."

"I wish Billy could feel like taking up with something nearer home," said grandmother. "We have so little time to stay in this world, seems if we ought to keep together."

"Oh! Billy will come back," said Lucy Maria, — "come back, and build that great house in one of our pastures."

"If Starry Banner would let him, he might in *Long*," said Matilda.

"'Course I shall keep making visits," said Billy.

"How much money will it take?" asked Aunt Phebe. "Let us make some kind of a reckoning."

"By rooming with another feller," said Billy, "Mr. Fry says I can get a place to sleep in for a dollar a week."

"And his board," said I, "could be got for four dollars a week, or for three if he went without his suppers."

"Could you do that?" Matilda asked him.

"I guess not," said Billy faintly.

"Then there are other expenses," said Mr. Carver, — "washing, fires in cold weather, lights, a lecture now and then, or an evening's entertainment, besides clothes and travelling-expenses. I don't think 'twould be safe to call the whole a cent less than seven dollars a week: that's three hundred and fifty a year. Better say four hundred, as expenses are sure to overrun."

"He'll have to sail pretty close to the wind," said Uncle Jacob, "to do it on that; but let it go four hundred."

"He'll get a hundred the first year," said I, "and have a hundred added every year if he *keeps going up*. We'll allow, therefore, for expenses, three hundred the first year, two the second, and one the third, — six hundred dollars."

"I'll agree to find two hundred of it," said Mr. Carver; "and, when the Corry-pond Lot sells, two hundred more. But we don't know when that will happen."

"I wouldn't wait!" cried Lucy Maria. "I'd begin to pile up the money to-morrow!"

"How?" asked Billy.

"Oh! go to work, and earn. Work between schools, work vacations, work evenings. — pick huckleberries, pitch hay, shovel gravel, peddle essences, go round getting subscribers to something, or grinding something. I wouldn't rest till I got where I wanted to be! Don't you know about Cæsar, — that great Cæsar you read about in history?"

"Well, what about Cesar?" Billy asked.

"When he was bound off to conquer a city, and came to a river, he swam it: never waited for a bridge to be built, but swam it."

This remark started a fresh discussion, during which L. M. took up a pencil, and began drawing something on the fly-leaf of an old spelling-book; and, when her picture was done, she cut it out, and gave it to Billy.

It represented a furious stream, in the middle of which was a crowned warrior swimming across with might and main. Away ahead in the distance were pictured out the towers and temples of the city he was bound to conquer.

"What's that on his head?" asked somebody.

"That's his crown: don't you see the peaks?"

"What's he going to do with a fishing-pole?" asked Billy.

"That isn't a fishing-pole: that's his spear."

"And what is that on his face? — something to protect it?" I asked.

"Dear me!" said L. M.: "can't you tell a Roman nose?"

"What's that string coming out of his mouth?" asked Georgie.

"Follow it up, and see."

Matilda followed the lead-pencil mark from Cæsar's mouth to the top of the paper, where it ended in these words : " Never wait for a bridge."

While we were laughing, and making our observations, the artist was at work on another drawing, which she presented to Billy as a companion-picture.

Here was a stream also, on the bank of which sat a miserable, disconsolate-looking man, with folded arms and with ragged clothes. Over the river were people

digging; and there was a great placard up : " Gold Mines!" A little imp of a boy, with a grinning face, was asking the man, " What are you waiting for? " And from the man's mouth came these words : " For the stream to run past."

" Here, Billy," said Lucy Maria : " I'll make you a present of these pictures. Pin them under your looking-glass, where you can see them every time you brush your hair."

"I shall see them pretty often then!" cried Billy.

The young gentleman's "upper growth," as he calls it, still continues troublesome; not so much on account of its color, which has greatly improved, as of three separate individual locks on the back of his head, near the top, which insist on "standing up to look over." He came home the other day with a bottle of bear's-oil, which had a most ferocious-looking beast on the label. The contents were very pink and innocent-looking. "But maybe," said Billy, "they'll be scared of the *bear!*"

Billy runs up tall. Uncle Jacob tells grandmother she must have her doorways cut higher, or they'll be smashed in. The proposition has also been made of putting irons on his head to keep it down, — flatirons. But Billy don't think his brain needs any flattening; says his thoughts are flat enough now.

I start to-morrow for East M—— to make Josephine a visit, but shall return time enough to go to Coot Pint with the rest. Expect, if you will, some very interesting letters from there. I should enjoy the good times more thoroughly if you and yours could enjoy them with us and ours. The *lover*, Wilson Bryant, will be there for a day or two. Glad of that; for next to being a happy lover is the sight of one.

Affectionately your brother,

SILAS.

I remember that the spells of talk, as grandmother used to call them, used to occur pretty often about that time. It was to be expected that L. M. would have her fun about Billy's grand house, speaking for its best front-

6

chamber, and all that sort of thing. Still she was as anxious as anybody that he should carry out his plans, and engaged to find him in shirts all the while he was *keeping going up*, till he got to the top, when, of course, he would order them from Paris.

Hannah Jane was the only one who spoke discouragingly; though I could plainly see, that, to grandmother, sending Billy into the wicked, swarming city, appeared almost like dropping him into the bottomless pit. These thoughts, however, were, for the most part, kept to herself; probably because she had so long been used to having her anxieties treated lightly, and to being in a very small minority. It is my opinion, that, if there were as many grandmothers in a family as there are grandchildren, we should have very different doings.

Our grandmother said little; but I observed that the anxious look settled itself more deeply into those three little perpendicular furrows between the eyebrows, and that her pale blue eyes were often fixed mournfully upon her grandson, as if he were slipping from her sight forever.

She called me aside one day, after the grand subject had been upon the carpet. I think grandmother felt me to be her friend and ally; perhaps because I sympathized with her somewhat, and did not always begin to smile when she began to worry, like most of the others.

"Mr. Fry," said she (and her eyes grew moist), "if you think there's any danger of Billy's going without his supper, I'd rather — sell my gold beads."

I stooped to brush the dust off my gaiters, — for on no account would I have had the dear woman see the smile that would come, — then cleared my throat, and assured her, that in the city, where people dined late, very late, it was no uncommon thing for them to go without suppers; and that doctors said this was a very healthy plan. Informed her, also, that some young clerks only paid for breakfast and dinner, and depended for suppers on what their folks sent them with their clean clothes.

I couldn't have done a better thing. Her face brightened at the thought of mending and airing Billy's clothes. And he would not, then, be out of reach of her cooking-stove! Pleasing thought! Her boy had seemed slipping away from her, the outside world swallowing him up like a sea; but she could still throw over cookies, jumbles, and doughnuts, with a well-grounded hope that he would hold on by them!

Hannah Jane, as grandmother used to say, always carried her mind with her, and, whenever a plan was proposed, began at once to think up all the difficulties.

"Billy," said she one day. "if I were you, I would get a place in some retail store about here, after I'd done going to school; then you'll have money coming in right away, and can be at home to be taken care of in sickness. 'Twill be up-hill work earning money between schools. I don't know of any thing you can do to raise money, without 'tis raising fowl, or going round selling lozenges, or digging flagroot, or some such thing. I don't believe you can do it; and then, if you do do it, and do get a place to suit you (which isn't sure), they say young clerks have to put up with every thing, and get next to nothing for it. And then, when you do get a foothold, suppose the firm should fail; or suppose hard times make them have to throw you over; or suppose you stuck by, and 'twasn't in you to do business after all!"

"'Spose your uncle was your aunt!" cried Billy.

"When I was a young man, and went a-courting," said Uncle Jacob. — "Now, what you all laughing at? Don't you 'spose I went a-courting once?"

"See mother blushing!" cried the girls.

"What you want to blush for, mother?" asked Uncle Jacob.

"Don't know, I'm sure." said Aunt Phebe.   "I have never had any reason to blush for that young man!"

"Good for you!" cried Billy.

"Yes," thought I: "it is good for you, and you little know how good.   Many's the wife and mother and sister would be glad to say what you've said!"

"Pay attention!" said Uncle Jacob.   "Now, I've got to begin again.   One time, when I went a-courting, — she lived in a kind of lonesome valley, you know, three or four miles from everywhere," —

"Yes, I know," said L. M., — "where Aunt Myra lives now."

"But 'tisn't very lonesome there now," said Matilda.

"Come! whose telling this story?" cried Billy.

"Oh, well! — if you don't want to hear," said Uncle Jacob, taking his hat.

"Oh, we do! we do!" cried the girls.   "Sit down. Go on, dear Father Jacob, you lovely Daddy Carver! We'll be like the dead hours o' night!"

"Now, how far had I got?" he asked, sitting down again.

"To three or four miles from everywhere!" cried L. M. promptly.

"Why, no; I hadn't got there: I'd only started."

"You hadn't quite started," said Matilda; "but we'll play you had."

"There wasn't much play about it," said Uncle Jacob.
"I started one afternoon, one cold afternoon in the win-
ter-time, up to Warren's Valley. Went that day because there'd been a heavy fall of snow and we couldn't
work."

"Complimentary, very!" said L. M., just above her
breath.

"I was poor, and was saving up money for a particular purpose, — a very particular purpose. She understood all about it. There hadn't been such a fall of
snow for some years; and 'twas worse her way, being

in a valley. I got on pretty considerable well for half a
mile or so; but beyond that there hadn't been a single
spade set to dig a track. The wind blew so, digging
tracks wasn't of much use. Dreadful sharp wind! The
men that had been trying to dig told me the roads were
piled way up over the fences, and that in the valley
'twould be over my head. I have thought of that day
many and many a time since. Had my doubts about
getting there; but told the men I'd go as far as I could,
anyway. 'Time enough to turn back,' says I, 'when I
can't get any farther!'"

"That's what I say," said Lucy Maria, "when they
tell me the walking isn't fit for a woman. I start; and,
when I come to a bad place, I *kite* right across on the
tip-ends of my toes before the walking knows I'm there!
Most always get there when they say I can't."

"'Tis wonderful," said Aunt Phebe, "how ways are
provided sometimes, when you'd think 'twould be a thing
impossible!" Uncle Jacob glanced towards his hat.

"Wasn't it? — I should think — how? what did you
do when 'twas over your head?" cried Lucy Maria, hur-
rying to put in a question.

"In some places I found chances to turn out, and go
across the fields: sometimes I climbed over a hill. In
one piece of woods, I swung along by the boughs: sometimes I walked across a pond."

"Dangerous thing!" observed grandmother.

"I know it," said Uncle Jacob. "The ice wasn't
above two feet thick; but I never broke through it!"

"It is to be hoped," I remarked, "that your girl was
glad to see you."

"She knows best," he answered.

"You don't expect me to remember so long ago," said Aunt Phebe. "Besides, 'twas a busy time o' day with us, — supper getting, fritters frying, milk-pails coming in."

"Caught, caught!" cried the girls. "If you don't remember, how do you know what was going on ?"

"Did you see him coming ?" asked Billy.

"Oh, yes!" said Uncle Jacob. "She stood in the doorway, watching out."

"Oh! I only went there to " —

"To let the cat in," suggested L. M.

"When you saw her standing there, wasn't you glad ?" asked Matilda.

"What a silly question!" said Billy. "Course he was!"

"How do you know?" cried Matilda. "Are you glad when you go to see Maggie ?"

"Course I am!" said Billy. "But I don't ever go."

"Mebby you'd like to!"

"Course I would. You won't ever have to stand in the doorway after a snow-storm to watch for Sto. Thompson. His boots are too thin: his hands would be cold."

"Now stop quarrelling, you two," said Lucy Maria, adding a few more scratches to something she was at work on. "There! I wonder if those are good likenesses ?"

It was a sketch representing a lonely valley, where stood a house half buried in something which the artist declared to be snow. A stalwart youth was staggering through the drifts; and in the doorway of the house stood a smiling maiden with outstretched arms. His arms were outstretched also. The smile — not to say grin — on each face was very expressive.

There were other small sketches, one of which represented a bold, defiant traveller, being expostulated with
by track-diggers, who were in various beseeching and
warning attitudes.   Another showed the same traveller
swinging along by the boughs.   In the third, his head
only was visible above the snow; while the wild winds
were tossing his hair, and saying to him, so she said,
" things unutterable."

"Not a bit unutterable!" cried Uncle Jacob.   "They
were telling me to go ahead.   And you may make just
as much fun as you're a mind to; but that day's work
was a lesson to me ever after.   Don't know how many
times, when taking hold of a desperate job, I've said to
myself, 'Begin, start!   Time enough to turn back when
you *can't* get any farther!'"

L. M. immediately drew a lead-pencil mark from the mouth of the traveller standing among track-diggers; which mark ended in the above motto.   The pictures were then formally presented to William Henry, to be pinned up with Cæsar and the other.

I am sure of one thing; which is, that, in giving so many of our conversations, I am leaving out too much of our every-day life.   Still, having owned up at the beginning to being incapable of doing this thing properly, I shall take unto myself no blame.

Bobby Short staid all summer, "and was really a help," Uncle Jacob said, — "handy to fetch and carry; a good-natured fellow."   Bobby would take any amount of showing how and good advice with a smiling face; which is high praise to give young people, or old people either. We couldn't help liking him; lively, quick-witted, always ready for a good time, or to do chores, or to be dressed up as old woman, monkey, young bride, dandy, elephant, or angel; and a jolly good laugher.   Lucy Maria said the *tickles* broke out all over him; and the *tickles*, the way he had them, were catching.   Just one look at his face when they were on him strong was enough to set you a-going.   They often set him a-going. "Bobby Short's *gone off!*" "Bobby Short's collapsed himself!" were frequent exclamations, when, in some violent paroxysm, he tumbled down in a heap, and rolled over.   His cheeks were as chubby as ever, his face as round, his eyes as black, his teeth as white.   I forget whether it was cocoanut, or punkin-seed meat, that Billy likened them to in one of his school-letters.

But, for all he was so lively, I never once saw him go

beyond bounds. Some lively boys are always putting
themselves forward; don't know where to stop. I've
found out that there's a good deal to choose between boys.
I belonged to that species once myself, but never thought,
then, that it made much difference to people what sort
of a boy I was: knew my folks had to scold sometimes;
but so it did have to rain sometimes, and blow sometimes. It didn't occur to me that we fellows had any
thing to do with folks taking comfort, or not taking
comfort. But, during my summer at the Farm, I often
thought how much our two boys helped along, not only
in the liveliness of whatever was going on, but in the
smoothness of it.

Now, though I've dwelt in Boyland myself, and know
just how the small sizes feel, and the large sizes, and
the half-sized, and the sufferings peculiar to each, and all
about their being found fault with and misunderstood,
and hustled out of the way, — oh my! don't I know ! —
still I must confess that there are boys who may be, in
truth, called nuisances. I have been on pleasure-par-
ties where the edge of the pleasure, as you might say,
was completely taken off by our having to grit our teeth
inwardly at some conceited, impudent fellows, who acted
as if they knew more than any of the older people
there.

Our two boys were not kept down at all. They were
talked with, consulted with, joked with. I've heard
Aunt Phebe say, that, if a boy had any gumption, he'd
know better than to make a fool of himself.

Bobby Short's mother particularly requested that he
should not be treated in any respect like company, but
should be scolded at just the same as if he belonged

there. It was a standing question at Aunt Phebe's whether Bobby Short had taken scoldings enough to be considered as one of the family; and he, on his part, was desirous of taking the whole quantity necessary to constitute him a member. Uncle Jacob liked to have him about the garden, because he had a real taste for such work. Billy, Matilda said, didn't know a radish from a carnation-pink, and liked tiger-lilies better than any other flower. But Bobby Short hoed her flower-garden, and set out slips, and never went into the woods without bringing home some pretty green thing or other.

There was one branch of farming, however, which even Billy went into heart and hand; namely, killing weeds. It was really inspiring to hear Uncle Jacob calling his forces together, and to see them marching off, weapons in hand, to meet the common enemy, four strong, — Uncle Jacob (captain), Bobby Short and Billy (privates), and Tommy (small private), with a hoe, as he expressed it, "of his own size."

I remember Uncle Jacob saying one day, very solemnly, "Friends, my family is larger than I can afford to keep. I grudge them their victuals; and some of them must be made way with." We soon found he meant *weeds*, which were devouring what the beans ought to have; though Aunt Phebe said she didn't know but weeds had the best right to the ground.

There is such a large pile of letters to choose from, and all so interesting (though some be my own), that it is a hard matter to select. Perhaps these about our camping out are as good as any. I shall put them in just as they come, small talk and all. Juliana liked her letters done that way; and I have observed that what pleases one is sure to please a great many.

Mr. Fry to his Sister.

DEAR JULIANA, —

If you received the two letters from Josephine's, you will not be surprised to hear that I am writing from a high cliff overlooking the sea, and have more air to breathe than I know what to do with. I'm craving, I am! I want to breathe it all in! The trees come close to the cliff, so that you can have woods-air and sea-air mixed. We chose this place because it is so handy to cunners. We like cunners for neighbors! Run down the bank, or slide down, jump into a dory, paddle off a few yards, and you can almost catch them in your hands.

We came to-day. Hope we shall have as good a time up here as we did talking it over and getting ready. Mr. Gossam was loath to spare Billy.

[I interrupt myself here to make an explanation. Billy told Lucy Maria one day that he was willing enough to swim across the river, like Cæsar (meaning the river of no money), but didn't know exactly where to make a dive first.

"Willing to do any thing?" she asked him.

"Course I am!"

"Mind, I say any thing."

"And I say any thing."

"Well," said L. M., "Mr. Snow wants somebody to help cart sand. There's a place to make a dive!"

Don't know as Billy would have made a dive in just that spot; only that he felt *stumped* to do it, as the boys say. Mr. Snow offered him twenty cents an hour;

and he took hold and worked away with a will.   And it
happened, that, while he was at work, Mr. Gossam rode
by.   Mr. Gossam kept the grocery-store just beyond
N'emiah's corner.   He stopped his horse, and said to
Billy, —

"Now, ye don't say yer doin' that 'cause ye love to."

"No, *sir!*" said Billy.   "For pay."

"Ye take hold mighty handy.   Don't ye want to hire
yerself out for pay, evenin's and Saturdays and vacations, to tend store ?"

That was the beginning of it.   Mr. Gossam made a
pretty good offer, and Billy took him up.

Now goes on the letter.]

He (Mr. Gossam) remarked to Mr. Carver the other
day, "Now, Mr. Carver, I don't mean to say but it's jest
possible that 'ere boy o' yourn may be beat as to bein'
slick in his manners, and tonguey; and I have seen
chaps that dodged about rarther more spryer, and could
ketch hold o' yer meanin' in less time.   But I tell ye
what: he's a young man ye can put yer finger on !   Ye
can know what to depend upon.   And another thing:
he isn't etarnally scared to death for fear he shall do
too much !"

Mr. Gossam offers him good wages if he'll stay there
all the time ; but Billy has something else in view.

What he has in view just this minute is *cunnering*.
Oh, but we've made a jolly beginning !   I must tell you
all about it.   Grandmother and Mr. Carver mean to
come up for a day at a time, but not to sleep.   They
two and Gus staid at home to take care of things and
shut the barn-door.   The shanty is engaged for a week.

There's a cook-stove in it, and a long table fastened to the floor, — it runs nearly the whole length, — and some coarse dishes. In a loft overhead are bunks filled with hay. Stairs come down from this loft right into the room. We've brought plenty of bedquilts. Ladies lodge above; we below, — on the table, benches, or floor: either will do with hay enough. The plan is to catch cod, cunners, and mackerel, and fry or chowder 'em right out of the water; that is, eat them as nearly alive as possible. I read the other day of some savage anti-cookery tribe who eat them entirely alive.

We brought "light victuals" enough to last: at any rate, Hannah Jane says there's to be nothing cooked in that line except a few cream-o'-tartar biscuits when the bread gives out, or a huckleberry-cake. Huckleberries can be had for the picking close by. I don't know what the bread is made of if it doesn't give out!

As you may imagine, we had lively times this morning getting ready and riding up. Dorry arrived night before last, bringing his sister, his gun, and his fishing-tackle; also a large amount of eatables, — such as Bologna sausage, boiled ham, confectionery, and various kinds of baker's trash. Also a basket of peaches, which "ought to be eaten right away," and were. Don't you think there's a double satisfaction in eating fruit as one may say *on its own account?* There's an absence of selfishness.

Dorry has altered some in his looks. He's a tall fellow for eighteen; slenderer than Billy, with rather high shoulders, square, and very movable, — expressive shoulders: Billy's are sloping. His (Dorry's) nose stands out in plain sight. He says, if he is ever hung for his beauty,

'twill be by his nose! But I like it: it is well-shaped,
and shows character. Tommy says he can move it up
and down, and move his ears too. Very likely. I should
like you to see Dorry. He has blue eyes and dark hair.
Such a comical face as he can put on! An awful hec-
torer, the girls say! I like to see the three boys together
tramping off, their arms over each other's shoulders.
Sometimes Tommy hitches himself alongside Bobby
Short; and then they make a pair of stairs.

Dorry can only be from home a week; and it seems as
if the fellow wanted to do every thing in a minute, and
as if he did almost, he's so quick-motioned. "Nine
years old, and going on ten," he says is his age; and he
acts just about that. His face can put on such an innocent look in the midst of roguery, you'd think, to see it,
he was just out of a prayer-meeting; and he has at such
times a way of drawing down his nose and chin that is
sure to set Bobby Short into convulsions. They make
racket enough, those three together! Dorry's laugh
doesn't break out in tickles, like Bobby Short's: it roars
out like a cataract. Billy's, I might say, gulps out like
water out of a bottle; perhaps I should rather say wine.

Dorry and Maggie, as I said, arrived night before
last. Bobby Short and Billy went to the station; and,
when they had gone, I took a walk out to enjoy the sunset, and seated myself under a rock they call "Apple
Rock," which juts out about half way up a hill, or knoll,
not far from the house: it is flat on top, and, in dried-
apple-time, sliced apples are spread there to dry. I
often go out and sit at its base among the bushes at
close of day: for no matter where I am staying, or how
pleasant the people may be, there are times when I like

to sit down out of doors all by myself, without a word being spoken.

While sitting there watching the clouds, my thoughts went back to the time when you and I were children, — *Jooly* and *Sily*. It seemed such a little, little while! I remembered just what my feelings were when I came home on a vacation, and saw, after months of absence, the old familiar objects, — the barn, the well, ponds, woods, and streams, and Frisk! Do you remember Frisk? You can't as I can. Impossible! For you were not a boy.

While sitting there under Apple Rock, thinking these sadly-pleasing thoughts, I was startled by the noise of shouts, laughter, and resounding footsteps overhead. Dorry had arrived! The three boys came tramping down the hill, and landed on the rock.

"A speech, a speech!" cried Billy. "Come, show off your college-learning! But stop till I go in and get the dictionary."

"Never mind: he won't put in no dictionary words!" cried Bobby Short. "Come, speech, speech!"

Half a minute's silence; and then "Hurrah, hurrah, hurrah!" rang out from above in trumpet-tones, — regular Fourth-of-July-oration trumpet-tones. It was Dorry beginning his speech. "Hurrah, hurrah, hurrah! Three cheers and a tiger-r-r-r!"

"Here I stand, and shout, and swing my hat! Hurrah, old apple-tree! I'll soon be on the tiptop of *you!* And blue hills away off there, I'll soon be on the tiptop of *you!* Afar I spy the pond: perch, pickerel, shiners, your time is short. If Mr. Golden-Robin is within hearing, I engage an egg, and will call for it.

Ha, old Longshanks, whickering! Alive yet, old hoss? you'll soon feel something alive on your back, sir! Cup. cup, cup, cuppy, cuppy! cut, cut, ker-dar-cut! Cropple-crown, Shanghai, Bantam, Leghorn, black, white, speckled, and gray! I know your tricks! Steal nests, do you? I'll find you out!"

"The cat!" Bobby Short whispered.

"Cat! S–s–s–s–s–scat! — you old cat, you! Who stole my fish last summer? Bow, wow, wow! Here comes Towser! Hurrah, Towser! Oh, good fellow, good fellow! Know me, don't you? so you do! Good doggie! Come, let's be off!"

They sprang over my head, tumbled upside down among the grass, picked themselves up, and away they went, and left me wondering whether I wished I were a boy again.

And away the same three go now, tearing down the bank, the stones and sand rolling after them. Wherever Dorry picked up that old Zouave rig, nobody knows. He says 'tis just the rig to wear everywhere, in boats and every thing. On making his first appearance in it yesterday morning, he was greeted with uproarious laughter from the crowd; Bobby Short *going off* on the spot. He came bringing all his good clothes on his arm.

"Aunt Phebe," said he, "can't you put these out of sight? — up garret, or in a dark closet, or on a high shelf; or dig a hole down cellar, and bury 'em up? I don't want to see any good clothes about: I don't want to know there are any good clothes within hearing!"

"So I say!" cried Billy.

And so we all said this morning, and acted according-ly. Aunt Phebe brought down all the *huckleberry-*

7

clothes from up garret. Oh, such faded gowns! such
funny old sun-bonnets! such hats and trousers! I put
on a suit of Mr. Carver's, — great deal too large! — but
then, as somebody said, there was plenty to take in. Billy
said I'd better cut some off my legs and arms, and sew
them on to his. "I wish," said he, jerking away at the
sleeves of an old linen sack, — " I wish, when they make
things, they'd put some *growing* into them! My arms
and legs are all sprouting out of my clothes, and Tommy's too!"

"I'm sure, I wish they would," said Aunt Phebe,
" and some *lasting* besides!"

That planter's straw hat I brought from the South does
good service now, giving me shelter, and likewise, I
trust, a romantic air in harmony with the landscape.
The first is quite necessary, unless I wish my light and
scanty locks bleached to total whiteness.

As for Bobby Short, he says he's been making old
clothes all summer. Not having any of the same, Aunt
Phebe put on patches of as near as she had. He's the
last person to mind trifles of that sort.

Not a word was said against Uncle Jacob's wearing
his old turned-up-behind black Leghorn, or having his
trousers tucked in.

"Do let father look just as bad as he wants to!" said
the girls, " and Billy too, and take the comfort of it!"

His checkered neck-handkerchief was done up stiff
and clean, and satisfactorily tied on, with its sails flying.
That, he said, gave the finishing touch, and seemed to
spread a dressed-up feeling all over him. Every new
one that came out, Bobby Short had to *go off.* Tommy
got into the spirit of looking bad, and cried because he

looked too well: so, to satisfy him, Lucy Maria turned his jacket wrong side out. Maggie said she was a good mind to cry too, on account of her boating-suit looking too well for the occasion, and proposed borrowing something; but I remarked, I trust with a proper gallantry, that we should all cry if aught so charming were withdrawn from our sight! There's much red in it. Don't you like red? I do. Perhaps for reason of my having been for a short time a son of Mars; or because red is the beginning of "Red, White, and Blue."

At length, after ten times more fun than can be set down here, we surveyed one another, and pronounced ourselves ready.

"But, oh, dear!" said Matilda as a few last touches were given, — "oh, how we shall look! We shall look like a family of scarecrows riding out! Suppose we should meet anybody!"

"Both turn to the right!" cried Billy.

"Pshaw! I mean how we should look! Might meet Mr. and Mrs. Benjamin Calloon, or some of those other city people, riding!"

"And what if we do?" cried Billy. "Road is wide enough; and, if 'tis in the woods, both back to a turning-out place!"

"You know well enough what I mean!" said Matilda. "They'd laugh at us."

"Let them," said Lucy Maria. "They come to the country to amuse themselves. We go with the country, and help them get their money's-worth. I'm always willing to help on a good time."

"I think," said Dorry (speaking from under a visor that stood out like a shop-awning), "that we ought to dress according to Nature when we're going right among it."

"Poh!" cried Billy.   "Can't we laugh at them when they put on their airs and tiptoe round?"

Then he began to mince across the room, chin up in the air. like Mrs. Benjamin, which set us all laughing. He held his right thumb and finger as if carrying a parasol, and the left as if holding up long skirts.

"So they laugh, and we laugh," said Dorry, tugging away at his trousers to make them cover up more of his boot-legs.

"And that squares the account," said I; "balances the books."

"It really does make me laugh sometimes," said Mr. Carver, "to see Betsey Lucas, — Bets she used to be called; but, since her marriage to Mr. Calloon, it has been changed to Bettina.   I knew her when she was a poor, destitute child, glad to do a chore for a cent or piece of gingerbread."

"And now," said Matilda, "she comes stepping about in her silk and her satins!"

"And her dingle-dangles!" cried Bobby Short.

"I rather think," said Uncle Jacob, "that Mrs. Betsey does feel lifted up some.   When she's speaking to her old neighbors with that high-pitched, smiling, cambric-needle kind of voice she keeps on hand ready-made, seems as if she were speaking down to 'em from a ladder!"

"Or shining down on 'em from a star!" cried L. M.; "letting the light of her chains and bracelets stream down on us poor wretches!"

"Now, I like to see pretty things," said Aunt Phebe; "and we ought to try to have charity."

"Oh! I believe in pretty things," said Lucy Maria; "and shouldn't care how good clothes Mrs. Benjamin wore, if she only had sense enough not to be proud of them."

"There's something in that, I'll allow," said her mother.

"I have often noticed in rich people," Mr. Carver remarked with his quiet manner, "that 'up-the-ladder' way they have of talking down to poor people. Mrs. Benjamin puts a good deal of *down there* in her voice. When she speaks to me as we meet occasionally, it seems something like this: 'How do you do, Mr. Carver?' (*down there.*) 'Are your family well?' (*down there.*) 'Nice weather for your hay.' (*down there.*) 'What a fine growing boy you have!' (*down there.*) 'Isn't it time he went to a trade?' (*down there.*) People that are book-learned get the same tone sometimes."

"Oh, you ought to hear Mrs. Benjamin talk to mother!" cried Lucy Maria. "Ladder? Cupola! Belfry! Weathercock! 'Excessively warm day, Missus Car-rver.'" (Here L. M. imitated the "cambric-needle" voice.) "'Excessively warm day, Missus Car-rver! Allow me, do, to sit down in your nice kitchen. Why, with three servants to do my work, my kitchen never looks tidy like yours, Missus Car-rver.' And she and mother used to be Betsey and Phebe!"

"Well, well," said Aunt Phebe, "we must try to excuse it. More than likely she was born silly, and can't help it: folks are not all alike. And then, again, they are. Now, I know some that I could mention that are mightily pleased with new clothes; and they live a good deal nearer our house than Mrs. Benjamin Calloon!"

Our conversation was interrupted here by the apparition, or rather the real shape, of Mrs. Paulina coming in at the gate.

" There ! " cried Lucy Maria. " Oh, dear, there's Mrs. Paulina ! How much shall we tell her ? Now we shall catch it, I guess, ' *spendin' so much time !* ' "

Mrs. Paulina came to look after Jacky.

" Such a little vexin' plague as he is ! " said she. " I thought I knew what dirt was before ; but he — he don't even look at the scraper, and jumps over the door-mat like a cork-stopple. Must be somewhere about your premises. He'd sooner chase after Billy than eat."

" He's been here," said Billy ; " but I sent him off. He was firing stones at a mark ; and the mark was on the fence : so the stones went right over into Matilda's pansy-vines ! "

" Clear bunch of mischief ! " said Mrs. Paulina. " What, are you all bound off? How long you going to be gone ? "

" We calculate on a week," said Aunt Phebe.

" Don't see how you possibly can spend the time," said Mrs. Paulina.

" We have to spend time every minute, long as we live," said Lucy Maria.

" Folks can't go and work too," said Mrs. Paulina. " If I go out one single hour, my work feels it. I'm hinderin' myself now, every minute I stay."

" Well, I don't know," said Aunt Phebe. " Sometimes I think, that, if it had been meant we should stay in the house all the time, there wouldn't have been so much out-doors given us."

" That's my mind exactly ! " I remarked. " Besides

the enjoyment, it really does us good, soul and body, to go out and observe the beautiful things in Nature."

"Yes, if anybody only had time," said Mrs. Paulina; "but we've got a sight of sewing to do. Mercy and Ella say it takes them about all the time they can get to alter over their dresses : you know folks have to look decent. But I'm crazy stayin' so! I must hunt up that boy!"

Just as she stepped out, Gus stepped in.

"Come, Gus, tackle up, tackle up!" cried Uncle Jacob: "'tis getting along in the forenoon."

"Yes, sir ; to rights, to rights!" Gus answered. "But the new whip's gone, and I lay it to that pesky Jacky!"

"Better lay it on to him!" said Billy.

"O Billy!" said L. M., "when he thinks so much of you!"

"Well, he's doing something forever!" said Billy.

"I know it," said Gus. "Can't nothing lay still a minute! Lors, that little critter don't make nothin' o' gappin' up new axen! Misses his hits, and chops right inter the ground, and spiles axen!"

"Jacky has a good deal of blame put upon him," said Aunt Phebe.

"Oughter!" cried Gus, — "oughter! Sich a master critter to get hold o' things! 'Tother day, he shun up a spout (he can shun up any thing): he got the rake down that I hid up high enough, I thought, and raked down summer-sweetin's with the rake!"

While this talk was going on, it suddenly occurred to me that I had seen a couple of boys, not long before, scampering towards the old orchard. I said nothing, but, leaving Gus to finish his grievances, walked quietly off in that direction.

"Go long! Git up! Gee! Gee there! Haw! Bry! Git up! Git up!"

"What can he be driving?" thought I. The crack of the whip, too, was plainly heard, and footsteps of some creature galloping.

I looked over the board fence, and there was Jacky driving the calf by his tail; while Tommy whipped up with the new whip. The calf went on a tight gallop, zig-zagging, Jacky holding on by both hands: though how he did so was a wonder; for Starry Banner jerked him over that uneven ground, making him stumble and pitch, describing arcs, trapezoids, and triangles,—scalene, right-angled, and isosceles. Beg pardon for putting such learned matter in a letter to a female ; but look into little Silas's geometry, and you'll find it all there, and worse. I sprang over the fence. He let go the minute I shouted; pitched heels over head in the grass; and bossy flew off in a tangent (*vide* Euclid).

Meanwhile Mrs. Paulina came into the orchard by another way, though not in time to witness the most interesting part. She hurried up to Jacky, caught hold of his arm, and marched him home. I then carried the new whip back in triumph. and brought down the house by describing the performance, which I did in much more glowing language than is set down here.

In my absence, the hay-cart had been brought to the door; and bed-clothes, provisions, and fishing-tackle were being stowed under the seats.

"Tumble in, tumble in!" cried Uncle Jacob.

And we did tumble in, — thirteen of us in all, besides Gus, who went to bring back the horses. Mother Delight and Mr. Carver and grandmother stood by to help,

and see us off. Mother Delight is going to stay at
grandmother's, and take care of Aunt Phebe's dairy, and
wait upon her milk-customers, and make butter. She
and grandmother will have a real good time, and are
depending upon it. Uncle Jacob may go down for a

day or two, and send Mr. Carver up. At any rate, the
old ladies will come once while we stay, and perhaps
twice.

The mosquitoes, I find. are a little troublesome. We
heard, before coming up, that they fairly drove away the
last party who staid here, or rather who didn't stay.

Mosquitoes, however, are small things compared with the ocean, the forest, this bold cliff, and fish right out of the water! Still, being forewarned, we came forearmed, and are fully prepared to keep them out of the shanty: so we are sure of one place of refuge, if worst comes to worst.

The girls are adorning the inside of the building with green garlands; also getting the bunks in sleeping-order, and setting the table. This last proceeding is the most interesting to me just at present. We have been here several hours, and our appetites are really fearful; but we can't eat a crumb of any thing, in consequence of having signed a pledge not to until dinner is ready.

Now one boat has just come in with cunners and rock-cod. Now the boys are hard at it "cleaning 'em." Now they dash up the bank with them. L. M. calls out, —

"Have them fried, Mr. Fry?"

"By all means!" I answer. "And by every possible means, — the most rapid preferred!"

While the meal is preparing, I will sit tranquilly beneath this greenwood-tree, and, leaning against its massy trunk, enjoy at once the balmy fragrance of the leafy forest and the roar of the sounding sea.

You will hear from me again very soon.

Affectionately your brother,
S. Y. FRY.

P. S. — Not quite so soon as this, I didn't mean; but I wish to confess, that, whatever one of the gentler sex might do, it is entirely beyond my masculine ability to be sentimental with the comic so constantly intruding. There go *the three,* pitching down the cliff through the

loose sand and gravel; Tommy almost crying because
he can't catch them, and trying to crawl down backwards.   He does look so perfectly comical!   At the last
moment, when starting from home, Tommy couldn't find
his straw hat.   Uncle Jacob picked up an old Scotch
cap of Bobby Short's, and clapped it over him.

"There!" said he, "it fits him like — like — oh, dear!
like what?"

"Like a too big thimble!" cried Georgie.   And so it
did, and does.

"Never mind!" said Uncle Jacob: "'twill keep the
sun out of his eyes."

"And out of his nose too!" cried Bobby Short.

"Tip it back more," said Lucy Maria: "there, **so!**
When grandmother comes up, she'll bring your straw
one."

It won't stay tipped back, though; and he "can't see
hardly any," he says.   There he rolls over!   Never
mind: he'll get to the bottom sooner.   It is his constant
aim to keep up with *the three*.   Can rolling over be
keeping up?   S. Y. F.

I was intending to give here my next letter to Juliana, describing our experiences at the Cliff; but Lucy Maria's to her
cousin Myra (cousin Joe's sister) is so much better!   I think
the female pen has a livelier way of hitting off things, a lighter
touch; probably because they are lighter-minded.

Lucy Maria to her Cousin Myra.

DEAR COUSIN MYRA, —

O My., and dear My.! I told you I would; and I
will.   Take it altogether, it was a decidedly comical

time, as you will find out before coming to the end of this letter. How glad we all should have been if you and Joe could have made it possible unto yourselves to come! The boys had such fun! and Billy came across a *squirrel-man*, and expects to make heaps of money; or rather, now I think of it, the *squirrel*-man *came across* him. But of this anon.

We started in the hay-cart, just a dozen of us, — father, mother, Mr. Fry, Dorry, Maggie, Bobby Short, *My Bettina*, William Henry, Georgie. we three girls, and Tommy. No: that makes thirteen, don't it? besides Gus, who drove. perched high in front. When before folks, he tries to straighten up; but it only amounts to tipping his hat farther back on the back of his neck. Gus must have had some beauty in his day: his face is quite a pleasant one to look at now. Dorry mounted on the seat with him, and, whenever there was a good chance, would steer the horses to where it was sideling. to scare us girls, and then scold at Gus about it; and. in rough places, he contrived it so that every individual wheel went over an individual stone every individual minute: so that, what with laughing and jolting and fright, our countenances had their expressions very much confused. *My Bettina* looked pale as a cloth, and just barely kept from crying. You know what a light skin she always had. She grows to look more like her mother every day. Has those same light frizzy curls.

Suppose you will wonder how *she* came to be among *us ;* and no wonder you will. This was the way: Mrs. Benjamin found out we were going, and asked mother if she would be willing to take *her Bettina*, as she was rather a weakly girl, and the air at Coot Pint might strengthen her. Now mark this, My. If Mrs. Benja*min* and a few friends were getting up a private party anywhere, and mother should ask her to take Matilda along, can't you imagine what faces would be made up about it? I guess the light curls would toss. " How intrusive!" " The *idea* of our taking her daughter!" Even if mother did offer to pay board, that wouldn't take away from the intrusiveness; would it? But I think Mrs. Benja*min* rather considered it a favor done us; that it was paying us a compliment to be willing to let *My Bettina* spend a few days in our society. if we are society: which, as far as I can find out, we're not; for Hannah Jane heard Mrs. B. say last fall that she hadn't been in society for four months. Poor thing! Hannah Jane suggests that there's a saving disposition at the bottom of the matter, as there are plenty of boarding-houses by the sea where she might take her girl to be strengthened. But let that go. I only charge her with this, — that although our calling on *My Bettina* in a friendly way would be considered presuming, still she is willing *My Bettina* should mix with us when good is to be got by it.

Of course we took her. Mother says what people *are* is no affair of ours; but what they need is. Mother would like to strengthen anybody's *Bettina*, and everybody's.

Hannah Jane thought the damsel might turn her nose up; but I said if she did. and did act ridiculous, — why, all the more fun. For my part, I like to have all kinds; then we can laugh at the silly ones, and with the funny ones, and love the good-natured ones, and get wisdom from the wise ones.

But I'm all off the track. You know I never do pre-
tend to write a regular letter, but just run on. They
say I'm easy to get off the track in other things besides
writing letters. I left ourselves on the road, being jolted
and scared out of our wits, and almost out of the cart.
That rogue would look round to us with such an innocent face, and declare that he turned out everywhere
there was a bad stone! True enough; but 'twas towards
the stone!

Between you and me, Dorry's growing handsome; but
mum's the word! Never wrong a young man by letting
him know you think he's handsome. It would make him
vain; and vanity is a blot on the character; and to blot
his character is to do him a wrong. You see, young men
haven't strength of mind to bear such things!

We arrived alive at Coot Pint. Oh, such a jolty
hill as we went down just before getting there!—a long,
steep hill, which had logs put across to take the steepness
out of it; and we had to jolt over those logs! Arrived
between eleven and twelve, but not much past eleven,
and hoisted a flag at the main peak of the shanty.
Found it quite a respectable affair, delightfully and ro-
mantically situated on the edge of a cliff, and looking
off upon the wide sea. I took up Tennyson and Shakspeare with me. It had an up-stairs and a down-stairs.
Up-stairs were bunks filled with hay ranged along the
sides, — say fifteen or twenty of them. We brought
quilts and blankets; and the first thing we did after
father and the boys went a-fishing was to make up the
beds. No: first we set mother in a chair. There was
one chair there that had been a rocking-chair, and was
partly a rocking-chair still. We set mother in that, and

told her not to stir; for we meant she should have a long time of perfect, perfect rest up there. Such a busy, workful mother as she has been always! and never took a long rest in her life! We pulled the chair, with her in it, up to the window at the end which looks off upon the spreading sea; and, oh! you can't imagine how spreading and blue and unspeakable the sea does look from that cliff. But I never describe; no use. We folded up her hands, and left her there with orders to watch the boat, and see that the boys didn't get drowned.

Next we made our beds; and next we unpacked the cakes and pies, and hid them where the boys couldn't find them. Suppose you will ask if there is any such place in the world. I don't think there is a place that would last very long. Maggie, dancing about the shanty (she's just like a bird set free), danced on to a board in the corner, — a loose board, that tiltered up; and, upon looking underneath, we found a little cellar-place about a yard across, and two feet deep, and just the thing. We put our pails and boxes in there, spreading hay over them for a blind, in case the wrong ones should tilt up the board.

Next we trimmed the walls with green boughs and wreaths and oak-leaf trimming. The girls went out, and found splendid red lilies growing wild, and brought them in by handfuls; also some ferns and pretty running vines. There were plenty of bottles lying about, left by former occupants; and we used those for vases. *My Bettina* took hold very handily in arranging them. She seemed to like flowers in earnest: so I put her down one long white mark. Always deal fair, I say: don't you ? In other matters she rather held back; stood about in a placid, lazy way, as if she couldn't imagine what she was going to do with herself. Being out of society, I suppose, is like being a fish out of water.

Next we rested a little, and looked at the white sails away off on the blue, and breathed some of Mr. Fry's air; though he told us not to, for he wanted it all. Poor man ! he's very delicate.

Next we pinned up a paper, headed "Meditations,"— a long piece of blank paper, with a written permission at the top, that whoever had any beautiful thoughts pressing upon them, suggested by the landscape or by any thing, might have the privilege of writing them down. This, you know, for a safety-valve.

Next we set the table. There was a long pine table on one side, with boards for seats. We found mugs, plates, knives and forks, in a little cupboard, and placed them round as far as they would go, and then the vases up and down the middle.

We had a kitchen ! One little corner was partitioned off, and that was the kitchen. It was just big enough to hold a cook-stove, a sink rather larger than a chopping-tray, and a woman. Underneath, Hannah Jane discovered a teakettle, two frying-pans, and a dinner-pot. These discoveries threw a home-like feeling about us. We brought our own coffee-pot and teapot, and a few dishes, — not too many; for we came to be rural, and determined we would be rural. Mr. Fry whittled us out a few forks and spoons : these last were of the shovel-species. We took his whittlings for kindling, and then sent him to pick up an armful of dry stuff to burn. Then Hannah Jane made a fire; and then we went down to the bank to meet the boat.

The fishers had grand luck. "Cunners, cunners! why, you could catch 'em by the hundred million!" they cried. Father and Dorry went farther off with their boat, and got rock-cod.

I was glad we hid the eatables : those creatures were so hungry! Hungry? — ravenous, famished! Threatened to eat us if we didn't reveal! Billy got down on his knees in that little kitchen, and pleaded for a quarter of a cracker — only a small, dry quarter of a cracker — with tears, real tears, — he knows how to make them, — in his eyes! Dorry told horrible tales of people who had died of starvation. He set the flag half-mast; and then they drew lots to see which should be eaten.

We stood firm. We said, "No : " the law of the place was, that every one should come to table with a perfect appetite. To take up their minds while we cooked the fish, I told them to carry the girls to sail; for Hannah Jane and I were all that could work to advantage. So Billy asked Maggie to go rowing. Does do me good to see Maggie. She seems to enjoy every thing, — every thing : whether she walks or rides or hops or runs, or whatever it is, you'd think 'twas the first time she ever did it, she's so earnest. Her face is full of animation : it is something like Dorry's, only not quite so much so. She wore, up there, a beauty boating-suit, that came just to tops of boots, — dark gray, touched off with scarlet; and red ear-drops, small ones; black lace on her hat, with a spray of coral (imitation of course) acorns; and a scarlet neck-ribbon tied in a sailor's knot. She has dark eyes, not dreamy, but starry; lashes between

8

long and short; and a fine color, same as Dorry. I like
to see the two together, he takes such good care of her.
When he found she was going rowing that day with
Billy, he went down and helped Billy help her in, fun-
ning all the time; but you could see there was real
brotherly love underneath.

We managed to get the whole crowd off the land, some
with Billy, and some went with father in the great boat
to take a sail. Mother went with him: and *My Bettina*
ventured at last; though she seemed rather scared to go.
Hannah Jane said, scared of tanning; but I told Hannah Jane she must not be so wicked.

We two made a splendid chowder! A man that was
staying at another shanty about a mile off happened
along, and showed us how he made them. And we fried
those fish, — oh, such a brown! Why, you could throw
them over the house! Rolled them in flour first. Our
table looked very inviting. Mother thought, and so did
we, that 'twas best to have pie and cake both, and the
plum-pudding grandmother sent, so the boys might feel
satisfied, and not be rummaging round after things they
hadn't had.

When every thing was ready, or little before every
thing was ready, we ran up the flag, as had been arranged; then stood on the bank and shouted, and
drummed on pans. It wasn't long, you may believe,
but very short, before they were tearing up the bank and
into the shanty like wild creatures. "Dear My.! and
oh, My.! and oh, dear My.!" If you want to enjoy perfect felicity, watch a hungry crew like that eating chowder, and cunners fried brown.

For a few moments they ate in *perfect silence*. A

whole page could express no better than these few words
the terrible intensity of their appetites.   And when, at
last, speech returned, it was not all at once, but by
degrees, a word or two at a time, thus: "Good chowder!" "Good cunners!" "Good pie!" "Good pudding!"   Short ejaculations like these first showed they
were coming to themselves.   Hannah Jane poured out
the coffee, and let Maggie put in the cream and sugar.
Maggie said she liked to, because it made her see how
good every cup tasted.   She got some coffee-stains on
her fluted trimming.   Too bad!   Even the boys left off
eating some time or other, — even William Henry.   He
made several trips to the kitchen.   Don't you remember
how we used to laugh at him for that when he was a
little boy? — how he used to run out to see if there were
plenty to fall back upon, before passing his plate for
more, so to be sure there was enough to go round?

When all were satisfied, then came the tug of war,
— clearing away.   "Oh!" cried Matilda, "how shall we
ever get cleared away?"   Matilda often wishes, when a
meal is over, for the floor to open and swallow the dishes,
table and all.

"Cleared away?" cried Dorry.   "Oh! I know how.
Attention, all!   Great plates round the right, and pile
up at Billy.   All pass 'em, and say '*Pass*' as they go by.
Now, attention again!   Small plates to the left, and pile
up at Mr. Fry.   Mugs to the left, — left! — and pile at
me.   Knives to the right, and pile at Bobby Short.
Forks to the left, and pile at Tommy.   Spoons to the
right, and pile at Miss Georgiana.   Now stand!   Attention, company!   Take up piles!   March!"

Mr. Fry went cap'n, and the rest in file behind.   Dorry had a mug hung on each finger and thumb, and held two in his mouth. We found this such a quick way of clearing off the table, that we've tried it at home since. Dorry wanted to wash the dishes, and made a dish-cloth with a handle long enough for him to stand in the other room and reach to the sink. We declined his weapon; but, as the boys insisted on helping, we let them take the knives out doors, — those we found up there. — and scour them in the sand. Billy hung about a while to see where mother was going to put what was left; but I whispered to Maggie and Mattie to say something to him about setting up the croquet. Dorry and Maggie brought a beautiful croquet-set.

Towards night, when it grew cooler, all of us—father, mother, Mr. Fry, and all — played "hunt the squirrel" and "tag." *My Bettina* rather held back. She isn't one of the mixy kind. Did you ever see a real lady? I never did; that is, not knowing certain sure it was a real one. She doesn't seem to me like a real one; though she is very ladyfied. What do you think of her taking her napkin, when we were all seated round the table, and wiping her plate, mug, knife, fork, and spoon, with some parade, though she'd seen Hannah Jane and me wash and wipe every one of them? Maggie seems to me more like a lady, for all she acts so wild. Don't mean exactly manners. Let's see now: what do I mean, I wonder? A lady at heart: how will that do? Now, she has a quiet way of taking things as they come here at our house, and don't mind taking hold too, and helping, for all she's used to living where the work is carried on out of sight. Hannah J. finds fault with that little extra fine touch, or accent, in her way of speaking, and thinks she may be rather too extra polite outside to be good all the way through. But I tell Hannah that Maggie has been brought up in that way; and it may come just as natural for her to be extra polite as for us not to. At any rate, mother approves of Maggie; and she can see through people about as well as anybody I know of. But this car seems to have switched off somewhere.

After we'd played and raced and had a lively time, we gave the boys a piece of apple-pie all round, and a summer-sweeting apiece (grandmother sent a peck, or so); for we had too late a dinner to think of a regular supper. They said apple-pie called for cheese; and we had great fun not letting them find out where we took the cheese from.

While we were playing, Mr. Fry left to finish barricading the shanty. You know, Mr. Fry is what may be called *sure-footed*; that is, he always goes prepared, and always wants every thing to be done in the very best manner. Perhaps he thinks he can do things in the very best manner. And I think, myself, that he can do as well as the general run.

[My modesty would compel me to skip the above, only that it does not seem right to let mere modesty break the connection. — S. Y. F.]

Well, Mr. Fry, learning that mosquitoes prevailed there, went prepared. He took up a large quantity of netting (very fine, close netting), a paper of tacks, trusting luck, for a wonder, to find a stone to pound with, and nailed up this netting at every window above and below. There were only two above. Did his work faithfully; for the mosquitoes had already made themselves felt, and were quite troublesome at dinner-time, though

we were too hungry to mind it much.   You see, Mr. Fry
has such a delicate, thin skin, that he is peculiarly sensi-
tive to stings of all kinds, bites, and bumps.   He nailed
up netting, as I said, at every window, and hung a stone
on the door, so it would swing to of itself.   Then he

threw down lots of hay from the bunks we didn't use,
and let Hannah Jane and me in through the least little
bit of a narrow crack; and we spread it on the floor in
comfortable bunches, and put a quilt or blanket on each
bunch.

Just before sunset, we all went up on a hill close by,

where we could look off on the water at our right hand, and over miles and miles of woodland at our left, not level, but sloping up to the sky far away in the distance, like seats at a circus. And, oh, what a sunset! But I never describe: I don't know how. It is no use for one person to try to make another person know and feel how beautiful any thing is: I've found that out. But, oh. it was so calm! and the shadowy twilight came in such a still, gentle way! Even the boys were hushed for a while. Mother said she felt like having something sung, — something not very noisy. So we sang, "Tenting to-night on the old camp-ground: " you know how soft that chorus is. Dorry's tenor is so sweet, it fairly brings the tears to my eyes in some tunes. Mr. Fry told us of things he'd been witness to in real "*tenting to-night,*" and one sad story about a young fellow — very young, scarcely more than a boy — who ran away from home, and was found dead after a battle, — his first battle, — stretched on the ground, holding in his stiff fingers the picture of his mother! It touched us so to think. that, in running away, he should have taken his mother's picture. They were not able to find out the boy's real name; but Mr. Fry knew what town he came from, — some out-of-the-way place, — and afterwards went to that town, and, by going to church, found the original of the picture, and followed her home. I can't tell the rest; but, altogether, it was a very sad story.

Then Mr. Fry, to change the subject, and brighten us up again, told about the contrabands. Such ridiculous stories! Mr. Fry is quite good at telling stories, and gave their talk exactly, I should guess; for it sounded natural enough. We got a-laughing, and laughed till

we cried; and Bobby Short *went off*, and rolled half way
down hill.

Then we sang some of the war melodies, particularly
" John Brown," *by request*, — Billy, you know.   Plenty
of room for his chorus up there.   *My Bettina* has quite
a pretty voice, but can't sing much without her notes, and
wasn't acquainted with those tunes.   By the way, Maggie flats, but not badly.   The mosquitoes found us out:
so we went in — squeezed in, one at a time — through a
narrow crack that Mr. Fry held open for us.

" Now enlighten the luminaries!" cried Dorry; and
we took out the candles.   Grandmother wouldn't hear a
word to our carrying kerosene-lamps, for fear they'd go
off.   The boys set the candles in raw potatoes.   We
lighted any quantity of them; and the room was bright
as day.   Set them in a row along the table.   Cut off
both ends of the potatoes.

We poked the hay up in one corner in case of fire,
and then made a thorough search, and slew every mosquito that had been left in.   You ought to have seen
father reach up and bang away, and Mr. Fry!   Mr. Fry
said one mosquito would keep him awake all night.
Father said their singing was what provoked him.   Dorry said that was only doing their best to make the operation pleasant.   Mr. Fry drove a nail over the door-latch
for the last time, and told Dorry, if he wanted to get out
again, he must tunnel out.   That fellow had all the time
been making believe he had left things outside, and asking him to open the door.

So Dorry began to jump about to find a place where
the floor was hollow to begin to tunnel; and we were
afraid he would jump on to that loose board, and then

'twould all be up! I didn't know what else to do to stop
him; so I said we were going to have tableaux; and, as
mother was sitting close by *the spot*, told her she must
be in the first tableau, all the time running it over in
my mind what it should be. And all at once "Past and
Future" popped into my head: you know that picture
hanging over the bureau? So we had mother for Past,
and Maggie for Future. Mother did as well as anybody
could possibly do. We made her cast her eyes down,
and look very thoughtful. Haven't you seen her sometimes, towards evening, when the house was still, sit
without doing any thing, or taking much notice, thinking? I never like to disturb her then. Maggie made
a very good Future. We told her to imagine she was
looking at some beautiful thing away off in the distance.

Then Dorry said, if he couldn't be in a tableau, he
wouldn't play; and I told him he might be Simple
Simon, catching a whale in his mother's water-pail; and
they all said that was exactly the part for him. You
wouldn't believe, Myra, that any human, sensible being
could look so like a simpleton as he did, sitting there
fishing in a water-pail! We put father's old black turn-
up-behind straw hat on him, and Bobby Short's jacket,
and a wide ruffle round his neck (made of newspaper).

Then William Henry and Bobby Short said 'twasn't
fair if they couldn't too. So we thought it over, and
then took those two and Tommy, and let them act that
going-to-bed stanza from Mother Goose, beginning, "To
bed, to bed!" says Sleepy-Head. Bobby Short, stuffed
out big as a barrel, stooped over, holding "the dinner-
pot." We dressed up Tommy in a funny rig, and let
him represent *Slow*, holding back Billy by the coat-tail.

We put a peaked, ruffled night-cap on Billy (made of paper), and gave him a candle to hold, as if he were just starting for bed. I told him to *yawn*. And he did yawn! Bobby Short caught a glimpse of his face, (though I charged him not to), and dropped *the dinner-pot*, and *went off* at the very beginning.

Myra, I have told you the light and trifling part; but now comes something really serious. We were so taken up by the tableaux and the fun, that I had hardly noticed there was trouble of any kind, until I heard Mr. Fry say, " What do you keep doing so for ? " Then I observed that we all kept slapping our faces and hands; did so, I mean, without paying much attention to it, being, as I said, otherwise occupied.

" What do you keep doing so for ? " Mr. Fry asked. But, at the same time, he was rubbing his own forehead.

" I felt a *skeeter*, I thought ! " says one.

" And I thought I did ! " says another.

" And I know I did ! " says another.

" I've been feeling 'em all along," says father, slapping his hands, " and hearing 'em, only I knew it couldn't be."

" Why, they're everywhere ! " cried Billy. " Here they are on the netting, trying to get out ! Thousands of 'em ! "

" You must be mistaken," said Mr. Fry, scratching his cheek, you know.

" O—h my goodness ! O—h ! Look ! Look up on the wall ! " cried Bobby Short.

" But how could they get in ? " says Mr. Fry.

" Tunnelled in ! " says Dorry.

And oh, dear, My.! It was the living truth !—the *skeeters*, I mean, — very living truth; for the room was alive with them. Mr. Fry couldn't believe it. They got in his hair (thin hair he has); but he couldn't believe it. They bit through his linen coat-sleeves; but he couldn't believe it.

Suddenly we heard "Hah, hah, hah!—hah, hah, hah!" I thought he was never going to stop. Dorry: he'd been exploring.

"What's the matter?" we all shouted.

Another explosion.

"What's the matter? What do you see?"

"The cracks, the cracks! They come in the cracks!" he cried.

True; dreadfully true! The walls were only boarded; and there was a crack between every two boards. And you know we lighted all those candles. Oh! I never saw a comicaler face than Mr. Fry's.

"Put out the lights, quick!" said mother, "and every one of us go straight to bed before any more get in."

The boys sprang for the candles, and puffed out every one, of course; leaving us in the dark. Father lighted one, and told us to hurry up stairs, and go to bed without any; for pretty likely they hadn't come in up there, where 'twas dark. Soon as we were safe aloft, he blew it out. We lay down just as softly in our bunks, so the skeeters needn't know we were there.

Down below, they were having all kinds of a time,— quarrelling for the hay, quarrelling for bed-quilts. You see, there was no time to arrange matters in the panic. Hannah Jane meant that every one should have a reasonably comfortable bed. There was only a layer of boards for the loft-floor: so we could hear every sound. Father and Mr. Fry thought the netting had better be taken down, and the mosquitoes let out. This was done. and the mosquitoes not only let, but driven. Oh, such whacking and banging! For, of course, those boys didn't make any unnecessary stillness. Then they shut the windows; then they opened them for air, and hung things up to keep out the enemy; then took the things down again; for it came on to be one of those hot, close, dog-day nights.

At last all was quiet, — oh! quite a long time. But I know those fellows were not asleep. Mother told us, at the first, not to lisp a syllable, or hardly move or stir, so they might keep still down below for fear of waking us.

Such an unnatural calm could not last. Presently we heard Bobby Short's tickle (repressed); then William Henry's chuckle (repressed too, fearfully!), and knew very well, by *not* hearing Dorry, that he was at his tricks, — sticking in pins, probably; pulling the hay from under them, to a certainty.

"Hush!" father said softly: "you'll wake them up up stairs."

Then I heard Maggie laugh, as if she were trying not to; then Mattie; then Georgie.

Mother whispered. "Hush, girls! if they hear you laughing, there'll be no whoa to them."

Then silence again for quite a long time; only sometimes Mattie would call across in a whisper, "Maggie, asleep?"

"No. Are you?"

And all the while we kept up a repressed but active slapping of face and hands. Oh, it was fearful! We drew the quilts close around our chins, and tried to cover our faces; and could, if it hadn't been for breathing: but noses had to be left out, anyway, and one hand to slap with: for, oh! they got in our hair, and bit our eyes; bit through two thickness of pocket-handkerchief that I spread over and tried to breathe through! And their dreadful singing! It rings in my ears even now!

And down below, — O Myra! down below! Why, I just lay and shook with laughter, hearing them *fighting 'em*, and hearing Mr. Fry groan, and the boys *carrying on!* Bobby Short *went off* very frequently; and sometimes we thought he'd never come back.

"There's nothing sneaking about them; is there?" says Billy. "They let you know they're coming."

Mr. Fry seemed to look upon it in the light of real suffering, and take it accordingly. But those boys! — some of their nonsense and squealings made the girls laugh out at last; and, after that, there was, as mother foretold, no whoa. When Dorry pricked the other boys, he'd slap himself, and say, "Gracious! what big ones! they bite through every thing!"

Billy declared he'd make up his bed on the table. Dorry wanted to sleep with him; and in a very short time both rolled off. Then there was a strange noise, as if a rock or log were being knocked about. Dorry said he was only "beatin' up his piller."

After a while, I heard the door open softly, and somebody step out. I went to the window, tiptoe (the window was near my bunk; and, to tell the truth, I had been there more than once, looking at the moon), and saw a ghost walking towards the cliff, — Mr. Fry, with a long white blanket on. Presently a second ghost stepped out, — father. The first ghost turned back; then the

two had a little ghostly talk, and agreed, I guessed, to go
down and try it on the rocks; for they vanished in that
direction.

"Now let's go to sleep," says Bobby Short, "earnest!"

"So I say!" says Dorry.

Billy declared he'd go out and sleep in the hogshead.
There was a tipped-over hogshead close by the house.
I went to peep, and saw him, with an armful of hay,
crawling in.   I kept on standing there; and oh the
wonderful moonlight on those woods and on that sea!
But I never describe.   Presently, when all was quiet, I
saw Dorry tiptoe along to the hogshead, and give it a
very gentle rock, as if rocking a cradle, accompanied by
"By-lo, by-lo," and ending, of course, in a turn way over.
Bobby Short took a sudden roll upon the grass; and Billy
crawled out, and shook the hay off.

"Let's go a-fishing!" says Dorry.

"Agreed!" says Billy.   And away they went, — all
three of them.

"We sha'n't sleep a wink to-night," said mother.
"'Tis two o'clock, or more, I know, by the moon."

Why, Myra, we couldn't!   'Twas impossible!   Why,
you've no idea!   Oh, and it was so hot!   But then we
didn't think much about the heat.   *My Bettina* actually
wept.   Her bunk was next mine.   I went to the poor
thing, and she begged me for a thick bed-quilt.   I packed
her up like a mummy.   Then the others wanted to be
done that way: so I did them all up like mummies, leaving
out on each a nose. and a forefinger to guard it, and told
them to imagine they were in a pyramid, and had gone to
sleep for forty centuries.   But pretty soon the mummies

began to sing, "Mary had a little lamb," and kept on with "Lightly row," "Twinkle, twinkle, little star," in the most solemn and steadfast tones. Now and then I would look out the window, and see a tall ghost or a short ghost stalking about, with nobody to lay it.

Well, morning came at last, as mornings will; and in August they are not so very long about it. Such a jolly frame as we were in, — mother and all! I'm so glad she's just the kind of mother that she is! Some mothers would go round with a dreadful doleful face, and groaning, after such a night as that. We went out into the cool morning-air, and saw the sun rise. The sunrise over the water! O Myra! But just keep calm, L. M.: you know, you don't believe in words.

We set the room to rights; swept the floor, and sprinkled it; brought in fresh flowers, and set the coffee going; and that smelt reviving. The boys caught plenty of fish, among them some delicious mackerel. They were full of their compliments and their "good-mornings;" hoped we had rested well, and all that. Said they came across a man sitting up straight in a dory, anchored about a quarter of a mile from shore, who had been actually driven off the land, and was staying there "out of reach of 'em."

We had a jolly breakfast. By flapping newspapers, managed to eat in some peace, but not much. Mr. Fry and father said they had had a very pleasant season on the rocks. After breakfast, father, mother, Mr. Fry, Dorry, Tommy, and the girls (all but Hannah Jane and me) went off rowing and sailing, — rowing, mostly, for reason of no breeze. I declined going. These moderate times don't suit me. I like it better when 'tis just a

little bit on the safe side of dangerous. Hannah wanted
to get things regulated.

Billy and Bobby Short said they meant to try for a
nap somewhere. I took my Shakspeare. I carried up
several volumes of poems, thinking it would be very
romantic to sit and read poetry right among the raw
material that poetry is made of.

Well, I tried it, — tried rocks by the water's edge,
tried seaweed, tried flat on the sand, tried green grass,
tried under the trees, tried up in the trees, tried walking; but always, and in every place, there would be a
cloud of dark-winged things between my eyes and the
page. The whole air was full. A mosquito-bath! I
told the boys, I believed the earth was passing through
a constellation of them.

It was a hot, moist, stagnant day; not a breath of air.
As I passed the shanty-door, the boys begged me to
come in and cover them over better, so they could catch a
nap before Dorry came back. They had piled some hay
near the door in the likeliest place for a draught: and
each had covered himself well as he could with a quilt.
They begged me to tuck it about their feet, to "keep
'em from getting up their trousers-legs;" and close under
their chins; and then spread another quilt over, 'cause
they bit through that one: and then to lay their hats
over their faces; and then put veils over their hats; and
then lay something heavy on the edges of the veils,
"so they couldn't crawl under." You see being smothered was a mere trifle, *compared!*

They lay perfectly still for quite a long time, and
would have dropped off, I do believe, if Dorry hadn't
come back. He left the girls picking Irish moss, — lots

of that there! — and came up to bring the oars. I
hushed him, and pointed to the *bundles*. Unluckily,
they wriggled just a little speck. That cute youth took
in the situation at once, and acted accordingly.

"I want to lay these oars down somewhere in a safe
place," said he, and dropped them gently on the *bundles*. The *sleepers* made no sign. Dorry walked about
in a careless, indifferent way, clearing up the house, he
said: now and then laying a broom, or a bucket, or a
bag of potatoes, — in fact, about every thing that could
be moved, — upon *the bundles*. Of course, the end of
it was, that Bobby Short *went off* at last like a pistol.

"Wake up, Billy! wake up!" cried Dorry. "There's
a man from Boston coming to see you! Here he is
now! Walk in, sir!"

I turned, and saw a stranger at the door. Dorry conducted him in such a way, that he had to step over the
bundles. "Put your foot there, and jump," says Dorry.
And he pointed to a hollow place between the two.

That was the squirrel-man. I'll tell you about him
another time. I want to make haste now, and get us
away from that place of torment, just as we hurried to
get away in reality. Perhaps you won't believe it, Myra;
but we were actually driven from our quarters. Imagine
ten million needles pricking twelve people, and keeping at it! Why, they drove us almost raving distracted!
People in the other shanties said it was a very unusual
year; and I should hope so! Some acquaintances, riding that way, called to see us: and we had such a funny
time doing the complimentary under the circumstances!

"Warm day!" (Slap.)

"Very!" (Slap.)

9

"Charming prospect!" (Slap, slap.)

"Lovely!" (Slap, slap.)

"Enjoy stopping here?" (Slap.)

"On some accounts." (Slap, slap, slap.)

As I said, they vanquished us. Maggie and Matilda and the boys would have been willing to try one more night; but I, if no other way offered, was ready to start, and run every step of the way home. The man that wanted to see Billy was going down past our place; and we sent by him for Gus to come up after us; and glad were we to see him arrive. Being determined to retreat with a show of glory, we adorned each hat, bonnet, and horse's head with a scarlet lily, and so went home in triumph. I don't know whether you will believe it, but, for days and days afterwards, we were continually slapping faces and hands from habit. Tommy's face bears the marks now. You see the poor child *slept* almost all night, he was so tired.

We made up for having to come down from Coot Pint by going somewhere every day while Dorry and Maggie staid. Hannah J.'s Wilson was disappointed; and, as he had arranged to allow himself two free days, we asked him to spend them here. So funny, H. having a lover! She don't seem at all the person you'd think would have one. Wish they were not quite so quiet and so common-sensical about it. With a pair of true lovers in the family, we are entitled to feel a great deal more romantic than we do. But they blush sometimes: that's one comfort. Mother scolds at me for saying things to make them: but why don't they seem more romantic? then I'd be on their side. Wilson is what they call a "boss-carpenter" now; began to be it last spring. We have our suspicions of a plan being planned that will call for wedding-cake. I can't think of it without crying; for I've always looked up to Hannah Jane. And mother — oh! what will mother do if one of us little birdies is stolen out of the nest? She won't let me talk about it. Better not mention this, as there is nothing certain.

Love to Aunt Myra: and be sure and remember me affectionately to Joe when you write; not forgetting the *accordion*, to which long life and breath never-ending.

From   LUCY MARIA.

To those who may think Lucy Maria's account exaggerated, I will say that the half has not been told; but let me add, in this connection, that none who are pining for sea-air, and fish right out of the water, need avoid Coot Pint on account of our experience there. That summer was unusually moist; and the very same shanty has been occupied by many different parties since, without the least annoyance.

For my own part, I have every reason to remember our *camping out*. Those girls teased me so! and Uncle Jacob — why, I could scarcely go anywhere without being earnestly advised to take some netting along.

There was one slight incident, rather out of the common course, which we did not tell the girls until some time after.

In bringing down the hay for our beds, we brought down, without knowing it, a mouse's nest. In the night, Uncle Jacob heard faint squeaks almost directly under his head, and, by striking a match, discovered four little baby mice about an inch long! This accounts for some of the *suppressed* racket in the lower room, and certainly for one of those *going-offs* of Bobby Short's, during which Lucy Maria experienced such anxiety lest he might never return. It was just after this discovery that Uncle Jacob and myself *walked*, as related above

We spent the remainder of the night sitting on the rocks, so enshrouded in blanket, that only one nostril was exposed. He was full of his stories and his drollery; and as much as I love sleep, and detest those insufferable insects, and as *thin-skinned* as I am, I would be willing to spend just as many hours, on just as many rocks, with just as many mosquitoes, could I be sure of just as entertaining company.

The man from Boston who wanted to see Billy was, as Bobby Short put it, "the man that keeps the squirrel-shop." He was, in fact, in the live-animal business, — squirrels, rabbits, birds, &c. Also bought skins. His place of business was in the city; but he was then staying at Coot Pint with a party who came there to shoot, fish, and enjoy themselves by land or sea.

Meeting with Dorry, and expressing a wish to find some boy who would catch squirrels and rabbits for pay, Dorry recommended Billy. I smile as I write these words, thinking of one of Billy's adventures while in the squirrel-business. If the letter he wrote Dorry about it can be found, I must certainly avail myself of its contents; for though I recollect perfectly well the bare facts, yet his way of telling makes them seem more real.

Meanwhile, from the pile of my own letters before me I select the following, not because it contains any very striking experience, joyful or otherwise, but because it gives some idea of the family life and of the family individually.

Mr. Fry to his Sister.

DEAR JULIANA, —

It is a fine September morning, baking-day morning; and I am sitting on Aunt Phebe's piazza, writing this epistle, hoping it may find you in better health than usual. Not being much given to meditation, but finding my chief delight in seeing and hearing, my location

exactly suits me : for. seated on this rustic bench. I can
see a great deal that is interesting without, and hear a
great deal that is interesting within.

If you could only behold this back, or rather this
end yard. you would behold there wheelbarrows, roller-
carts, two hay-stacks, vehicles of all sorts and of all
ages. a plough. a drinking-trough, a hogshead, boxes,
barrels, and baskets. dogs lounging, cats racing, hens,
roosters. and many other things.   In the barn-door some
of the animals are standing for a tableau, — were you
aware. before, that they knew how to get them up? — a
lamb, a cow, and a rooster, representing innocence, use-
fulness. and watchfulness.

There goes poor little Rover.   While we were camping out. Jacky cut off the end of his tail.   Tommy was
overcome with grief.   Do you know how quick cats are
to notice any change in the familiar objects about them?
Bring home a new piece of furniture. and they will
smell of it, and rub against it, and walk round it, as if
trying to get acquainted.   Georgie's cat. Mary Ann,
observed Rover's loss, and bestowed upon him so many
of these little extra attentions, that he flew into a rage,
and made her feel very sensibly the indelicacy of noti-
cing a personal defect.

And, now, isn't this singular?   For some time after
the mishap. Rover seated himself every evening at a
particular spot by the board fence, and there whined
and mourned his loss!   We suppose the deed was done
on that spot; and we know that Jacky was the doer, because Rover snaps at him, now. every time he comes in
sight.   Tommy. however, is anxious to keep on good
terms with Jacky, because Jacky is a *bigger feller;* and

as the *big fellers* won't play with him (with Jacky), for
certain reasons, he is very glad to go with Tommy's set.
Besides, he seems to consider himself entitled to a sort
of *outside* place here: I suppose because the Mr. Carvers took an interest in getting a place for him, and in
finding Tim a house to live in. Then Billy, you know,
was, in a manner, his discoverer.

It is all true what I intimated in regard to his father;
though this is not known beyond our two families, and
only to the older members of these. I hope the school-
children won't find it out. They torment him enough
already. Poor friendless child! He has no claim even
upon Tim, except that his father and mother and the
old man came from the same village in Canada.

The neighborhood boys plague Jacky. They say he
wears a little bag, — a little round leather bag, — fastened
to a string which hangs around his neck, underneath his
shirt; and that he will never let anybody see it. One
story is, that Tim's a Roman Catholic, and that what the
boy wears is something sent him by the Pope of Rome.
It is odd that he won't let any of us see it, — not even
Billy. Billy befriended the little fellow strongly at first:
but lately — well, I can hardly blame him for getting out
of patience; Jacky does do such provoking things! But
then he is so devoted to Billy! There's nothing he won't
do for him. Likes to hang about him; and will jump
to fetch and carry at the slightest hint. 'Tis really
touching to watch the poor fellow, especially after he
has spoiled some of Billy's things, or provoked him in
any way, — to see him trot along by his side, darting up
those quick, eager glances, as if trying to find out
whether he were to be borne with or not. The little

rogue has a bright eye, and a decidedly brisk, lively manner, and, when not at work, seems always just in the very midst of a good time. His smooth, pale face is an expressive one; and it wears, at such times, a look of entire satisfaction : the greater the mischief, the more entire the satisfaction. I never saw a better-natured boy, or one more anxious to please. He is helpful of his own accord. In doing you a favor, his eyes shine, and he seems in a perfect glow of delight. Quick-motioned too, and quick to observe ; sees what is needed in a flash, and is off like a flash to get it: but he seems not to know truth from falsehood.

O Juliana! you are a woman, with the fine instincts of a woman. Pray tell me how a boy like Jacky should be treated.

Grandmother feels for him. "Poor little child!" she says : "he's always so willin', and looks so pleasant!" You see, grandmother has a chronic propensity to give apples to little boys; and this propensity is by no means checked in Jacky's case ; and I more than suspect him to be familiar with the flavor of her molasses cookies. The girls have even accused her of baking turn-overs on purpose for him. "They taste so good to a child that never has any!" she says; "and he's so ready to do an errand !"

But, then, you can't trust him. He would run a mile to fetch me a bottle of ink ; but it might reach me, as one did, with the cork pushed in, and half empty. If grandmother gives him one apple, he is just as likely, when her back is turned, to help himself to another. And as to mischief, — why, just as great composers are born with music in them, so he seems to have been

born with mischief in him. Why, he's really an object
of curiosity. You never know what he won't be up to.
Set the grass on fire in Long Pasture the other day.

Say, what shall we do with this child? — this ten-years-
old boy? Whip him? It appears almost as if we
might as well whip a marigold for being yellow, or for
its smell.

Now, there's Bobby Short. He staid with us over
two months : always made himself agreeable ; and would,
I know, never be guilty of an unprincipled act. This
seems due to no effort on his part. Bobby Short is
so constituted, that ugly ways and dishonorable acts go
against his grain. If not honorable, he would not be
Bobby Short.

Now comes the puzzling question : Shall we commend Bobby Short for those qualities that are a part of
his nature? Shall we, any more than we commend the
damask rose for its fragrance, or for its being pink?
Well, rather more, I suppose. Still there is sufficient
uncertainty as to the amount of praise or blame due to
make this a question worth thinking about, — a question
which it would be well for boys and girls to think about
when they look down upon the outcast street-children ;
or for us elder ones, in fact, when looking down upon the
outcast anywhere.

Have you made up your mind how Jacky shall be
treated? or hasn't there been time to consider? Let
me suggest, that, when you do consider, you consider
this forlorn child, not as Jacky, but as your own boy in
Jacky's place. This may help you to a decision. Don't
hold him off to look at him. Bring him close to
you.

I hear the little fellow's shrill voice now *"counting
out :"* —

> "Intry, mintry, kutry, korn.
> Apple, seed and, brier, thorn.
> Wire, brier, limber, lock.
> Five, mice, in a, flock.
> Sit and, sing. In the, spring.
> O—u—t, out!"

And now another : —

> "Iggary, igary, ogary, on.
> Fillissy, follissy, Nicholas, John.
> Queeby, quoby, Irish, Mary.
> Spinkalum, spankalum, buc!"

He has run away from work. I haven't the least doubt;
and will probably *catch it* when Mrs. Paulina finds him.
Still, as I said before, he must pay his way.

Juliana, this has not even begun to be the sort of letter I sat here for to write. My intention was to put
down whatever I heard within, or saw without ; thus giving you a double entertainment. 'Twas Rover turned
me aside, — brisk little Rover, flying at the hens, and
driving them into the water-trough. That water-trough !
I could write letters by the dozen on its varied experiences. It is the general rendezvous for cattle, fowls,
and children. Indeed, I believe I might sit here a month
and write letters, taking, each time, a different object for
a subject.

The talk inside goes on lively. Aunt Phebe has
missed a piece of plum-cake she put away in the buttery.
The girls *blame it on to* their father. He owns up at
last ; says he thought may be the cat might get it !

Besides, knows they wouldn't have any so good on the supper-table. "And if we do," says he, — "I never knew it to fail, — but, if you set on extra nice cake, company is sure to be there to eat it up!" Says company always does come when they have good things. L. M. tells him he puts cause for effect.

"If 'twere not for company, you wouldn't get any," says Matilda.

"And so," says L. M., "you ought to be grateful to company, — not reproach them."

Matilda has just passed out with a handful of withered flowers. She never puts these in the stove; says it makes her feel badly to see the fire taking hold of the poor things: so she carries them out to die among their kindred. Matilda's face, and light, braided hair, make me think of those pretty German girls we saw at Newark. Her figure, also. Lucy Maria is slender. She is graceful in her motions; has merry, twinkling eyes like her father's; and much of that hearty, sincere look which seems to run in the family. When I say her eyes twinkle, I don't mean to say they twinkle every minute of their lives. At times, at very many times, they have a mild — well, call it sweet expression. But I should think you might tell by my letters just about what kind of a face hers is. Its shape corresponds with her figure. All three of the girls have remarkably fresh, pure complexions. I suppose L. M. has the most real beauty. Her mouth, as William Henry said once, speaking of a pleasant lady in the cars who treated him to oranges. "is like the mouth of a picture." I call it an amiable mouth. The lips meet in such a pleasant way! and, even when it is quiet, there's always a ghost of a smile playing about the corners. I acquired this habit of judging of the dispositions of people by their lips, in travelling. If you are ever able to travel in a horse-car again, you just watch the passengers sitting along in dumb show, and notice the difference in their ways of closing the mouth.

Hannah Jane is large, well-formed, and looks like a bunch of clear common sense. She has a round face, and light brown hair like Matilda's. Lucy Maria's is dark. Hannah Jane thinks less of dress than either of the others; is careful, thoughtful; never makes a joke, but laughs very cheerfully when one is presented. I think she is rather more apt to judge hardly of people than L. M., or is not so apt to weigh fairly. L. M. likes to look on all sides of a question or a character. She takes this from her mother. Her wavy locks she takes from grandmother. They say grandmother had beautiful hair once. The color, alas! has faded; but the *wave* is still there. (*Vide* Dorry's description in Wm. H. Letters.)

Aunt Phebe, in the midst of rolling out pies, has just laid down a rule : " *Never think strange.*" They were talking about Mrs. Paulina.

" How *strange* it is," Hannah Jane remarked, " that Mrs. Paulina doesn't send back our three-pint pail ! "

" That's because you are young," said her mother. " Now, I have lived a good while in the world, and I have '*thought strange*' and *wondered at* people so many times, and found out afterwards that they had good reasons, and been *wondered at* so often myself, when I had good reasons, that I've come to this rule : ' *Never think strange.*' If we could look into people, and see all their whys and why nots, it would alter the case; but we can't."

"I shouldn't think you'd stand up for keeping borrowed things!" said Matilda.

"I don't," said Aunt Phebe. "Keeping borrowed things, as I have seen them kept, is next kin to stealing. All I meant was, that Mrs. Paulina *might* have been hindered in some way from bringing back our pail."

"Maybe," said L. M., "she's keeping it to rub up bright. Hope she is!"

"Maybe she has put it away in such a safe place," said Aunt Phebe, "it has gone out of her mind. I've done that myself."

"I guess Jacky went huckleberrying with it!" said Georgie. "He took her coffee-pot once."

"Oh! I know," said Lucy Maria: "Mr. Slade has gone after white sugar in it! Billy said he came to the store, a while ago, after two pounds of white sugar. Told Mr. Gossam he guessed he'd get 'two pounds, so as not to keep runnin'!'"

"How much white sugar anybody uses," said her mother, "depends on how they've been brought up."

"That's so!" cried Uncle Jacob from another room. "People's habits mostly do depend something on how they've been brought up."

"So we ought to have charity," said Aunt Phebe. "A good many reasons may hinder bringing back a three-pint pail. Now, carry that three-pint pail into other things, and have charity!"

"How about dandies?" asked L. M. mischievously.

"You have her now!" I thought; for dandies are her

especial abhorrence. "Well," said she, "if you can tell *anybody* by their outside looks, you can tell one of that kind; because you seem to know right off that the outside is all there is to them. I never see one of those silly-looking (what your father calls *dandified*) *coots* without wanting to do *so!*" (I peeped in just in time to see her puffing with her lips, as if blowing a feather away.)

"Good for you, mother!" cried Hannah Jane. "I'm glad to hear you come down square on somebody!"

"Still," added Aunt Phebe in a hesitating voice, balancing a pie on the ends of her fingers to trim the edges, — "still I may be wrong to judge them. 'Tisn't impossible but that even they may have human feelings. But I know one thing: I don't want our Billy to be one of that kind."

"Precious little danger!" the girls thought.

Poor Aunt Phebe! What with her fears of not having *charity*, and her scorn of all deceit and outside show, she is brought to sore straits.

Now Tommy has come in with wet feet and trousers; says he got caught in a mud-puddle. Now he's crying to go to the show this afternoon. His mother says, "No: you went to the circus last week. Little boys can't go everywhere."

"There he runs in to grandmother's!" said Matilda.

"I gave grandmother her charge this morning," said Aunt Phebe, "not to give him any money."

Tommy has a bank, in which are cents untold; but he can't get it open. It was made so at his own request. Billy has a bank too; that is, he is getting together quite a little pile of money. Has trapped a good many

squirrels, rabbits, and woodchucks, and sold a number of
skins.   Means to "*go into it strong*" next month.   Shall
keep you advised of his success, and of any remarkable
incidents which may transpire, for the entertainment of
little Silas (if there be any *little Silas* by this time).   I
suppose that ancient veteran has forgotten how it feels to
feel little.

Billy is anxious to leave school at once, and devote
himself wholly to making money, — *right away*, — so as
to go into a place by the first of January.   Mrs. Benjamin came to the store the other day to get a bottle of
spiced bitters for *My Bettina*, and, in talking with Billy,
told him that learning wouldn't be of any use for a
business-man.   Mrs. Benjamin don't approve of poor people acquiring much knowledge.   She remarked to some
one, that she thought it very foolish of Mrs. Jacob Carver to allow her girls so much reading-time.   Don't know
what she would have said if the girls had bought their
piano!   Did I tell you, that, after their father lost his
wood, the girls made him take what money they had
earned towards buying one?   He felt badly about using
it : but the woodcutters needed their pay ; and the girls
told him they shouldn't take any comfort playing, thinking that the men he owed might be going by, and hearing them.   Said 'twould always seem out of tune ; and
they'd rather begin all over again.   Mrs. Benjamin says
Lucy Maria might clothe herself handsomely by putting
her time to better use, instead of reading, and making
pictures.   I suppose, this, reduced to its lowest terms,
means that it would be better for Lucy Maria to wear
more flounces. and paint fewer roses.

But Mrs. Benjamin isn't the only person who talks

in this way. I once heard a lady say (and she was considered by most people, and by herself, as rather a superior lady), that, in her opinion, it was a waste of money to provide high schools for the middle and lower classes. "It is not well," she said, "to educate such children above their level: it will make them look down on their parents." O foolish *superior lady*, not to understand that the truly educated never look down on anybody! Now, I think that poor people need learning more than the rich, because they have fewer advantages of other kinds.

In speaking of *level*, I suppose she meant *level of money*. Yes: I know she did; for I distinctly remember hearing her say that learning was for those who could pay for it. She couldn't have meant level of mind, because you find no more good minds in the wealthy class than in any other. Mr. Carver thinks, that, some time or other, — say just before the millennium, — all the learning of the earth will be free to all the children of the earth. Some people want the community to be arranged in layers, and kept so, — the zeros at the bottom, then the hundred-dollar ones, then the thousand-dollar ones, then the ten-thousand, fifty-thousand, hundred-thousand; and so on. Of course, all such persons would dislike the millennial arrangement, because that would tend to forming the layers on a different plan: mind would come to the top, and money go down to zero.

Were this letter addressed to a stranger, that stranger might infer that the writer avoided all chances of making money; but you, my dear sister, know that your brother has never been opposed to our family finding a pot of gold!

Speaking of money always brings me back to Billy; for he has the money-fever strong about this time. The squirrel-man, finding his squirrel-boy so eager, told him of an *Irish-moss man*, who would pay for as much of that article as he would send on: and, as Billy has no time to go himself, he hired Quorm to cart some; and his father let him pay in vegetables. So here we have Irish moss whitening and drying. Requires considerable labor to cleanse it; but then, the nicer it looks, the better the pay. Billy is pretty persevering.

Now Mr. Carver has come in; and they are talking about the Corry-pond Lot. There's a prospect of selling it. Some great man is going to build some great factory near there, and land will go up. Aunt Phebe is calling me to come in, and take my turn-over before Uncle Jacob gets it. Such a call I must obey. So no more at present. From your loving brother,

S. Y. FRY.

I smile again in copying the sentence speaking of William Henry's squirrel-adventures, — one of them was so comical! My letter speaking of it must be somewhere in the pile, unless Juliana has mislaid it; or possibly Billy's own letter, written to Dorry about that time, may be procurable.

The mention, as above, of the Irish moss, and of Tommy's desire to go to the show, brings to my recollection the manner of his getting in to that show, and likewise his coming home at night.

We were sitting out-doors, some of us. after tea, near where the moss was spread to dry; and, very naturally, the talk ran on the blanc-mange it might make, and the

parties where it might in that form be passed round.
and the pretty girls who might taste it, and so on. —
just our Summer-sweeting kind of nonsense, — when
Aunt Phebe came out, asking what had become of Tommy; for the child had not been seen since dinner.

I immediately thought of the show, knowing very
well that grandmother couldn't have stood it to hear
him cry for any thing so long as there was any milk-
money in the porringer. I mentioned my suspicions:
but Aunt Phebe said she had been to grandmother; and
Tommy did not even ask her for any money, but went
off in a great hurry with Jacky.

Soon after this, the young gentleman appeared, offer-
ing himself as a candidate for supper; and a very needy
candidate he seemed. Tommy had been to the show.

"How did you get in?" was the unanimous question.

"Oh! *I* know."

"But we want to know too!"

"I went in — I went in taking hold of somefing."

"What something did you take hold of?"

"Of a seat."

After further questioning, it appeared that Jacky had
managed to get himself employed by the proprietors in
various ways; and that, out of pure friendship, he let
Tommy "take hold of" a settee, and so passed him in
free as one of the helpers.

"I sho-o-o-d wight by the door-man," said Tommy,
acting it out with his hands; "and he didn't say nof-
ffin'!"

After this explanation, silence reigned among us for
the space of some seconds. A few individuals looked

10

rather smiling than otherwise; but all appeared to feel
that smiling was not exactly in order. Aunt Phebe's
face wore a very grave expression. "Tommy, that was
cheating!"

"'Tis go-un to be again to-night," he stated in a
somewhat doubtful tone of voice.

Aunt Phebe led him away. In about half an hour
after, I saw Uncle Jacob driving off with Tommy in the
riding-wagon. The *door-man* was found, and received
his quarter.

Many people would have thought it folly to take so
much trouble for such a small sum. The sum was small,
I know; but the principle spread over all creation. Aunt
Phebe said she did detest meanness of every sort and
fashion, and all kinds of *underhandednesses*, sneaking
ways, and getting things out of people for nothing! and
she wanted that ground into Tommy while he was young,
so 'twould never wash out!

I remember, that same night, of hearing L. M. say
with a comical groan, —

"Oh, dear! there's poor Tommy being led off to have
his 'talking to'! When I was a child, how I did dread
one of mother's 'talking to's'! Mother does know how
to make poor little sinners feel terribly ashamed!"

Aunt Phebe's "talking to," and the general bearing
of the family towards him, made Tommy feel himself
such a great way below par, that he was glad to raise
himself up to good fellowship by getting me to open his
bank, and paying his father the quarter.

The following letter is selected because it contains a number of interesting items, I think. If boys want to skip the

sticks of wood, squashes, corn-cobs, and clothes-pins, they can do so. There's no law against skipping. if we except that against girls skipping in the street; and I, for one, am sufficiently friendly towards them to wish even that law abolished.

Mr. Fry to his Sister.

DEAR JULIANA, —

I think this fine bracing weather must be welcome to an invalid like yourself. October is *one* of my favorite months. It gives us as much warmth as is agreeable, and as much coolness; as much daylight as we care to use, and as much fruit as we want to eat.

We are all going on happily here, — all up and stirring, particularly Billy; for the Corry-pond Lot is sold. That "place in some large firm" seems very near; and I am not sure but he discerns afar off the towers and turrets of his grand mansion.

I am writing at grandmother's, in my own room. Only one reason prevents my wishing you were sitting here too, enjoying this beautiful prospect. The one reason is, that I then could not or should not be occupying this stuffed arm-chair. My duties as a man and a brother would forbid.

This is a cosey, comfortable, ancient room; and it just suits me. The furniture does not match, to be sure; but it matches my frame of mind, whether that be gloomy, bright, or serene : and so various are its contents, that even were the curtains dropped, shutting out out-doors altogether, I could find plenty inside with which to occupy my mind. Why! the bed-quilt alone gives me never-ending entertainment; for though I often begin at the head, and try to study out the figures and the

beauties of every square. I am certain, before reaching
the foot, to be lost in the mazes of shapes and colors,
through which the quilting, though it does have such a
straight-forward air. is no guide whatever.

The window-curtains are full, and are made of
large-figured — extremely large-figured — copperplate;
the figures being composed of immense peonies, and
other flowers that I don't know the names of. A wide
ruffle runs across the top, hanging down; and this ruffle is trimmed with white tasselled fringe, that was net-
ted by grandmother's mother. The bed-curtains, also,
are trimmed with it; and are looped up in a great many
places, or several. The floor is painted green, sprinkled
with white drops, — a very cool, agreeable floor for sum-
mer-time. Since the weather has become cooler, grandmother, for fear of my having cold feet, is continually
dropping down braided mats. By the bedside, fire-
side, in front of the arm-chair, at each window, before
the glass, wherever a person would be likely to sit
or stand or walk, the floor is covered. That before the
glass is not braided: it is made of lozenges, — many-
colored woollen lozenges. The rug in front of the fire-
place is really handsome; being wrought by hand, with
carpet-yarn, different kinds of brown. This was done
by William Henry's mother; as, likewise, was the silk
patchwork cushion on the low chair, and a white stand-
cover, which looks like lace. There are other specimens
of her handiwork besides, every one of which is a mar-
vel of neatness and delicate finish. I like to have
these in the room. It may be imagination; but they do
really seem to throw her gentle influence about me.

William Henry's mother must have been a saintly,

lovable person. They always speak her name tenderly, and in a subdued voice, as if her memory were very sacred. How true it is that a beautiful character never dies! And what a blessing 'tis 'tis true! Sometimes, sitting here alone, I shut my eyes, and, by remembering the picture in Billy's room, try to bring before me the face and form of this deeply-lamented Harriet, of whom it is said by all, *"You couldn't help loving her!"* I am sure the memory of her is a blessing; and, if **a** blessing, a help.

The responsibility of filling the place of such a mother weighs heavily on grandmother. There has been, however, as you may imagine, no lack of love and of tenderness. And certainly a mother could never have hoarded up with more tender care every little relic of his babyhood and early boyhood, — his first shoes, his little cap and feather, a bright plaid frock, even his first jacket and trousers, all tattered and torn. The girls declare that grandmother saved all the broken dishes that Billy ever broke till they outnumbered the whole ones! I can imagine his having made sad havoc among crockery-ware, and among other ware, and everywhere. Indeed, this very room bears marks of his youthful presence, — pin-scratches on the window-glass, a few nails driven in in unnecessary places, dents in the woodwork, and a hack or two on the tall mahogany bedposts!

By the way, how much there is in one's surroundings! These tall mahogany bedposts give me a very kingly, or at any rate a very princely, feeling of nights. There is a frame-work overhead, which touches the ceiling; though, to be sure, it need not raise itself

far to do that. This frame-work is covered with white
dimity curtains. The bureau and table covers are
of white *dimity* too. I like to keep saying *dimity;*
for I never saw any *dimity* before, knowing it to be
dimity; and I think it has a very meek, innocent sound.

The arm-chair is covered with *copper-plate:* so is
copper-plate a new word, too, to me. It has an artistic
sound; and I like to say this over too, but not so well
as I do *dimity.* This last — this *copperplate* — is
purplish, I should say, were there not a future possi-
bility of your coming here, and calling it something
just the opposite !

I really hope you will be able to travel as far as
here by another summer. The change would be a
benefit; and then I want my little niece to see Georgiana. The worst of it would be my having to give
up, not only this chair, but this room; for, having once
set foot within its four walls, you would refuse to leave
it for any other, match or no match. The chamber in
Josephine's new house, which she so kindly calls *Uncle
Silas's room,* is. I am aware, a pattern-chamber. The
bed is flat, low, and level; the pillows are models of
weight and size; and the *pillow-shams* are perfection
in their way. which is sham. The covering of the
divan (a trunk, I believe), the window-curtains, the
spread, and. I might almost add, the carpet and wall-
paper, are off the same piece of — patch, she calls hers.
Nothing could be neater than those dove-colored sprigs,
— if they be dove-colored (it is dangerous talking of
colors to a woman, and a German-worsted woman at
that). I enjoy Josephine's room: it is satisfactory. Its
neatness arouses all the neatness within me. Its fitness

is a silent discourse on the desirableness of a well-balanced mind.

But, happily. a man's capacity for enjoyment is not limited to the walls of one apartment. I enjoy both kinds, as you may know from the fact, that, until beginning this letter, the question of these things matching. or not, had never entered my mind. Not match? They do; or mingle, at any rate. What matter if they present every color you can find in a ray of light? Don't they all unite, and form a perfect whole? Their very unlikeness causes them to correspond with each other and with my own feelings. Now, there's a sameness about Josephine's dove-colored arrangements (if they be dove-colored); and whether you feel sour and sad, or merry and glad, this sameness is fixed before you like a dead wall. But here there are sombre colors for your dull moods, and plenty of red, yellow, and blue for your lively ones. These last three, and others, are in the wall-paper, which is a very dark ground *diamonded* off with posies. This wall-paper stops at the fire-place; for there the woodwork reaches to the ceiling. If I am ever staying here when William Henry is away, I mean to ask grandmother to let me take down that picture of his mother from its place opposite his bed, in the little sink-room chamber, and hang it in this vacant place. I like so much the expression of those earnest eyes! They seem to look out from a pure and truthful soul. Perhaps *pleading* is a better word for them than *earnest*. When William Henry was a little boy, about four or five years old, he told his grandmother one night, after a rather naughty day, that his mother's face talked to him. He was in bed at the time, and, as he spoke, turned away from the picture.

" And what does it say ? " grandmother asked.

" Say, ' *Do* be good boy ! ' " he answered, half crying.

Grandmother thinks the picture has always had an influence over him ; though he may not be aware of it.

Georgiana has something of that same earnest expression in her brown eyes. I would like you to see Georgie. She is older, rather, than your little Mary, but not so tall. They would play nicely together. She has chubby cheeks, the oddest little puckered-up mouth, — rosy mouth, — straight eyebrows, and brown hair, which grandmother keeps back out of her eyes, and tied in some way that fetches a bow behind each ear. She's young of her age : and I am glad of it ; old little girls are such painful creatures to have about !

I do wish little Mary could see Georgiana's baby-house ! It consists of space, up garret, partitioned off by chests, barrels, spinning-wheels, old fire-boards, yarn-winders, and other things. Here alone, or with her little playmates, Georgie carries on her house-keeping, — sets her tables, makes her beds, keeps school, and gives parties ; and here her numerous children are dressed, undressed, scolded, coaxed, trotted, spanked, and rocked to sleep. The cradle is the same in which Billy and herself were rocked.

Besides her dolls (and what she likes better than dolls), there are all her stick-of-wood, squash, clothes-pin, and corn-cob children. These are invaluable in case she feels like keeping an academy or giving a large party, as the number need not be limited.

There are several *residences* in the garret, in each of which dwells a separate family. Thus Mr. and Mrs. Brick live by the chimney ; Mr. Brick consisting of a

pair of tongs and a straw hat, and Mrs. Brick of a
shovel and sun-bonnet.   Mr. Window is a forked stick
of "refuge oak," rejoicing in one arm (a rare possession),
and a beaver.   Mrs. Window is a fair, split-pine matron,
with a gorgeous head-dress and a trail.   Capt. and Mrs.
Knothole are the boot-jack and press-board.   Dr. Beam
and his wife are respectively the lower end of a broken
pitchfork and an old pair of bellows.   All are fittingly
though scantily attired.   The school-ma'am is slim, being composed wholly, when I saw her going up one day,
of a yard-stick, an apron, some dandelion curls, and a
veil.

There is no lack of grandmothers, because there is no
lack of necked squashes.   A row of these venerable
characters, in old women's caps, is comical to behold !
Neither is there any reason why Mr. and Mrs. Brick
and others should not have large families ; as, for these,
clothes-pins and odd forks, corn-cobs and odd knives,
are all that is required.

The garret-stairs are near my door ; and sometimes,
of a rainy day, I sit and laugh and laugh at the proceedings above, till I feel just about, as Dorry said,
"nine years old, and going on ten."   Mrs. Knothole
sends out her invitations, and would be " happy of your
company to tea."   These invitations are accepted ; and in
due time the guests arrive.   Mrs. Knothole throws open
her house literally, being obliged to take down the walls
for a table.   The talk runs on various subjects, — weather,
cookery, behavior of their children, forwardness of their
infants ; and the conversation is frequently interrupted
by the squalling of said infants, who, of course, have to
be hushed up, patted, carried about, and take oil, same
as live ones !

At a proper time the banquet is spread, where, if one may believe all one hears, every delicacy of every season is served. Tea is poured out: and the happy company are helped to bananas, apricots, strawberries, cocoanuts, jelly, roast turkey, and gooseberry-sauce. The remarks on all these fairly make one's mouth water. The politeness of hosts and guests, the complimentings, are beyond all account ; but, on the other hand, the cruelty of shutting up their naughty children in the warming-pan is dreadful to think of !

Sometimes the cat, Mary Ann, permits herself to be arrayed in hat and shawl, or in night-gown and night-cap, and then rocked in the doll's cradle ; and sometimes even Tommy, when driven to it by a lack of *fellers*, or by his love of dressing up, will let himself be "sent for," and will appear as "the doctor," with cane, spectacles, ruffled shirt, and medicine-trunk. One day, he was called to Mrs. Dr. Knothole's visitor. the "belle of Boston," — a slim stick. dressed up like Mrs. Benja*min* (by L. M., no doubt), in the height and depth of fashion, — with fine shaving curls, ribbons, laces, flounces, feathers, flowers, and a striking chignon. The unfortunate lady had fainted !

I should like to go up some day and make a sketch of the proceedings, to send little Mary : but my first step on the stair would break the charm; and, in the twinkling of an eye. host, hostess, and guests would resume their inanimate condition.

I did, however, take off my boots, and *peek*, one afternoon. when the party was almost done, the table cleared away, and the company sitting around the fire for a sociable chat. The fire consisted of a pair of andirons set against the chimney. The guests were ranged in a sort of semicircle against a background of chests, spinning-wheels, fire-boards, and other furniture. The boys and girls, being spry, had perched themselves on yarn-winders, spindles, wheel-spokes, chair-backs, &c.

It was the grandmothers that undid me; made me turn back in a hurry with what Billy would have called "a *squelch*," and flee to my room. I hardly think they heard me.

Now, even while I write, the little girl comes across the garden, tugging a bright-yellow, crooked-neck individual. soon to be arrayed in fitting apparel; viz., a ruffled nightcap. Lucy M. declares that Georgie feels a motherly feeling toward every one in the field; and hardly dares to taste of a squash-pie, lest she should be eating one of her own children's grandmothers!

The specimen about to be added to the community overhead looks big enough to be a great-great-grandmother. Now she stumbles! Down it goes; and down she goes! Jacky runs to the rescue. I saw him hanging about the house before I came up, — waiting, I suppose, to see whether Billy were here, before daring to come in. He has been devoted to Billy from the first. Used to run his errands, and follow him about like a little dog: and so he would still; only Billy declares, after long experience, that he "*will not have Jacky round!*"

And I hardly wonder at this. He is so provoking! Last week, he carried Billy's ship — the large. full-rigged ship Cousin Joe made — off to the pond, and got the shrouds in a muss, and broke her yards. He never gets mad, whatever you do or say to him. Were Billy to give him a good shaking. as happened after the shipwreck, and shake him to rags almost, he might whimper a little; but, if Billy wanted an errand done the very next minute, he'd brighten up, and be off in a twinkle. The other day, he was the means of a rabbit getting away. Billy says, "My red hair does get so mad!" I tell him his hair isn't red enough to get mad now!

The poor child seems forlorn enough. Mrs. Paulina sent him away long ago. Grandmother pities him, and lets him creep into the house of a rainy day, and hang about her stove; and gives him cookies on the sly.

"What makes you, grandmother?" Billy asks: "'tis only tollin' him round; and more than likely, when you give him an apple, he's got his pocket full, that he helped himself to."

"Poor friendless child!" says grandmother. "Everybody's down on him; and he's got no home that is a home!"

The little rogue has quick feelings. When Billy does give him a pleasant word, his pale face lights up in a moment. Did you ever hear of quick-motioned eyes? His are. They dart quick glances at you, as if to make out in a flash what you mean to do to him, or how he stands with you. I suppose this comes of his having been *pounced upon* so many times. Billy let him carry his squirrel-trap the other day; and he did trot along by his side happy as a king.

There he goes off with Tommy and a large pumpkin. Tommy is to have a Jack-o'-lantern; and Jacky will be head workman. Tommy is Jacky's firm friend; but the larger boys plague him more than ever. That *secret* about his father is no secret now. The matter leaked out at last; and the children got hold of it. This has revived the matter of *the bag*, and has added to his other nicknames that of "*jail-bird.*"

Have you decided yet, you kind-hearted, reasonable woman, how this child shall be treated? Is there any way of saving him from growing worse as he grows older? If born bad, is it fair for everybody to be "down on him"? Still everybody ought to be down upon all wrong. How shall we make him understand, that, while we scorn and detest thieving, we feel only kindness and pity towards the thief? Another question: *Do* we feel kindness and pity towards the thief? I think Aunt Phebe does; and grandmother, of course. Aunt Phebe says she has made up her mind that bad folks are more to be pitied than poor folks or sick folks, or any other kind; for what can be worse than to be so made that you like sin?

Hurrah! Billy's home! Do you want to know how I found out without seeing him, or hearing his voice? By the rummaging sounds from below. Our Billy is a rummager. When the fit is on, he wanders here and there, opening and shutting, ransacking bureau-drawers, climbing to top-shelves, scattering newspapers, undoing bundles, not with the view of finding any thing in particular, but just to see what he will come across. Grandmother follows him like a calm after a storm, bringing things to their level again.

There he goes with certainly as much as a quarter of a pie! In all my travels, I never met with anybody so utterly and constitutionally hungry as William Henry. "I never see a plum (raisin) but I want to put it in my mouth," was a juvenile remark of his, they tell me. He might extend this remark far beyond "a plum."

Now he walks off, talking, between bites, with Storey
Thompson. Georgie runs after him. He's teasing her
with something, — a letter. Now he holds it up; and I
guess, by their motions, he is telling her to "*speak for
it.*"

She spoke for it, and now comes back with the letter;
and the boys walk away. Storey gets plagued as well as
Jacky. The *fellers* call him " Kid-Fingers " and "Cuppy," and "Storey Thomp, full of pomp." He has been
seen, sometimes, sawing wood with gloves on, " all on a
summer's day; " which accounts for the first nickname.
The second came about in this way : —

One morning, Gus was killing a fowl for the market; and, after being deprived of her head, she ran a few steps, as fowls do sometimes; which semi-posthumous proceeding took her under the barn. Storey, being present at the time, called out, "Cup, cup, cuppy!" and threw down a handful of corn to make her come out! So, now, the boys call him *Cuppy*.

He wants to go *squirreling* with Billy. We have great doings in trap-making. Billy is going down to Corry's Pond, Saturday, where Quorm has promised to set some traps. I am to keep store for him; expect to enjoy my part. There are some queer old coveys that come to the store, and sit and talk, and tell stories.

. . . .

Always your brother,

SILAS YOUNG FRY.

P. S. — I have just drawn from memory this sketch of Mrs. Knothole's party; which please give little Mary. — S. Y. F.

In copying the above letter, many, oh! very many incidents come vividly before me, — some so comical, that, in recalling them, I laughed out, here all alone by myself; while others were of a serious nature, — sad, even.

Poor little Jacky! It was not a very long time before he found *a home:* and I trust the angels can answer better than we the question I asked my sister. "How shall he be treated?"

There were circumstances connected with his passing away which made that event a sorrowful one, particularly for our two families. These circumstances will be found related farther on, just as I set them down at the time, in writing to my sister.

The letter which Georgiana was made to *speak for* came

from Etta, a young sister of *My Bettina*, — the same little girl who brought cocoanut-cakes and other niceties for our Fourth-of-July dinner. She was about a year older than Georgie, and sometimes, while in the country, came to play with her. For a number of weeks, they went to school together; and their intimacy came to the pitch of promising to write letters to each other.

I have just come upon one of these very entertaining epistles. Perhaps it may as well go in with the rest. Girls will be interested to read it. But first we must have Billy's squirrel letter.

William Henry to Dorry.

DEAR OLD DORRY, —

I expect you will laugh; and laugh away, then: who cares? I guess you wouldn't if you'd been there. Don't doubt you would, though! But, if you had been me, you wouldn't. Matilda will write about it to Maggie if I don't to you: so I might as well; and here goes.

I expect I ought to be glad that I heard something down there that wasn't such a very good thing to hear; but it would be a lie to say I was glad all over. My conscience is glad; but the rest of me isn't. Wait till I get there, then you'll see.

It happened just about two weeks ago; and I should have written before, only for feeling so strained and sprained, especially my arm, — the one that I write with. But I may as well begin, and put her through; for 'twould be just like Lucy Maria to make it all up into verses, and send you a copy. She isn't a cent's-worth too good to do it: though I must declare that she hasn't laughed at me half so much as I expected, or as much as she could; and hasn't made any picture.

I feel bound to state here, that William Henry gave that lively young lady more credit than belonged to her. She did make a picture, and she also wrote an amusing account of his adventures, after the manner of some old writer, — Dr. Johnson, I think; yes, it was Dr. Johnson, — beginning in this way: "William Henry, the son of Mr. Carver, left Summersweeting Place early in the morning. His heart was full of hope, his head was full of plans, his hand was full of traps. Dew-drops glittered on the plain; the sun rose bright in the eastern sky. He pressed rapidly forward across the meadows, and saw at length the ox-cart standing before him."

Out of consideration for his feelings, however, this account, and the picture, were only circulated privately. — S. Y. F.

[Now goes on the letter.]

I had to walk a mile across the fields to get to Sam Long's, — a man you don't know. Sam Long was going after wood, quite a good ways by Quorm's, and so let me ride to the place where he turned off. I carried lunch, and some new box-traps, and a box with places parted off, for the squirrels. Sam went to within half a mile of Quorm's, and then turned off; and I got off and footed it.

Quorm was working on baskets. I started on one; but it was one-sided. When he got ready, we went out to *catch 'em.* Quorm had some nets; and he threw these over a couple of trees where he thought there might be squirrel-nests, to snare 'em. I chased lots up trees; but they go down the other side just as easy! Don't you remember that one you most got that first time you ever came here? If 'twasn't for their getting out on the ends of boughs, a feller might do something. Quorm says that's where they always build their summer nests;

11

and their winter ones in the middle, in hollows. Summer residences and winter residences these fellers have. They don't seem shy in any sort of degree on the ends, but tilt away there all in plain sight; for they are so cute, they know you can't get them. I guess, if I scrabbled up one tree, I scrabbled up forty, and more too! I found one winter nest, he said it was, — an old one, out of repair, and out of use. 'Twas in the middle of a tree, in a crotch between two branches, in a hole; hid so that, looking up from down below, you couldn't see it. That nest held stuff enough! I threw out dry leaves, moss, and grass enough to make a good-sized haycock.

Besides snaring 'em. Quorm said he knew where one had a hole in the ground; and we'd try to dig him out. The hole was under a bank, where I never should have seen it. We dropped a stick down, and found 'twas just about three feet straight down; but there seemed to be no live animal inside. He said you couldn't tell; for the critters burrowed all ways. We dug down, and followed the burrows; but he'd stepped out, — gone out the back-door, I s'pose. But such a pile of provisions as we arrived at! I knew they hid away nuts and things, but had no idea they went into it so strong. Quorm says they are so craving, they'll keep lugging off and hiding away as long as there's any thing in sight. Regular old misers! In that hole we found, now, without stretching, half a peck of corn (good measure), half a peck of mixed grains, and about the same of grass-seeds, and a great pile of acorns and walnuts!

Now you see, old Dorrymas, I kept round with Quorm that way a good part of the day, digging down, and climbing up. About the last part of the afternoon, there came along a carriage with some ladies in it; and one of the ladies wanted to buy a basket: so Quorm said he'd leave me there to go it alone a spell; and, when I got tired, I might come to his hut, and have some roast rabbit. He roasts 'em on a string.

I read once in a book, that, if you want to see wild things in the woods (birds or any thing, bugs or any thing), you must sit down stock-still as a mouse, and not stir hand nor foot, and nigh about hold your breath; and I knew that myself before I read it: so I sat still, up against a tree-trunk, and kept my eyes and ears open. Gracious! what lots of bugs and crawlers, and all sorts of "critters," there are, that keep just out o' sight of folks! Gracious! that tree-trunk was all alive when I looked close!

There were squirrels in sight, and out of sight. I could hear them up in the tree going "Chip, chip, chip!" like chickens. Guess that's why they're called "chipmunks." Can't explain about the "munk;" but anybody that's gone to college ought to know. If some of 'em had only been just about half as spry, I should have been better off than I was.

I got up, and walked along; thought I'd be looking out for walnuts and squirrels at the same time. Found a tree where they hung thick enough, and filled my bag full. Went up trees, chasing squirrels for nothing, till I got about mad.

One little striped rascal scampered along a stone wall. Now look out for this one, Dorrymas! He's the rogue! He's the feller as did it! This botheration, he raced along stone walls and other things (this wasn't in the thickest woods), and I after him, much as half a mile,

through thick and thin, — but more thick, — in awful
places! — briery, boggy places: for I was determined I'd
have that one; for 'twas in a barer place, and no jumping
from tree to tree. I saw that squirrel drop four nuts!
— three out of his mouth, and one out of his paws.
When I first saw him, his cheeks pouched out like
Bobby Short's when he had the mumps. Guess Bob
would like to have dropped his mumps out.

Now I'm going to tell you something that is a good
deal better reading about than feeling. I s'pose you've
known times when your "sweet William" got his spunk
up. All I've got to say is, Add this time to 'em. No,
it isn't: I've got more to say, and the worst of it. He
led me such a chase! But at last he made for a tree that
stood entirely and individually all alone by itself. Now!

Up he went, lickertycut, and I after him like a cat
up a spout, and je—st got a glimpse of his tail whisk-
ing into a hole quite high up. I got up as high as I
could, and tried to run my arm in; but, the hole seeming
too small, off with my sleeve, and jammed her through
quicker'n lightning. Had to stand tiptoe; for the hole
was about level with my shoulder. Something bit my
forefinger. Now laugh! You wouldn't if you'd been
where I was: and I wasn't just where I was very
long; for the bough I stood on split off, so it left nothing
but the hub, that I could only keep my toes, one foot at
a time on, and cling hold with the arm that wasn't in
the hole. You see, I couldn't pull the other arm out;
and that was what's the matter! You see, when it went
in, it jammed in in a hurry: but the hole being so high,
and so small round, and me settled down some after the
bough gave way, and having to cling hold by my toes

and all the rest of me, I couldn't seem to get much purchase; and every pull seemed as if 'twould take the flesh all off my arm: so there we hung, — he inside, I out.   But I made out to squeeze him so, I guess he never bit again !

Well, there I staid; couldn't do any thing else but stay.   Yes, I could: I could holler.   But, you see, I didn't exactly like to holler.   You know (course you do) anybody in such a fix had rather get down himself. First I'd pull a spell, then hang on a spell.   But when it came to be sunset, and I thought about Sam Long meeting me at the turning-off place, I began to yell, "Help, help!   Quorm!   This way!   Here I be! He—lp!"

At last I didn't care who saw me, or who made fun of me, or who knew it, if somebody would only come. 'Twas a pretty straining undertaking to hold on under so many circumstances!   So, to take up my mind, I began to count my feelings: "Cold, one; tired, two; hungry, three; mad, four; sorry, five; lame, six; hoarse (hollerin'), seven."   When it grew dark, things began to look dark, I tell you, old Dorrymas! and the jokey part — what little there'd been — was nowhere; and I knew grandmother *had begun*, and how anxious my folks would be.

Want to know how I got down?   You know Mother Delight.   Well, Jake Bruel and Tom Bruel are her grandchildren.   Their mother is the one that Mother Delight calls "My darter Angeline."   Their father's name is Pete Bruel; and their grandfather is Old Pete Bruel.   He comes up sometimes, and puts his horse in our barn for nothing.   Guess you've seen that old

scalawag of a beast. They all live down Corry-pond
way. After I'd hollered a spell, Jake and Tom happened to hear the invitation I'd been giving out for
somebody to come and see me, and came. I sent 'em
after Quorm. They went, and found Quorm and Bunkum looking after me, and brought 'em along.

This is the way they took me down. I'll tell you; so,
if you ever have to, you'll know. Bunkum climbed up,
and raised me by my shoulders; and Quorm held my
legs; and I pulled my arm out, — biggest part of it.
Left some of the outside flesh of it in there, and some
shirt-sleeve.

You may know I'd had a serious time, when I tell you,
that, as soon as they set me down on the ground, I
tumbled down all in a heap, — fainted; and. next thing
I knew, I was being lugged off in Quorm's arms. He
took me to Bunkum's hut. It was nearer. Bunkum
lives in more real Injun fashion than Quorm does, and
farther into the woods, but nearer to where I hung
out my sign, — L. M. calls it *hanging out my sign*, —
"William H. Carver. Dealer in Squirrels." Does to
laugh over now; but 'twas no laughing-matter that
night. Even when I got to the hut, I couldn't stand up
alone, I was so weak and strained. They dropped me
into a bunk in the corner; rubbed stuff on my arm
(melted up in a quahaug-shell); and gave me something
good to drink, — hot and sweet, and mighty good. and
stillin'. I guess; for I felt sleepy, and went off to sleep.

Don't know how long I slept, but waked up by rolling
over on my arm. Felt stiff in my joints. Couldn't
have kicked a football over a hen-house. Heard a great
jabbering going on, and looked over the edge, and saw —

don't you remember, that time going to Coot Pint, of
one little, two little, three little, and more little, ragged,
barelegged Injuns popping out of the bushes as we went
along the Corry-pond Road, and Uncle Jacob saying
that folks called 'em *swamp angels?* Don't you remember that little one in a tail-coat big enough for
two? and that other, in a white beaver stuck on the
back of his head? and one with great man's boots on?
They were Bunkum's little Injuns; and there they
were squatted in the middle of the floor, parching
corn. They'd pushed back the coals, and put their corns
on the hot stone. In Bunkum's hut, the fire-place is
in the middle. 'Tis a place hollowed out in the ground,
with a great flat rock at the bottom, and a hole overhead
for the convenience of smoke. They were close round
the fire. stirring their corns. and jabbering; and back of
'em sat Bunkum and Old Pete Bruel. Quorm wasn't
there. Old Pete likes to be round with the Injuns.
hunting and fishing and drinking. I'd give something
to know all he knows! All the hunters want to get Pete
to go with 'em. He's always lived down that way, and
knows a good deal about wood-lots, and who owns which.
When folks want to know about old boundary-lines,
they go to Pete.

  Well, these two sat there, mighty chatty, tipping up
the jug pretty often. Bunkum is a real Injun. He
was in his shirt-sleeves, — red flannel shirt; collar un-
buttoned, and stretched open. Old Pete is a short-
legged, bald-headed, red-faced old fellow. He was
rigged out in two or three layers of old coats. Little
small eyes he's got. They two sat there guzzling
and chuckling, — Old Pete with his hands on his

knees; and, after a while, I found they were talking about me, and who my father was, and who my grand-father was. And this is what I'm coming to. Old Pete said he and my grandfather used to run ranges together, and used to know more about wood-lots than any other two.

This was true enough, I guess. You see, the old ranges were run when land wasn't of much account, and were only put down as running from such a pile of stones, or such a rock, or such a blasted tree or notched tree: so no wonder boundaries got doubtful, after a while.

But what most concerns me is this; and it does con-cern me a good deal. They got a-talking about our Uncle Wallace Lot, and about its being sold; and says Old Pete, chuckling, and slapping his knees, " He, he, he ! he, he, he ! 'Twasn't Mr. Carver's to sell ! 'Twasn't Old Wall's to give him !" Then, " He, he, he ! Chuckle, chuckle, chuckle ! "

I can't tell you all the talk, because I haven't patience to ; and my arm isn't so dreadful limber yet. But Pete told Bunkum that " Old Wall," as he called him, had to go to law with Sam Long's grandfather about a range; and that he (Pete) was called up for a witness, and lied in court so to help " Old Wall " get his case.

You see, I was hearing it all, looking over the edge.

" What'd you do that for ? " I hollered out.

You ought to've seen how it sobered down that old feller when I yelled at him ! And how he stared !

" What d'ye want to lie for ? " I hollered.

" Oh ! you keep still," says he.

But afterwards I got it out of him.

"Old Wall was rich," says he, "and found work for a good many hands. I was poorer'n poverty, and had a little family about me, and couldn't get nothing to do without he let me have work. That 'ere range, if it cut off that 'ere lot, would have to run so's to take a good

slice off his property : and he gin me to understand, that, if my talk went agin him, no more work."

"So you lied !" says I. "So whose do you call that lot ?"

"Lors !" says he, "'twon't make one bit o' difference. I sha'n't never tell." (Course he wouldn't ! Might be

taken up for perjury.) " You needn't let on nothing about
it. Them Longs is well off. 'Taint all one an' as if
they was poor tudies. They've got no eend o' woodland ! " says the old scamp.

I can't sit up straight, and make my arm go long
enough to write any more, only just to say that I got a
chance home early next morning with Dr. Sweetser.
He'd been down to see Angeline's child. Didn't get
very many squirrels. Lost two by the little Bruel
scamps looking in the box and lettin' 'em out.

From your friend,

SWEET WILLIAM (HENRY).

P. S. — I'm saving that squirrel for Maggie. I've got
a tip-top cage for it ! — S. W. H.

The day, and particularly the evening, of William Henry's
unlucky expedition, was not one to be forgotten. Grandmother
not only " began," but kept on. I went to Sam Long's. Sam
had waited fifteen minutes at the turning-off place, and then
concluded that Billy had " stepped on a piece," but didn't
overtake him.

Grandmother, Mr. Carver, myself, and the supper-table, sat
up till after eleven, expecting him to arrive every moment in a
state of starvation. Then we gave him up. Mr. Carver told
grandmother, that probably Billy found squirrels so thick, and
got so earnest, that he took no note of time ; and, having missed
Sam Long, would either stay all night at Quorm's, or come
afoot ; and if the latter, why, a great fellow of fifteen might be
trusted to find his way without walking into a pond, or getting
run over. So grandmother retired for the night ; though I suspected her of placing bandages and other appliances where
she could lay her hand on them in case of Billy's being brought
home drowned or damaged.

The young gentleman arrived early next morning, not in the best of spirits, as may be imagined; and, through the day, he showed a greater degree of seriousness, I thought, than his unlucky expedition would account for. This was explained when he told his story about the wood-lot.

Of course, there was but one course to take, — give the Longs their property.

The next letter is one of those mentioned just now as having been written to Georgie by Mrs. Benjamin's little girl, Etta.

Etta Calloon's Letter to Georgie.

MY DEAR GEORGIE, —

My sister Bettina she says I am not big enough to write letters; but my Uncle Willy says I am too, — big enough. I like my Uncle Willy. I don't like my sister Bettina; she orders: and I don't like my brother Clarry, that's just my size: he makes fun, and dunno how to act. Clarry would be better to be a girl: for you can tell girls things; but you can't tell boys things. And he always puts his feet somewhere. And two little sisters could dress just alike; and, oh! wouldn't that be perfectly splendid! I used to rather be a boy, so to drive hoop, and run out and do things, and holler: but now I'd rather be a girl; for mother says 'tisn't lady-like to run; and boys don't have so many pretty clothes as girls do. And I guess Clarry better be a boy; for mother couldn't get very much time to make his things. Mother's new machine hems ruffles perfectly splendid! Mother's going to let me have five ruffles on my new pink silk. Mother thinks I seem quite like a young lady since I began to go to dancing-school. Since I began to go to dan-

cing-school, I have my hair braded up nights, — little
brades, you know: wet 'em some, and then unbraded
again in the morning, when I get up; and it bunches
out all round, way out, — lovely, mother says. My Uncle
Willy is nothing but a man, mother says: so no matter
what he says: he don't know. He says looks like a crazy
Jane's porcupine — no: I guess Crazy Jane and a porcupine. I hope they'll do back-hairs up high's they do
now when I'm a young lady; for mother says 'twill be
very becoming to my style, but 'tisn't to Bettina's style.
Mother says my style is going to be anteek style. My
new pink silk is perfectly splendid! and its sash is going
to have ends to it behind, and hang down behind, ele-
gant!

I have to have a great many dresses to wear to dancing-school, because all the girls have on different dresses
every time: and mother says she'd be ashamed to send
me with the same dress on; and so should I too. But,
if you alter the trimming, then 'tisn't any matter. We
dance the German. Sometimes I get little boys: I
think little boys are horrid! Anna Myrick says she
thinks their mothers oughter be ashamed: but they will
keep coming; and we can't help ourselves. But sometimes I get a lovely great one! I couldn't go last time
'cause I'd worn every one of my party-dresses: and
mother couldn't get time to sew on my ruffles, because
she had to sew on eighteen dozen little buttons on to her
new lilac Mosumbeek that she was going to wear somewhere; and had the nuralgic in her face. Grandma says,
when she was a little girl, little girls didn't have but two
gowns besides the meeting-gown, and wore one every
week. Grandma said she wonders how many gowns
little girls will have when I'm the grandma.

I put on her specs, and her cap on my head, to see how I should look then; but she said I was too chubby. Grandma said she had chubby cheeks once. I wonder how they got so as they look now; and I asked her; and she said I should know, child, quite soon enough.

Isabel Turner is going to have a party in two weeks, just like a grown-up party, with a band of music and frozen pudding and citron-cake and ice-creams and salad, and dance the German, and white kid gloves; and, oh! won't it be perfectly splendid? Sit up late as grown-up folks we shall! and do just what grown-up folks do! And three more girls I know are going to have 'em too. All we girls that are going have splendid times, recesses. talking about it; and makes the other ones that can't go feel mad. Mother's begun to get me ready. Mother says 'twill take every minute; and all the girls' mothers don't do any thing but make things; and mother don't know but her head'll go crazy. Bettina wants mother to help her, too, for her ball; but she won't very much. She can't; for she's got to get me ready. Mine will be white, with Cloony lace, and rose-color under the Cloony; and rose-color French kid boots, because she thinks my feet look best in boots; but not the gloves, — they're white.

Mrs. Turner, the one's mother that's going to have the party, wants me to dance the hornpipe alone; and I expect to tremble just like a leaf before so many. — all looking at me, and some of their parents and friends! Mabel Pinker will too. She's going.to wear blue. My Uncle Willy don't want me to, and my Uncle Willy says 'tis a bad plan. And my father don't, either. But mother says we are so unsuffisticated, it won't hurt us. I hope I

spelt that great word right. Father says he wants me
to be a good speller. He says he thinks I'm a poor
speller now. But mother says I shall outgrow that.
Oh, won't it be perfectly splendid! I can't think of
nothing! Only two weeks! — Thursday, Friday, Saturday, Sunday, Monday, Tuesday, Wednesday, Thursday,
Friday, Saturday, Sunday, Monday, Tuesday, Wednesday.

My new hat's got a real ostrich-feather on it. I called
on Mabel Pinker yesterday with it on. All the girls
make calls on each other now, and, when they're out,
leave our cards. — quite small ones, with lovely edges to
them. And the boys do just like gentlemen, — raise their
hats when they see us. But Clarry won't. Mother don't
know what to do with Clarry 'cause he acts so. He
dunno how to behave. Can't think of any thing more
now. Wish you would write another letter to me, and
tell me more stories about that Jacky that acts so. It
makes my Uncle Willy laugh. My Uncle Willy says
he'll buy some of your great brother's things that he
sells. How does Grandma Squashy do? and little
Dicky Corn-cob? I told Uncle Willy, and made him
laugh. He wants to come to Mrs. Brick's party next
time she has one, and will come if she invites him to.
My Uncle Willy says he should like to live next house
to Mrs. Brick, so to go to her parties.

> Write soon.
> > Your affectionate friend,
> > > ETTA CALLOON.

I afterwards became acquainted with Etta's "Uncle
Willy," and found him a lively, companionable young

man. The "great brother's things that he sells " were
the various articles which Billy undertook to sell, and
did sell, on commission, after the sitting of the cooking-
stove council had taken place. These articles consisted
of maps, pictures, and a kind of soap for cleaning coat-
collars, the name of which just this moment escapes me,
but which I can cheerfully say that no unmarried man
should be without.

After Billy's disappointment in regard to the wood-
lot money, he seemed very low-spirited, for him. It put
him back ; and, as grandmother said, he never could
bear putting back. Grandmother became quite con-
cerned for his bodily health, on the ground that he
allowed a *cut pie* to remain untouched, all in sight ;
though, in my opinion, *incapacity* was the true cause of
so erratic a proceeding, or want of proceeding.

I do think, however, that the poor fellow was at that
time really "worried and plagued in his mind." This,
perhaps, too feebly expresses his condition. In a letter
to Dorry, written about that time, he says, —

" I shall die if I have to stay round here ! 'Tis dull as
putty ! 'Tis all putty ! Gracious ! I shall die if I don't
go somewhere, and go to doing something ! — if nothing
but blacking shoes ! I'm sick o' hanging round here !"

I have seen other boys in this same state of disgust.
Nothing pleases them. *'Tis all putty.* 'Tis grubby.
Like caterpillars in their " *chrysalises*," they are burst-
ing to plume their wings and soar away.

We recognized this pre-butterfly condition of Billy's,
as one brought on by the workings of Nature, and therefore not to be lightly regarded. Solemn council was
held around Aunt Phebe's cooking-stove. Previous to

this, however, we older ones had decided among ourselves that the young man really did possess some business-knack; as, for instance, in hiring small boys to work for him, and making a profit on their labor. His operations in *bayberries* (sold for making bayberry-tallow) were on a tremendous scale! Hired boys worked in well here, — in the picking, — as also in "snaring," "trapping," and in the "*moss-business.*" His head, in fact, was running over with schemes.

Another business-trait which we noticed was his exactness. He would not pay the little chaps one mill over their dues, or one mill under. A separate account for each was kept in a very mercantile-looking account-book.

Being the one grown-up boy in the family, it was but natural, that, at so important a period of his life, he should have frequently come under discussion. I remember Mr. Carver's expressing a hope, at the council referred to, that Billy's devotion to money-making would never draw him into narrow, mean ways.

"*No!*" said Aunt Phebe in a low but decided tone.

"You can't be sure," remarked one of the girls.

"Yes," she answered in the same tone: "I feel sure. I've watched him with a motive: and I've trembled for fear of seeing him take advantage; for fear of our not being able to respect him; for fear of finding something in him, — something that went *bias.*"

"But you can't tell, by these little matters, what he'll do by and by."

"Yes, you can! Five cents can show a thousand dollars' worth of meanness."

"That's true," said Mr. Carver.

"The greatest hinderance in his way," continued Aunt

Phebe, "is his being so quick to flare up. He can't bear much; and he'll have to."

This trait and others having been duly discussed, the following was declared to be the sense of the meeting : —

First, That William Henry's inclination for a certain calling was strong enough to warrant his following that calling.

Second, That Mr. Carver was unable, without considerable sacrifice, to meet the expenses of such "following."

Third, That offers of pecuniary assistance be declined (this in reference to the offer to William Henry of a small loan from myself, and of a larger one from Davy's father). Reason, the undesirableness of placing a heavy load upon the shoulders of a young fellow just starting up hill.

Fourth, That said William should wait until he had earned enough to pay at least two years' expenses.

Aunt Phebe was afraid that this last was too hard on Billy. He might get discouraged, she said, or unsettled in his mind. For her part, she was willing Jacob should sell a piece of land, and give Billy what it brought, right out and out. Mr. Carver said, if a boy's purpose could be so easily shaken, or, he would almost say, could be shaken at all, that boy would never succeed as a business-man. What he wanted was that Billy should get used to clearing away difficulties, and to jumping over them. Six months' practice of this kind would be a good apprenticeship to any sort of business. As for outside names, and rich men's names, and great men's patronage, he did'nt believe in any thing of the sort.

12

"No!" cried Uncle Jacob. "You don't want Billy to be boosted up, or hoisted up, or sent up on a kite."

"Just so," said Mr. Carver.

After some further talk, it was decided that William Henry be allowed to leave school, and to earn money by all ways and means that seemed to him good; such ways and means being left to his own finding out.

The matter of Billy's leaving school caused more talk than we have room for here. The chief thing which reconciled us to this step was, that the subject of our conversation showed a decided taste for natural history, — liking to dip into such books as treated of the habits of animals and of insect-life.

"Now," said Mr. Carver, "if he should carry out this liking, and inform himself on these matters, as he will have good chances of doing, I don't see why we should say he gives up getting any more education."

"For my part," said I, "I believe it is just as important to know how all the different kinds of spiders build their nests as to know the capitals of all the divisions of Asia and Africa. I had a knowledge of the capital of Afghanistan once; but it never sank into my mind, or influenced my life to any great degree : but a little book on insects, read in my boyhood, impressed me so deeply, that now, if I have any sense of the wonderfulness of the overwhelming amount of *life*, of *living*, that goes on around us, it is wholly owing to that book."

"And besides," said Lucy Maria, looking up suddenly, "as he grows older, this liking of his may lead him on to other things; and so he may get a very good kind of education, after all, if he wants to."

I had wondered that Lucy Maria should sit by and say so little. But observing, at last, a half-suppressed smile on her face, I glanced at her portfolio; and, by so glancing, discovered, that instead of copying poetry, as I had supposed, she had been engaged on a set of drawings *illustrating* our conversation.

The two first illustrated the remark of Mr. Carver's relating to the overcoming of obstacles.

One of this pair represented a resolute, not to say defiant youth, in the act of starting upon his travels over a decidedly rough road. The rocks, the pitfalls, the steep ascents, depicted by the imaginative artist, were awful to contemplate. Deep chasms yawned; dark mountains loomed in the distance, around whose perpendicular sides the road ran like a needleful of cotton.

But the rugged chap was good for it. He had thrown aside his jacket, stripped up his sleeves, and, with the aid only of a balancing-pole, seemed ready to spring forward. Observing that to this balancing-pole were attached sundry letters of the alphabet, such as " P," " I," " U," " II," and others, I asked their meaning; and was told by the obliging artist, that said pole, though common-looking enough, was in reality a choice mosaic, and that the letters stood for perseverance, integrity, unshirkfulness, honor, &c.

The mate to this picture showed us a youth of what may be called the cosset species. He was well wrapped in coats and comforters, ear-pads and mittens. Two men with garden-rollers smoothed the way before him, a third was leading him, and a fourth held an umbrella over him.

The other pair of pictures *illustrated* Uncle Jacob's remark about *"boosting;"* and the first of these was quite amusing.

A lazy young fellow was preparing to climb a mountain; and several well-meaning individuals were intent on boosting him up, some of whom used, for this purpose, long poles flattened at the proper ends. One fellow fastened a pair of wings to his shoulders; while another was getting a derrick ready to *hoist.* But the funniest was an odd-looking man, who came tugging along an immense kite, evidently with the intention of tying it to the young fellow, or the young fellow to it. Its bobs were letters of recommendation. The kite itself was labelled, *" Patronage."* Somebody had attached a bag of gold to each ankle; with what motive it was hard to tell, as they only served to weigh him down.

The *companion-picture* to this represented a smart climber going up a precipice at a fearful rate, clinging hold by fingers, thumbs, toes, and even teeth. And I observed that the rugged rocks projecting here and there, or an occasional stump, seemed to be of more real use to him than all the other fellow's contrivances. By the furled flag strapped across his shoulders, I judged that he meant to go all the way up.

The Cookstove Convention *resolved* that these four drawings be presented to William Henry Carver, with the request that they be added to the collection of pictures by the same artist already in his possession.

. . . I give the following letter, because parts of it are closely connected with the one which comes after : —

Mr. Fry to his Sister.

DEAR JULIANA, —

I asked Aunt Phebe for the recipe for that pudding. mentioned in my last as being very innocent. and, at the same time, sufficiently nourishing for the stomach of an invalid : and she says there isn't any need of any recipe ; says, just put a third of a cup (not a grain over) of rice (raw) into a quart of milk, with a dust of sugar and a trifle of salt, and let it stand in the oven till the rice is soft. One grain over *a third* will go that grain towards defeating your object ; which is to obtain a thick, delicious cream. This cream, if not made too sweet. has a rich cocoanut-flavor. Instances have been known of people sprinkling sugar on what they took out in their plate.

Mild, delightful weather we are having, — hardly cool enough for a fire ; but how pleasant it is to see one ! I am writing in grandmother's little charming sitting-room, where the sun shines in all day, and streams across the carpet. She has made a fire in the Franklin fireplace, set the tongs and shovel in their "*jamb-hooks*" all right, and says I must take as much comfort as I can. The brass andirons, the brass balls on the " frame " (fire-frame). and the brass-headed shovel and tongs, are suns, too. in their way, and almost put my eyes out. Grand-mother has just set a row of apples along the " frame." I should bite into some of them but for their being so handsome. Their beauty will not save them long, though : 'tis only skin-deep. after all.

This is the carpet's last day down, or the sun would not be allowed to stream quite so unobstructedly. Lucy Maria is in the kitchen, helping to mend up the old one; and, after that is put down, grandmother is going to take the comfort of the sunshine.

Billy is getting some things together to take over to Ellertown, — a small manufacturing village on the other side the pond, — just the place to sell his commodities; and there is to be an auction there to day, which will draw crowds. He expects to meet Benjie, — a Crooked-pond schoolmate, who comes there to-day with his uncle. Instead of going all the way round, Billy means to row across the pond, — a much quicker way, and a pleasanter.

Ever since the sitting of the Cooking-stove Council, this enterprising youth has been, in the words of Mother Delight, "a new creetur," — soliciting agencies, buying "rights," and *pitching in* strong. How I do enjoy the vigorous style of his goings-on! The house fairly resounds with his footsteps and the note of preparation, — meaning *whistling*. His face, though bright and beaming, takes on the earnest, thoughtful look of one who means business.

"Bring on your bundles!" he has just cried out from some height or depth.

Besides his own things, he has a package for Mother Delight, — a new gown, large-figured, and very bright-colored: maybe delaine, maybe alpacca, maybe all-wool. Oh! now I know: L. M. has just called it by name, — "Tycoon rep." She told it to Mrs. Paulina, who is examining the goods. This dress is a present from several families where the old lady goes nursing and visiting. The girls of the neighborhood are planning to go to Ellerton and make it up for her, — mean to carry their suppers, and have a jolly time in her one little room. I offered my services as threadneedler, but have been declined.   Mother Delight is fond of high-colored, large-figured goods.   They say the shopkeepers never take down any of their *plain* stuffs to show her.

I've been stopping to eat apples, and to fix the fire; and I have also mended one hole in the carpet.   Used to mend when in the Army of the Potomac.

Billy carried his luggage to the skiff, and has come all the way back to get his other hat.   The idea of his starting off with that old straw one!   Grandmother meant to keep her eye on him; but he went down cellar to fill his pockets with apples, and slipped through that way.   Changing his clothes is a catastrophe he always avoids and eludes when possible; but I will give him the credit of never being unwilling to change his hat.   It is easy to do, he says, and shows respect to his brains.

"Do spruce yourself up a little," L. M. has just said, "and go decent!"

"I am spruced up," he says: "don't you see this good hat?"

"Oh! you're just like an ostrich," says L. M.   "Put your head under a good hat, you're all right then.   Only makes your other clothes look worse.   See the spots shine up!   I really don't think that rig looks decent to meet your friends in."

"'Twill do for my enemies, then," says Billy.   "Everybody that don't buy is my enemy."

"Do change your coat, at least," said L. M. in a coaxing tone.   "Come: I would.   Come: grandmother'll feel a good deal better.   'Twon't do to depend too much on people's being near-sighted,"—alluding to one of Uncle Jacob's sayings, that you can always allow for some people being near-sighted, and others not taking notice.

Billy has changed his clothes, and now is blacking his boots. Now he has rushed up stairs for a clean collar. Poor fellow! He finds. that, in sprucing up, one thing leads to another. I do hope he won't come through! How he does stave about overhead! To be sure, he's in a raging hurry.

Now, grandmother thinks it has got to be so late, — half-past ten, — he'd better eat his dinner, instead of carrying a dry lunch in his pocket. Billy don't feel hungry a mite, but is willing to go through the ceremony.

"Can't you eat a little of this good pudding?" grandmother asks.

"Don't risk it very near him," says L. M.

Billy thinks he may worry down some of it, give him sauce enough.

Off at last. Grandmother is exulting that he ate the pudding, and won't get faint. How he goes it over the fences! Lucy Maria has just made the remark, that the superior sex can be made to eat very poor pudding, and not know the difference, if you only give them sauce enough to go with it. Says it is really touching, sometimes, to see how her father is imposed upon in this way.

I'm going now to help Georgie find "a new man." Billy broke the other bootjack yesterday, pulling off his boots in a hurry; and "Mr. Brick" had to come down to resume his former duties. We are going to have an apple-paring bee next week, for paring apples to dry. The *parers* will bring their machines, and we expect a lively time. Georgie was delighted with the "Miss Cherubina St. Clair" that little Mary sent her. She always delights in paper-dolls. Tell little Mary that

"Miss Cherubina" is invited to Mrs. Knothole's *grand reception*, and will grace the occasion with the *trained party suit.* I go now to find out, or hew out, a new Mr. Brick.

Affectionately your brother

SILAS.

Mr. Fry to his Sister.

DEAR JULIANA, —

I suppose you have been for some time expecting a letter from me, and one of a very amusing sort. But really I have had no heart for any thing amusing. We are all rather under a cloud just now. Since I last wrote, Jacky, the mischievous little Jacky so often mentioned in my letter, has passed from among us, to find, we trust, "a home." His sickness was short, — less then two weeks.

I say we are under a cloud, not merely because we all felt interested in Jacky, but because William Henry is in a manner connected with this occurrence. He doesn't talk much about it: but I know he feels badly enough, — perhaps with reason; I can't say with certainty. The little fellow had not seemed quite like himself, grandmother thinks, for several days previous. I will tell you some of the circumstances.

. . . Billy swallowed his dinner that day, as I wrote you in my last letter, and rushed off, literally, in a tearing hurry. At least, we felt sure, watching him from the windows go over the bushes and briers, that it would be a tearing one.

On arriving at the pond, as he told us afterwards, the skiff was nowhere to be seen. He raced up and down along the shore in a not very calm frame of mind, as you may believe. Pretty soon, Matilda drove along in the riding-wagon. She was going for bright leaves; and Gus was driving. Gus said, the wind being the way 'twas, he guessed the skiff got loose, and drifted across. Gus's guess sent Billy at a full gallop round the pond. But before he got quarter way — 'tis about a mile round it — he met a man, and asked him if he'd seen his skiff. You see, Mother Delight's bundle and all Billy's things were in it. The man said, "No," but said he saw one going towards the island, not long before, with a boy sculling. "You better go back and holler," he told Billy.

The island is only a little bunch of earth and rocks, with a few bushes and scraggly trees. You can row all the way round it in five minutes.

Billy ran back, and hollered; and, nobody answering, the man said he might pull his skiff down from under the bushes, and so paddle off and find out what the matter was.

But we knew nothing of all this till late in the evening. We were sitting around the fire at grandmother's. Aunt Phebe and Uncle Jacob were in there, as very often happens. We were rather making fun of Uncle Jacob. He met Quorm going home late, with four brooms unsold, and took the lot to pay in potatoes, — four stiff barn-brooms, made of white-oak slivered up or slivered down.

"What can a person like you want with four brooms?" Aunt Phebe asked.

But all declared that they hailed them gladly, as forerunners of a coming neatness in the yards, especially in the great end-yard where every thing stays. He is often petitioned to *clear up;* but says he likes to have things round, so there'll be something to look at when he looks out the window.

As it grew towards nine o'clock we began to speak of Billy, and wonder what kept him so late. Grandmother *had begun,* of course.

About half-past nine, I should think it was, there came a knock at the back-door, — a very peculiar knock, as if some one were pounding with a stick. I went to the door, and found Tim, who wanted to know if Jacky had been here; he hadn't seen him since morning. I took him into the sitting-room; and, while we were trying to think where we had seen the boy last, a carriage drove up, and stopped. Some one jumped out: the carriage went on, and in came William Henry. Benjie's uncle, it seemed, had remained over night at Ellerton, and had taken them both to "the Corners" to hear the "bell-ringers," and had come round by our place to drop Billy.

Billy was in fine spirits, and began telling about the performance, and about his good luck in selling, and about some funny old fellows at the auction.

We asked him if he saw Jacky any time in the fore-noon. He looked hard at Tim; and I noticed that his countenance changed.

"Why!" he exclaimed, — "why, I thought — didn't he swim ashore?"

"Where did you see him last?" we asked.

"On the island," said Billy; "but I thought he'd swim right ashore."

"He darsn't," said Tim. "He no more darst put hisself in that pond than nothin', he's so scared o'

snakes. Snakes is all he is scared on; but he's scared
to death o' black snakes."

Then Billy told us about missing his skiff, and borrowing one, and rowing off to the island. You see, he knew
pretty well who the rogue was; for Jacky had set a box-
trap on the island, with the idea of catching a squirrel.
It had long been the little fellow's ambition to catch a
squirrel to give Billy. He stood to it there was a squirrel's nest on the island; said he had seen one sail across
on a chip. Billy treated his story very lightly; but I've
no doubt 'twas true. Once, when standing out on picket-
duty, I saw a squirrel sail across a stream myself on a
chip. He used his tail for a sail; and, when safe over, he
took his sail for a towel, and wiped his feet with it.

"Don't believe I was two minutes rowing off," said
Billy. "All my things were in it, you see: and she leaked
some, and I knew it; and that was what made me so mad.
I was afraid he'd let the things get wet; and so he did,
some. When I found her, I found some of 'em in the
bottom, but couldn't see Jacky anywhere about. Expect he got scared, seeing me coming so swift, and went
and hid. At last I caught sight of him under some
bushes, and hollered away at him. 'Come out here, you
rascal!' says I. 'I'll give it to you!' So he crawled
out slow, and I grabbed him by the shoulders, but didn't
do any thing to him, 'cause he trembled so. His arms
hung down without a mite of life in them! So I only just
sat him down *hard*, and came off. Didn't do any thing
to him."

"Didn't he cry?" Georgie asked, tears standing in
her eyes.

"Yes: bellered like a good feller. But I told him he
liked the island so well, he'd better stay there."

"Why, Billy!" grandmother exclaimed.

"'Course I thought he'd swim ashore," said Billy.

"He darsn't," said Tim. "He's scared eenymost to death of water-snakes!"

Tim opened the door to go. We followed him out,— Mr. Carver, Uncle Jacob, Billy, and myself. No: Billy did not follow; he went ahead. Never ran faster, I think, even in the old Crooked-Pond races. We were not slow ourselves; but, by the time we reached the shore, he had already landed on the island.

I shall have to put off the finishing of this letter

until evening; for grandmother has just called me to dinner; and I don't like to keep her waiting a minute, especially when we have company. Mother Delight is here spending the day. You can have no idea of the enjoyment I derive from her visits. I depend on my afternoon with these two. Wish you could hear for yourself how entertaining they are; Mother Delight, in going her rounds, collects so many items.

Five minutes later. — On the whole, I have concluded to send this, as my long silence may have caused you some anxiety. You will hear again very soon, — perhaps in a day or two. Mother Delight has brought a wonderful piece of news: Jackey's father has come.

In haste, your brother

SILAS.

Afternoon. — No chance of sending this to the post-office: so don't feel disappointed at not getting it. Dinner is cleared away; and I have brought down my reading and writing, so as to sit with the old ladies, and hear them talk. Nothing pleases me more than to have Mother Delight come to spend the day. I always had a liking for old ladies, — they are so sympathizing, so protecting! always wanting to do up your unlucky fingers, or make you a poultice, or tie something around your neck. I'd sooner have Mother Delight come into the house than a whole opera-troupe. Wish you could see her. I know 'twould cheer you up. Why, her entrance really seems to light up a room. Everybody in it smiles. Can't help it, her own bright expression is so catching. "Why, here's Mother Delight!" they exclaim. "Now take your things right off! We'll put another piece of meat in the pot, and get the old rags out," — alluding to a saying of hers, that folks always ought to go a-visiting time enough to have another piece of meat put in the pot. The "rags" are rug-rags. Many families save up their old duds on purpose for her to braid as she goes her rounds.

I call the old lady handsome. In the first place, she wears a cap. I do hope, Juliana, that, if you ever are an old lady, you'll wear caps. Come, say you will, and I'll promise to give you a pair of gold-bowed specs."

Now she is braiding her rags. Grandmother has sat down near her to pare apples. We are going to have "apple-grunt" for supper. Not the faintest idea have they of the pleasure I derive from their conversation, or how deeply I am interested in the reminiscences of fifty years ago; and also in the reasons why Ella Slade has just turned off her beau; and in Mr. Snow's cider-press giving out; or that I have to turn away my head and smile as the fact is stated that Mr. Joe Long's eldest daughter is going to marry a man who has told her to furnish the house without thinking the least mite about the cost! Gossip, is this? Why, it's only stating interesting facts. Do as you'd be done by is fair. And I'm sure I'm willing to have it spoken of, and smiled at, if I ever tell my lady-love to furnish our house without thinking the least mite how much the things cost. Bless you, Juliana! what a frame of mind a man must be in to make such a remark!

Now Mother Delight (I believe I told you how she came by this name) is telling something rather funny, and of quite an exciting interest. She pauses in her braiding, and leans a little forward. Grandmother pauses in her paring, and does the same. 'Tis good as a play. If I could only sketch them to the life, I'd certainly hang up the picture in some gallery of art, and as certainly make my fortune.

Mother Delight is the more rotund of the two, — round face, quite a color, short curls in front (black mixed with gray), bright black eyes, and wears a cap, — a cap with gay little bows in the — the — what are they called? I heard the name just now. Something to do with a cat. Could it be "tabs"? Yes; but I don't see why. Not a large face, with wide, spreading features. Were I to describe her nose exactly, I should say it was a very small "cherry-picker," very slightly cherry-colored. Mouth small also; and, when she is intent on her work, the lips drop apart.

Grandmother has a slender figure, but is no taller than Mother Delight. Her eyes are blue, her features comely. You see in her face wrinkles of a twofold expression, as if smiles and worriments had taken turns making marks there. I should say that grandmother's principal trait was simplicity, or childlikeness. She is always willing to be told of new ways of doing things, new cures, new recipes; gets lost in wonder that the world has grown so wise. Seems, sometimes, like a little child, that thinks everybody but itself knows everything. Grandmother's cap is different from Mother Delight's, — comes farther forward. Isn't there, or wasn't there ever, such a thing as a "sheep's-head nightcap"? I don't believe I made it up. If there is such an article, it fits close to the head. That's the way grandmother's does. And hers has a ruffle round the edge, with not very much cloth in it — in the ruffle; and just back of it — back of the ruffle — runs a piece of striped ribbon about an inch and a quarter wide, that comes down and ties under her chin. Mother Delight's doesn't tie. Her's is more jaunty. Her chin hasn't any conveniences for tying things. You will wear a cap, won't you, when you are — well — say eighty or ninety? and I'll get you patterns of both these to cut them out by. How intently grandmother listens! She believes every word. Wish you could see the sweet, childlike expression of her face. They say she was very pretty once. Her complexion must have been exquisitely fair. She has just showed Mother Delight her string of gold beads, and told her all the particulars of her father's bringing them home from London. There they go into their box, — "the same box they came in," — and the box into its drawer. These gold beads are a standing, not joke exactly, but byword, in the families. Whenever money is needed for a special purpose, they say grandmother offers to sell her gold beads.

Later. — It is nearly tea-time; and I will make one more attempt at closing this letter. The conversation of my dear old ladies has been delightfully entertaining. yet not wholly amusing: for at every pause, almost, their minds would revert to poor little Jacky; and various modes of treatment were suggested by which his life might have been saved. The arrival of his father (and such a father, and from such a place) will of course, in a little neighborhood like this, occasion some talk. Oh that it had happened sooner, if only by one week! No doubt, the man is bad; but, then, even tigers are attached to their offspring.

13

I will sit down early in the morning and begin another letter which shall tell you further particulars about Jacky. We did not find him on the island; for, after waiting till nearly dark, he swam ashore.

Once more, your brother,

S. Y. FRY.

I remember perfectly well having written another letter about Jacky at that time; but, as no such letter can be found, I will try to fill the gap from memory.

After being deserted, as was told in the preceding letter, Jacky remained all day upon the island. I learned from some little boys who watched the proceedings from shore, that, as the dory rowed farther and farther away, the poor child cried and screamed, " Billy, don't go leave me ! — oh, dear, don't go leave me ! " long after Billy had landed on the other side. A larger boy, who passed by in a skiff later in the day, told him he wasn't a-going to take him off. That island was a good place for rogues.

So there he staid till nearly dark, and then swam ashore, and ran home crying (so the folks said who lived about there), and trembling with cold, — with fright too, no doubt. Tim being away, these people warmed and fed him, and saw that he went comfortably to bed.

Very soon after this adventure, we noticed that Jacky seemed to droop and hang about in a listless way, as if all the life had gone out of him. He would creep in at grandmother's back-door, and crouch over the stove; refused her cookies; and not even Tommy could arouse him to any mischief. The only thing which would bring a smile to his face was a kind word now and then, or some little attention, from Billy.

At last, we missed him for several days. Some one said Jacky was sick. Aunt Phebe went over to Tim's, and found the child in bed with fever.

He died after two weeks' illness. William Henry was, as we all knew, very unhappy about it; blaming himself, and perhaps with reason. Fever prevailed in the neighborhood at that time; and Jacky, being far from robust, and not fed on particularly wholesome diet, was very liable to disease. Still, the exposure probably had much to do with it.

The following extract from one of my letters contains some interesting particulars : —

. . . I have seen his father, but have not talked with him yet. There is nothing attractive about him, unless it be his very evident grief. Sad, sorrowful people, always, I think, draw us towards them. In trouble we are akin. And, after all, we two may not be so very wide apart in other things as would appear. I find in myself germs, at least, of the same selfishness, — self-seeking, — which, in his case, led to crime ; and, with the same bringing up, I might have occupied the very next cell to him. We *good* folks take too much credit for our goodness. We look down upon the *bad*, so called, as being a separate and distinct species, with which we have nothing in common. To use Mr. Carver's expression, we put too much "*down there*" in our manner towards them, — especially towards the poverty-stricken, unedu-cated sinners. Now, let me ask you, is a rich man who refuses to pay a debt of a thousand dollars, because the law allows it, any better than a poor man who steals fifty?

I spoke of Jacky's having no friends; but it must be owned, for the credit of human nature, — at least, of feminine human nature, — that he received, throughout his sickness, the very best of care. It was told from family to family that he had several times called out, "Mother! mother!"

That call went straight to the heart of every woman in the neighborhood. They were every one anxious to fill the vacant place, — left their work, and attended him night and day. Mrs. Paulina put aside her washing one forenoon before it was half done, fearing help might be needed, and walked over there. I met her in the path. "Poor child!" she said to me, — "poor child! They say he calls for his mother."

. . . Billy has been in a very unhappy frame of mind. During the last days of Jacky's illness, he hardly did any thing but walk back and forth between the two houses. Of course, he can't help remembering how very fond the little fellow was of him. One day, when he was within hearing, Jacky talked constantly, as if he thought himself on the island, trying to hide. He would clutch the bedclothes, and pull them over his head, trembling as if with fright, — seemed to imagine they were the bushes. If I touched them, he would cry out. "Don't, Billy! don't, Billy!" And sometimes he would be fighting imaginary "black-snakes."

Billy doesn't say much about his feelings; but we know all the same. That morning, when word came that Jacky was dead, he left the room abruptly, and we did not see him again for some hours.

The funeral was at Mrs. Paulina's. There was a large gathering of neighbors : hardly one staid away. I suppose all felt how sad it was that the poor child was to be buried without a single person of his own kin to stand as mourner. Yet many tears were shed. Now that he was gone, we all remembered his willing disposition, his sprightliness, and his utter friendlessness.

Saturday eve, just at twilight, in passing through the graveyard, I saw Jacky's father. Matilda had made a wreath of white chrysanthemums for the grave; and I took my sunset walk in that direction. It is the custom here, I find. for people to decorate the graves of kindred and friends on Saturday nights. The church is close by; and on Sundays, between meetings, you may see men, women, and children walking among the graves. How much real good feeling there is in human hearts, after all ! Jacky's grave was almost covered with wreaths and scattered flowers.

I let Tommy go with me that night. He had made up all himself a little bunch of red berries and sweet-alyssum. In Tommy, Jacky has a sincere mourner. The little fellow held fast by my hand as we entered the graveyard. walking at a slow, steady pace. quite unlike his usual hop-skip-and-jump. Near the grave I saw a man sitting, — a poorly-dressed, ungainly-looking person. The moment he raised his head, — it was bent downwards, — I knew it must be Jacky's father. He scarcely noticed us. We laid our flowers on the grave. and walked quietly on. Somehow, I felt as if a stranger had no right to speak to him; that his sorrow was as sacred as anybody's sorrow. But afterwards, reflecting upon all the circumstances, I felt that he might have

been grateful for a word of sympathy, and turned back
to the grave. The man had gone. I shall, however, see
him again, and mean to have some talk with him. . . .

The following letter from Lucy Maria to her cousin seems
to come in here better than any of mine which have been preserved : —

Lucy Maria to her Cousin.

DEAR MYRA, —

I meant to have returned these Bombay pictures and
Joe's letters long ago. Wish we had a Joe to be sending home letters and pretty things all the time; but

then, if we did have one, 'twould be pretty hard sending him away to sea, especially a Joe like your Joe. How just like himself he does write, don't he? and as if his pen were alive as he is; which is saying a good deal. Wishes he could wake up and find himself in our buttery, where he used to climb to the upper shelf after goodies. I don't doubt he does. Wonder if he didn't make a better sailor for all that practice in climbing. We saw his vessel marked in the paper last night. I do feel so sorry you can't all come to Thanksgiving this year! I had set my heart on having a family party; and 'twill seem quite lonesome with only just ourselves. Oh, what a wicked girl I am to say, 'Only just ourselves'! Oh, how much we have to be thankful for that we have each other! O Myra! when I think of my father and mother and grandmother, and Uncle Carver, and the rest, and think what a blessing it is to have them all, it almost makes the tears come to my eyes, especially when I remember that I may not always have them. I suppose you will wonder what makes me write in this sober way. I suppose it is because I have in my mind, while writing, a forlorn, lonely man who is just now in our neighborhood. He is the father of that little friendless child I wrote you about; and he came too late even to see him buried. I do pity him so! Mother says she thinks that such kind of people, when they do have feeling, take trouble harder than any others; for they can't reason themselves into being resigned, and it makes them desperate.

They say he married a pretty, amiable young girl in the place where Tim and he used to live, — an English girl. It was some place in Canada. I suppose this story

about the pretty English girl came from Tim. I don't
doubt 'tis true.   Little Jacky had a beautiful white
skin and bright eyes, and was a pleasant-dispositioned
boy.   They say this man thought every thing of his
wife ; but, after her death, he drank, and went all wrong.
Mr. Fry has had some talk with him ; and it seems, that,
while he was shut up, he thought a great deal about
Jacky, and had planned things to do for him and with
him.   He says that boy was all he had in the world,
and he doesn't care for any thing now.   Mr. Fry told us
that the man said to him, without looking up from the
ground, — he always looks downwards, — he said, " I
long, and I *long ;* and it seems as though I couldn't be
denied."   Mr. Fry says he never saw such a pitiful,
heart-hungry look on any human face.

The man stays with Tim.   Takes no notice of anybody or any thing, unless 'tis our Tommy.   Seems to
like to have him about ; I suppose because Mr. Fry
told him what good friends Tommy and Jacky were.
Mrs. Paulina wonders at mother for letting Tommy go
near him.   Mother says she don't think herself he's
the most suitable companion, but says she'd a good
deal rather have him go there than with that smooth-
faced, deceitful little Neddy Shedd, that looks so spick
and span.   Besides, a man that likes to have a child
about him can't be wholly bad.   And as for Tommy, he
don't care who or what a person is, if he can only get
somebody to whittle.

How the man is going to be supported, I don't know.
Tim can't keep him ; and he'll find it hard to get work.
Mrs. Paulina says she can never feel it her duty to em-
ploy him ; says wickedness ought to be frowned down.

So do I think wickedness ought to be frowned down, but don't believe in trying it on one kind of folks, and not on another. Why don't Mrs. Paulina frown down Mr. Calloon? I know what he has done, and so does she. But, if Mr. Calloon should come into her house, it would appear to her like a very great honor. She would show him into the best room, and give him a slice of her best cake, and take his eating it as a kindness done her. So 'tisn't wickedness that she frowns down.

Mother Delight says folks ought to look at the souls of people. Mother Delight works for all sorts, rich and poor, and is quite an observing person. You know rich folks are more apt to show out just what they are to hired help, — sewing help, or any kind of help. They let back-door folks see the back side of their characters. Mother Delight says, "Strip the clothes off, then take the flesh off, then take the bones off, and look at their naked souls; and then you'll know." Myra, could we bear such a stripping? It makes me tremble.

Afternoon. — I left off to make the pudding-sauce, and peel taters. Father's just brought home half a barrel of sugar. Says we say so much about his using up so much sugar, he's going to find his own, and don't know as it's any thing more than right. He brought mother your mother's letter, with the pattern of the new black silk in it. Grandmother had one from Billy. He is doing much better than we or he expected. Says he stops at every house, and always asks if there is another family. I don't doubt it. I don't believe he skips by one little shoe-shop. Whenever Billy does any thing, he does a good deal of it.

He'll probably go to Dorry's. Says Tom Cush is at

home now; and he wants to see Tom. We think that
silk will make up handsome. I call it an extra good
piece for the price. Make your mother have it made
somewhere near in the fashion; for I don't know as old
fashions are any better than the new. They were new
ones once; and the new will be old before long. Mother
says she would have a black silk, if she had anywhere
to keep it, when her butter-money gets piled up high
enough. She ought to. Hers is nine years old. Billy
means to go out and see the Two Betseys before he
comes back. We depend on hearing from him there.
He writes in good spirits now, — much better than at
first. Billy did feel badly enough at the time of Jacky's
death. We couldn't say one word to him. That poor
child would almost have given him his right hand if he
had asked for it. But Billy got entirely out with him.
Billy's a good-hearted fellow. . . . Nobody can be perfect, can they? or can they? Myra, do you suppose,
that, if anybody did their best, they could? I suppose one thing against it would be, that people soon
find out they are good, — they themselves, I mean, —
and begin to take pride in it.

When Tommy came home to his dinner, he brought a
curious-looking little wash-leather bag. Said the man
had gone away, and given him that "to keep for his own
to keep." I remember that the boys used to plague
Jacky about some kind of little bag he wore round his
neck; and there was a story round that it had a "charm"
in it from the Pope of Rome: I'd a good mind not to
begin his — Pope's — name with a capital. I must
confess to having wondered a trifle about the matter
myself. 'Tis' really quite a curious little affair; and

there's something to tell about it, which I will tell you, and show you the article itself, when you come to make that visit. Just the minute Joe gets home, we want you both to come together, — not forgetting *the accordion.* Father has rolled up some late pears, each in a separate paper, and hid them somewhere, so Joe can have a taste of them. Some say they keep best under ground.

This letter and package go by Mr. Snow. I've picked out a big red apple to send you, of the kind you like. Tried and tried to find one perfectly fair. Looked over as much as a half-dozen barrels, quarter of a yard down, — call it half; but every single handsome one had a *nubby* spot, or a speck, or a worm-hole. Mother says you can't expect more of apples than of folks; and she says an apple or pear that has a little speck of rot in it is better-tasted; for 'tis just when they get to their ripest and best they begin to decay. Myra, I've been thinking it over; and 'tis just so with flowers and grass and other things, — even people; that is, with their bodies. How about their minds when *they* get to their best? or don't they ever? Oh mystery, mystery! Let's come back to apples, — to this solid, handsome, round beauty, that we can look at all over, and see the whole of it. But oh, dear! this apple is just as much a mystery, if we stop to think how the tree went to work to make it. Never mind. Take it: 'tis your own. Eat it, and be happy. What do we do with all mysteries? Swallow them : so Uncle Carver says. I suppose the red cheek is where it turned to the sun. That shows what looking on the bright side will do. Don't you remember when you and I were little tots, and you and Joe were here visiting with your mother, how we two hid away apples, and he kept getting them "to meller" 'em for us; and, when he ate one, made us think 'twas the cat, or tried to? That must have been as much as — oh, dear, dear! — much as fifteen years ago. That ever I should come to saying fifteen years ago! But it must be so; for we couldn't have been over four then; and now we are — hush! But yes: between ourselves it may be spoken, seeing we shall both plunge into the chasm together, — the chasm of the twenties! Twenty years old! Oh, I never thought I should live to be twenty years old! No more teens for you and me, but ty, ty, ty, now, till we die, each one worse than the one before it. Oh, how dreadful it will be when it gets to be for-ty, fif-ty, six-ty! — when your life is lived, and you haven't any thing more to do! O Myra! I don't want to grow old, do you, and have wrinkles and crows' feet, and eyes sunk 'way into your head? Wonder what looking sort of old ladies we shall be. I've read, or dreamed it, somewhere, something like this, — now, how shall I get it into words? — that people's dispositions or feelings or passions, or the workings of their minds, from childhood up, were so many sculptors at work on their faces. They begin their work early, and keep at it, chiselling, chiselling, chiselling. Lots of these busy sculptors there must be, if every little fret makes its little mark, and every scowl and every smile. Grown-up faces do look as if they had been worked upon; and what a difference there is in them! Take, for instance, Mother Delight's and Mrs. Paulina's. I guess very different sculptors have been at work on those two. Mrs. Paulina makes great worriments over small plagues, and hurries and scurries from morning till night, never stopping to read or to look at a pretty thing. She'd think 'twas a dreadful waste of time to stand still long enough to see the sun set. And as for buying a picture, she'd as soon think of cutting off her finger. Matilda carried her a bunch of flowers one day, and she set them out on the sink-room shelf. Said flowers made dirt, dropping their leaves off!

Mrs. Paulina's *little sculptors* haven't put many loving, gentle, cheerful touches into her face. But Mother Delight's have into hers. Gracious! Mother Delight's little sculptors must have had a jolly time of it chiselling her face. Makes me think of what mother used to tell us children. She said, that, if we kept our faces cheerful and pleasant all the time, instead of wrinkles would come *twinkles* and *crinkles*. But what puzzles me is how to keep cheerful and pleasant all the time.

Many thanks for that jar of sweet pickles. We all liked them but father: he thinks the vinegar spoils the sugar. Says he'd rather have his sweet and sour separate. Mother tells him they do come mixed in life. Send the recipe for doing 'em, please. We've got lots of hard pears. Won't 'lasses-sugar do? I don't want to dig a well in that half-barrel the first thing. Send recipe, please, for the picklelily too. Is it pick-a-lily, or picklelily? Are you going to have your velvet bonnet done over again? I am mine. They're twins, you know. I tell the milliner, — she didn't seem to think much of the bonnet, — can any mortal being look more contemptuous than a milliner? — told her, of course it could be done over; for it always had been. Send more of Joe's letters: do. I haven't said half I meant to.

From your cousin, with love,

LUCY MARIA.

P. S. — They say females put the most important matter in the postscript. We expect soon to have a wedding in the family. Hannah Jane will be married in December. I put it here at the end, so that, in case of your showing the letter, this piece (of news) can be cut off. That's one reason. I know Aunt Myra likes to read letters; and I don't want even she should know quite yet. Another reason is, that I feel too sad about it to talk about it. L. M.

I think others besides L. M. have been puzzled to know how to keep " cheerful and pleasant." *Patience* is the best herb I know of for bringing on these symptoms. If I have not tried it myself, I have heard it recommended very highly. Aunt Phebe told me once that she had always got along better when she tried to be patient, especially when her children were small. Said she used to pile up a mountain of patience every morning to begin the day with, and stand on top of it.

If no letter turns up speaking more particularly of the *wash-leather bag* which " the man " gave Tommy " to keep for his own to keep," I shall say a few words about it myself presently, as it contained something quite curious. Meanwhile, here we have news from William Henry.

William Henry to his Grandmother.

MY DEAR GRANDMOTHER, —

I got your letter with the others' notes in it all right; and felt all right, too, when I got them. It does a feller good to hear from his folks. Don't get a-worrying. I haven't coughed or sneezed as I remember of. Can't write back exactly the kind of letter you wanted me to. Couldn't get sheets of paper enough. But tell L. M. I've saved up six men and women to tell about when I

come, and something for her to make rhymes about: and
tell Matilda I saw a queer-looking flower in a hot-house,
red and yellow, and grew all in a bunch; and I've got a
bulb of it for her. I guess 'tisn't a girl's flower, though :
girl's don't like so much looks to a flower, I s'pose. I
sell to more women than men; for the men are away at
work, where they ought to be, of course. Some women
slam the door in my face; but, if they only let me get
one foot and leg inside the outside-door, I fight my way
along very well. I call the door-mat my Rubicon.
Women are quicker to buy than men. I tell you, this
selling-on-commission business is quite something after
all. Quite interesting business. Every one that comes
to the door has a different look; and I'm learning to tell
by faces who'll buy. I bet with myself what she'll do,
when she first opens the door; and I most always win.
'Tis good as playing euchre. Say now, for instance, I
knock at a door. Woman opens it. 'Tis a two-handed
game. Let her face, say, stand for the backs of the
cards; for I don't know exactly what's behind it, or
whether she'll be easy to believe things, or hard. They
have a good many excuses, — are poor, or have been
cheated by peddlers, or haven't got time, room, &c. Say
we'll call these excuses their trumps and their bowers.
Now, you see, if I only had what folks call *a good address*,
— which means, I s'pose, good-looking, and easy to talk,
— why, then I'd hold the blank card, that takes bowers
and aces and every thing; for the blank card is highest
in the pack. But when we play euchre at home, you
know, — no, you don't know; but the rest do, — and the
pack isn't a euchre pack, and don't have a blank card in
it, we take a two-spot of diamonds, and use that for the

blank.   The two-spot comes nearest to nothing of any
other card.   So you see, that, seeing I haven't got what
I called just now the blank card, I've got mixed up so,
I've most forgot what 'twas.   I know, — *a good address ;*
which means, I guessed, good looks, and easy to talk.
Why, I do this way : I make it seem as if my things
were so first-rate and tip-top, that they don't need so very
much said about them.   I look the one I'm playing
against right in the eye, and say a few words, just the
earnestest I can scare up, — the ones that state my case
exactly ; and I call that way my blank card.   So, you
see, playing euchre does me some good, anyway.

I tell you, there's lots of money to be made by this
selling on commission . . . But don't tell, will you now,
how much profit I make ?   And I have a good time out
of it, too, seeing the country and all kinds of folks on
the road, and in houses and stores and little shoe-shops.
Guess I shall learn to talk.   Some of 'em are regular
jokers.   Sometimes I run foul of other peddlers, and we
have jolly times making up stories about our things.   I
bought some sticking-plaster of one, which please find
enclosed.   He said 'twould stick like a brother.   Better
give it to Tommy, and tell him to cover his fingers and
thumbs all over with it beforehand.

I've got some funny things to tell Lucy Maria and the
rest of you about a place where I slept last night.   A
little mite of a house, in an out-of-the-way place.   Poor ;
but I never got into a higher feather-bed.   She was very
much pleased when she found out I had a grandmother,
— couldn't quite believe it.   " You have ! " says she ; " got
a grandmother ? " and, after that, took extra care of
me.   Said her grandchildren were all scattered away.

I suppose she did things for me for you.   Put my overcoat to the fire, and all that.   It had been sprinkling.
She called houses *housen*.   The old man was a queer
old covey.   Wait till I come, and I'll tell you lots.   He
let me ride.

If I staid in all the rainy weather, as you want me
to, I should lose too much time.   I guess rainy weather
was made to use.   If we didn't use it, there'd be a good
deal of weather wasted.   I can always find some place to
dry myself; and my boots are thick; and I've got an umbrella; and I've learned how to hold on to it, I hope, after
a while.   My clothes seem to hold together so far, — all
but stockings.   It don't agree with stockings.   When
I felt my great toe running against the inside leather, it
didn't feel very good; and so I pulled the things all out
of my bag to look; and I took that great fat needle you
stuck in that piece of flannel, all threaded with thread,
and pulled it together by the edges.   Oh, weep not for
that boggle!   You can unboggle it again, and darn it
with yarn, when I come.   I sponge my clothes night
and morning, partly on their own account, and partly
on account of all you Summer-sweeting folks.   So you
may be easy about my looks, excepting one bodge of
white paint that I got on my sleeve off somebody's gate,
where they ought to've stuck up, "Beware of paint!"
It won't sponge off; but that isn't my fault.   I sponge it
enough.   'Tis a bother; for I have to stand sideways to
people, especially ladies: and 'tis an even chance I shall
forget to; for who wants to keep a bodge of paint on
their mind every minute?

I think I shall make a good deal of money this trip.
I spend precious little.   Generally pay for my grub in

14

my articles. By next spring, I hope, I can begin to try for a place. Dorry's father told me what the best firms are; and he mentioned the same ones Mr. Fry did. He thinks 'twould be about as well to go and offer myself without any recommendations. Says they can tell by the general looks of a chap. I wonder what my general looks are. One thing is sure: I can't alter me in that respect, and have got to take myself just as I find me. Do you 'spose anybody else will? He says (Dorry's father), that sometimes, the worse a feller looks, the better his chance is; that these handsome, slick, glib talkers are apt to feel too smart. and think too much of themselves, and too little of their employers' business. Expect he said that to encourage me. He says, that, if a feller really means to do his very best, he is sure to get along, or pretty sure. And seeing it's you, grandmother, I'll own up that that's the horse I mean to ride on. I wouldn't tell everybody, but don't mind telling you.

I enjoyed myself very much at Dorry's. Guess who Dorry asked to come too. Bobby Short! Dorry says he wishes he had my chance to travel all round and pick out a pretty girl. I told him I'd rather sell to their mothers; for their mothers' eyes don't put a feller out so. Dorry's father talked some very good talk to me, and gave me some very good advice; and I took it very kind of him. Dorry he had to add on his nonsense, advising me what to do when I went to the city, — how I must tip my hat to ladies, and steer out; and what tailor's I must go to; to have my hair cut, and must have it parted behind; and lots more. I don't believe Dorry's mother likes me very well. Don't you remember when she found me practising making bows before her best looking-glass, ever so many years ago? I can't make such a wonderful sight better bow than I could then. Gracious! I couldn't make such a bow as two fellers did that came into Dorry's one night, to save my head. Now, do you really believe that toeing-in has any thing to do with making a handsome bow? or are we all connected all over? I don't toe-in half nor quarter so much as I used to, I don't think; do you? Dorry says I've got entirely over it. I'm glad all you folks preached to me so much about it when I was small.

We four—Dorry, Bobby Short, Maggie, and myself—played euchre. Maggie and I were partners. Dorry cheated like sixty, and made Bobby Short laugh so he couldn't tell what trumps was. Bob didn't tumble off but once,—on account of people present, I suppose.

Tom Cush came in to see us. Tom knows lots. Carries books to sea, and piles of papers; and Dorry's father says he is an extremely well-informed young man. He talks as well as anybody. When he's in port, he takes pains to go and see every thing worth seeing. He goes mate.

We three all slept together in one room, and kept awake most all night telling things. At last, Bob went off,—not laughing, but to sleep. He was in another bed. 'Course, we'd been throwing pillows a spell, for the sake of old times; and Dorry and I agreed to pull hair in the morning, whichever waked up first. After Bobby Short went to sleep, we two got sober, and talked over old times and old schoolmasters. Talked over other times too,—times that haven't come yet: and Dorry told me what he meant to do, and to be, and to have; and I told what I did.

Keep easy about me. I won't catch cold, certain true. Better direct that bundle, if you please, to Crooked-pond Village : I shall be there by that time. Direct to the Two Betseys' shop. Love to all.

Your affectionate grandchild,

WILLIAM HENRY.

William Henry to his Grandmother.

MY DEAR GRANDMOTHER, —

I am writing this in the Two Betseys' shop. I arrived here last evening a little after dark. Came in just as if I'd been any other peddler, and talked with 'em ever so long about my articles without getting found out. At last I took out that old *pocket-comb,* you know, that I brought, with those two B's scratched on it, and asked if they had any combs to sell like that. The Other Betsey said they had, and took down some from a box. I said they were not exactly the same; for mine had two B's on it, scratched with a darning-needle. That brought down the house. Lame Betsey hopped up, and came pretty nigh walking without any cane. I pulled my hat off; and they began to talk both together just as they used to. I know they were glad to see me. They were dreadful sorry I had been to supper; but I told them I'd come to breakfast if they'd have flapjacks good as they used to.

Instead of the old ladder, there's a good pair of steps now leading up to that loft overhead. They said there was a comfortable bed up there; and 'twould be such a pleasure to them if I could content myself to sleep up there ! I wanted to stay; for it seemed more like home than anywhere I'd been.

They wanted to know if I was too big to be called Billy, — wanted to know if they must say *Mr. Carver*, I was so large. I said, no; Billy forever. Once a Billy, always a Billy. But they can't quite go the Billy, — call me William, or William Henry.   *The Other* gets it

William Hennery. I told them all about what I was planning to do. Fact, there wasn't much finishing-off to that loft. Bare beams overhead, and wide cracks in the floor. One little four-paned window. Not much like Dorry's rooms! After I went to bed, I heard Lame Betsey say, "He's away from home, and may not like to speak: hadn't you better ask him if he's got clothes enough on his bed?" So *The Other* put her head up the gangway. — she always does what *Lame* tells her to, — and asked me. "Yes, plenty," says I, "thank you!" Clothes enough! Much as forty puffs on, or comforters, or whatever they may be. Now, speaking about having clothes enough over me, I wouldn't feel anxious any more about that; for I can always spread my overcoat across. Dorry's mother didn't say a word about my warming my feet before I went to bed; but, my! you ought to've heard the Two Betseys! "Now, pull your cheer right up to the fire, William Hennery," says *The Other*, "and heat your feet hot;" and asked me if I had the habit of eating any thing before I went to bed. I could have done the thing; but thought I'd better not, not being certain how much they had on hand.

We've just been to breakfast. *The Other* said she was proper glad I took pains to remember her flapjacks. I told her 'twasn't the least mite of trouble. She fried a pile; and they wanted me to put sugar and molasses and butter and every thing on them. Said they were so glad to have company! Said it seemed more like living like folks to have company; and there was hardly anybody in the world they could expect to come and see them. A little chap came in, while we were eating breakfast, to buy a slate-pencil. That seemed natural. *Lame* says, *The Other* most always has to leave her meals to putter with some little cent's-worth. The little boy made me think of Jacky. I've seen two or three little boys that made me think of him since I've been away. I have wanted to tell you that I was much obliged to you for not saying any thing to me about that, grandmother.

You can't begin to think how clever the Two Betseys are to me. Asked me if I hadn't any stockings that wanted the holes darned up in them ; and gave me such a tip-top breakfast ! — flapjacks and dip-toast and sausage-meat and pie ! Pie for breakfast ! Said they knew it didn't make much difference to boys when they took their pie. Begged me to have a cup of coffee ; but I stuck to water : and *The Other* said, if I wanted to, I might soak my crust in her cup. Now, could any thing be kinder than that ?

After breakfast, I told 'em, just for fun, I guessed my hair wanted the ends of it clipped off. And they've got out the great shears, and spread the apron over the chair-back; and, when this letter is done, I'm going to have the operation performed, for the sake of old times. *The Other* says she used to be a *dab* at hair-cutting. They both inquired for your health and your rheumatism, and how much work you could do; and, I tell you, I cracked you up to *ninos !* Wanted to know if you kept fowls ; and, if you did, said I must tell you to give your hens "kyan pepper." Said that would make 'em think 'twas summer, and time for them to lay. *The Other* said she'd had a great deal of trouble with her setting-hen getting unsettled. I told her to put her under a barrel. She said she was so forgetful, she might never think to let her out. Lame told me a funny egg-story that I know you will like, especially the remarks. 'Twas about a man that came round taking pictures when she was a little bit of a girl. He did their father's, and he paid part in work. He was a cobbler and shoemaker.

The picture hangs up here. 'Tis in a red frame about a foot and a half by two. They took the muslin up so I could see plainer. I don't know what ails it; but that cobbler looked funny, if he looked so. But they think a good deal of it. Sort of made me laugh, though I managed to cough it off. They were afraid I'd got cold; and pitied me so much, I felt ashamed.

Lame said he ate dinner at their house one day, and they had bacon and eggs for dinner; and she cut all the whites off her eggs, and only ate the yellows. The man asked her if she didn't like whites; and she told him, no. Then he told her he would send her a hen that would lay eggs without any whites to them, — all yellows. "Now, what color should you guess that fowl would be?" says he. She said, "Yellow." He said, no, clear white; for the yellow would all run to eggs, and the white go into the feathers. Said it had a very sweet cackle; and she must listen for it, and look out for it coming along a winding path that wound round the hill. "And I was *cooty* enough," says she, "to stand and look out of the window, time and time again, for that all-yolked fowl."

"But it didn't come," said *The Other*.

"No," said Lame; "never." Then she didn't talk for about a minute, — seemed to be thinking; sort of sober. At last, says she, "No, no, it didn't come; but I'm not the only one that's looked for things which didn't come." Then says she, "I don't want to damp your courage, but only want to try to keep you from being too much disappointed. That's all. You mustn't expect too much: you'll have to take things as they come."

"And take eggs as they come too," says I.

" Yes," says she : "you won't find many fowls with a sweet cackle coming along the path, that'll lay eggs just the kind you want."

I asked them if they'd be so kind as to tell me how they both came to be named Betsey; and they told me all about it. But wait till I come. *Lame* was christened Elizabeth. Do you know how that name of Elizabeth first began? She told me : t'was made from " *The little Beth.*" I know all about the ones they were named for, but don't want to stop to tell every thing now : only 'twas two grandmothers. I wish the Two Betseys could come to our house. Oh, you and Lucy Maria and all of you ought to see 'em talk! When I'm telling any thing, they keep looking at each other every minute to see if each other don't think 'tis wonderful, — but I can't make you know how, without you see it done, — and keep saying, " Do tell!" " Did you ever!" " Why, how you talk!" " I never!" And, as soon as one begins to tell any thing, the other one pitches in, and they go it together, else keep asking each other questions. " What day was it, you?" " Name was John, wasn't it, you?" " Come of a *Thurdsday*, didn't he, you?" They call one another *you*. Seems as if they felt kind o' lonesome telling any thing all alone. *Lame* knows the most, I guess; for *The Other* minds her. When I came below to wash my face, — there weren't any fixings up aloft, — *The Other* hung up a clean roller-towel, and asked me to wipe my face and hands on the back side of it, — she always did, — because, when *Lame* ever came that way, she was pleased to see the towel look clean.

I'm going out now to take a walk round and see

who's here. Want to see Gapper Sky-blue. "Wedding-cake" don't keep now. Sha'n't trouble old "Brown-bread." Shall go to Gapper's and buy a cent's-worth of 'lasses-candy. Before I put my coat on, when I was washing my hands, *The Other* took that bodge off the sleeve with some of my own stuff. Funny I never thought of doing that! Now, when I want to make folks buy, I can show 'em the place where that was taken out.

I must stop writing now. Don't you be worried. I haven't forgot half the things you told me yet. Give my best love to the girls. Tell Matilda that button-hole she made wasn't quite big enough. I tried to get my head through, and 'twouldn't quite go through. I am **a very** good boy.   Your affectionate grandchild,

WILLIAM HENRY.

There are two things I wish to speak of here. One is the " little bag " mentioned by Lucy Maria in her letter; and the other is something else, — a little surprise that surprised my Summer-sweeting friends very pleasantly. I will begin with the first.

Tommy came home one day, as Lucy Maria stated, bringing the small wash-leather bag which Jacky used to wear around his neck. This bag was circular, and was about two inches in diameter; being sewed together more than half-way round with black silk in very fine stitches, so that the sewing resembled a cord. The remaining part was closed by means of a string running through holes made on both edges. When this string was drawn out, and the bag opened, we found inside a sort of a map done on parchment. At least, it was called a "map" in a short piece of writing folded up at the back. It had something the appearance of a locket; that is, it was set in a narrow rim (silver, we thought), with a thin " dented " back of the same metal, and was protected in front by thick greenish glass. The folded paper at the back seemed to be a fragment of a letter; which letter, judging by this specimen, must have been written a very long time ago, when capital letters were common stock, and everybody helped themselves. In these days we have to be stingy of capitals, certain meddlers having taken it upon themselves to dictate where and when they shall be used.

Fragment of Letter.

"TO MY DEAR SON.

"*The Carrier fetched by the Coach, yestereve, a Parcel, in the which we were well pleased at finding a sample of your Handiwork, done at School; the same being a Chart, or Map, of Kent County. My Son, it giveth us untold Pleasure and Satisfaction to feel that your Time is spent to such Profit, and your Grandfather's bequest used to good Advantage. My Son, your Grandfather was a Road Surveyor; and though I, his son, do by no means follow a so distinguished Profession, nevertheless has come down to me some Portion of that good man's Skill and Dexterity, whereby I am enabled to lay out the small Chart which accompanieth this; which Chart showeth the true Course of the Line running between the two Countries of* Honor *and* Dishonor. *My Son, you will observe that said Dividing Line runneth Straight, without one small bend. Should any Surveyor exhibit a Chart on which said Dividing Line maketh even one little curve, such Surveyor proveth himself a Bungler and an Impostor. My Son, you will observe, that, should a Traveller in the Country of H. take but one step over the Dividing Line, he steppeth into the Country of D. And my*" — (remainder torn off).

The chart, enclosed in its *locket*, looked something like this : —

There being neither date nor signature, we could only guess that it had belonged to some relative, far back, of Jacky's mother, the pretty young English girl, who, no doubt, had preserved the relic with great care for the benefit of her boy.

Oh, how joyfully she must have welcomed him when that which we so ignorantly call Death united them once more! Who knows but she came to meet him ? That cry of " Mother, mother ! " in his last sickness, was, perhaps, not the utterance of confused recollections, but a greeting.

I have a strong desire to meet with " the man " once more. In the street, and in cars, I often find myself looking at ill-dressed, and what are commonly called the lower class of men, hoping to recognize him. This shows my taking it for granted that he did not improve. Yet why does it show that, since some rogues go well dressed ? *

* Since writing the above, I have seen " *the man,*" and got from him many particulars.

I spoke, just now, of a pleasant little surprise. It was a surprise to all but Lucy Maria. She planned the whole thing.

It will be remembered that William *Hennery*, in his letter written from the Two Betseys' shop, suggested the idea of these very worthy women going to see his grandmother, — merely mentioned it, having at the time no thought of such an event really taking place. But L. M. had no sooner heard this letter read than she made up her mind that the Two Betseys should come. This seemed a wild idea, to be sure; but it just suited L. M. to bring things about which no one else would think of undertaking. People often speak of " sleeping on " their plans and their perplexities. Lucy Maria *baked* or *ironed* or *sewed* on hers, or perhaps took them through sweeping-day. The coming of the Two Betseys was *ironed* upon; and then, having, as it were, warmed herself up to the subject, and smoothed away all the difficulties, this irrepressible damsel set herself down to compose a letter.

Lucy Maria to the Two Betseys.

My dear Two Betseys, —

We never saw you; but we believe in you with all our hearts: that means something more than just believing, doesn't it? — means something warmer; means something more kindly. But we want to see as well as to believe. Seeing is believing; but believing isn't seeing. Now, when Billy comes home, why can't you both come with him? Do, won't you, if you can't stay more than two days? but I think 'twill take all of a week to get acquainted with the two families of us. We should all be so glad! You have no idea how it would please grandmother. Grandmother! — why, she would cover her entry with cloth of gold, if she had any, for the feet of those who had been so kind to her Billy.

Anyway, she'll lay down her new braided rug. I've heard her wish a great many times that she could be acquainted with you : and mother was saying, only the other day, that she did wish she could see Billy's Two Betseys; said, whenever he was with you, whether at school or since, he had seemed to be in a sort of grandmother air, which boys don't often get away from home.

Now, I know just what your excuses will be : so I'll set them up for you, and knock 'em all over. We'll call them *fourpins.*

1. Can't leave the shop.
2. Too old.
3. Can't afford it.
4. Shall make too much trouble.

Now see them fall down!

You can get Gapper Sky-blue and Rosy to stay in the shop and live there while you're gone. (One down.)

As for being too old, that's no excuse, so long as you're both in tolerable health. On the contrary, it is a strong reason for coming; for, the older you are, the less time you will have to enjoy this pleasant world, and especially us pleasant people (!), and smaller chance we have of knowing you. Now, it stands to reason, that, if there's but little time left, you ought to make the most of it. That's what I tell Hannah Jane and all of them when grandmother talks about going down to Maine to see a cousin she never saw, but who has always been writing for her to come down. I tell Hannah Jane, that, if her time is short, she ought to do every thing she is inclined to, and have every thing she wants. Dear old, good grandmother! 'tisn't often she'll own up to wanting any thing! (Two down.)

Thirdly, please find enclosed two package-tickets; and be sure and fetch with you a large trunk, and we'll cover the remaining expenses with butter, beans, or other farm-things of the eatable sort, that we can give, and not feel it a bit, and be glad to. I know just what father's and mother's ideas are about such matters. They believe that things grow to be eaten, and given away; and, if they take comfort giving away, why can't you let 'em take it? Pray, don't grudge them that little bit of comfort. Now, if you have got a great box of money hid under your floor, — even if you have, I know you won't take offence at my offer, but will only look at my motives. Anyway, there are three down.

As for trouble, you wouldn't make much. Of course, you would stay at grandmother's. — she wouldn't hear to any other plan; and she'll be proud to show you some of her cooking. Besides, we keep an eye on that spry young old lady, and don't intend to let her overwork herself. She don't like to give up the care or the work either: so we make various excuses for sending in things all cooked. You know, there are four of us healthy females here, at home most of the time, all able to work; and, if you'll only come, we'll lay a railroad across the garden, and the freight-dépôt shall be in grandmother's buttery. I do like to stir up the good things! Work? what's work? What's one man's work is another man's play. I calculate it would be play for a lawyer, — that is, a "Philadelphia lawyer." — play for him to take the scrubbing-brush, and scrub our floor; and, I tell you, scrubbing floor is quite interesting business. I really like to get a tub full of nice soap-suds, roll up

my sleeves, and vanquish dirt.   As board after board
comes clean, you can see that you are doing something, and have lived that much time to some purpose.   Good time for doing up your thinking too.
Sometimes I make believe the spots on the floor are
the wickednesses of the world, or my own, and that I
am scrubbing 'em away.   Yesterday I planned exactly how to have my winter-dress made while I was
sweeping the chambers, even to the buttons and French
folds.

I am so glad one of you is lame! — on our own account, I mean.   Mother says 'tis very good to have an
invalid in the family, — makes the rest more kind, more
unselfish, and better every way than they would be
otherwise; but, you see, there isn't one of us willing to
make herself an invalid for the sake of the rest being
better!   (Four down.)

Now, all your fourpins are knocked over; and you've
nothing to do but put on your things, and come.   No
matter what sort of things they are : we don't dress up
much ourselves, — couldn't if we wanted to.   So there's
nobody here to be afraid of; and as for while you're
travelling, — why, it isn't at all the thing now to make
much of a spread in what you wear to travel in.   English people don't; and of course we ought to go by
their rules.   At any rate, if we want to please *them*, we
must.

There are not many people, especially many strangers,
whom I would urge so to come.   But I know you are
exactly the ones we should enjoy a visit from.   We have
no great attractions to hold out, — a hearty welcome
you will be sure of: and as for Billy, I don't know but

he would do what he sometimes threatens; viz., jump over his own head! — which feat is becoming more difficult every day he lives. And as for being strangers, you're not: we've known you ever so long. And by the way, my calling you the Two Betseys you won't mind, will you? for Billy never told us any other name.

One reason why I want you to come now is on mother's account. Mother lost a very dear little child once, — a beautiful little child, so people have told me. It happened just at this season of the year. She never speaks of it; but we notice, that, when the time comes round, she seems, at times, more serious and thoughtful than is natural for her to be. Father and I usually contrive to make her go on some little visit, or to have some company staying at the house, so as to keep her from dwelling too long on her thoughts. Thus you see, that, by coming, you will be doing us a kindness, a real kindness; and you have such kind hearts, that I know you will think such an object worth coming for.

Trusting to see you soon, I remain, very affectionately, your friend,   LUCY MARIA CARVER,

(Billy's cousin; lives next house to Billy.)

The above letter L. M. sent in haste to Billy, with orders that he should read it, and enforce the contents, but not mention the subject in his letters home, unless writing to her, as she wished to surprise the folks; and not even to let them know what day he should come himself.

Although Lucy Maria had been tantalizing us with a "very good double-headed secret," which she claimed to have in keeping, still none of us suspected the nature

15

of it; and I, for one, fell into the trap innocent as a dove, that family got up secrets and surprises so easily; as, for instance, by arranging a sudden visit from some of their cousins, or making mother a stylish head-dress, or a plum-cake for father's birthday.

They came to town, Billy and the Two Betseys, by the late train, as had been arranged; Lucy Maria meeting them at the station. To avoid all suspicion, she took the horse in the afternoon, and went to visit some friends two miles off.

It was after seven o'clock when they arrived at the house. We had been to supper, and cleared away. Grandmother and I were sitting there, reading. Georgie was tending a very small-sized long-necked squash-baby, which had a bad cold, dosing it with medicine from a gill porringer by teaspoonfuls. The baby had a bib on. It made no fuss about taking its physic. Mr. Car-ver had gone to the post-office.

Billy, it seems, had his orders to wait in the entry. The carriage, by the way, stopped before reaching the house, so that we heard no sound of wheels. But we did hear talking in the entry; and presently the door opened, and Lucy Maria appeared, with a shawl over her head, as if she had just run across.

"I'll ask her," she said, speaking to some one outside. Then, turning to grandmother, she said, with just her natural every-day voice and expression, "Grandmother, here are two travellers, two old ladies, travelling in this part of the country, and don't know where the hotel is, and want to know if they can be kept here over night. Of course you can't have 'em!" she whispered. Then, turning to the entry, she spoke to them in rather a stiff,

constrained manner, as one does when talking to strangers, " Won't you step inside ?　My grandmother will
let you sit down and warm yourselves, I've no doubt;
and then, if you'd like to go to a hotel, some one will
drive you over."

They stepped inside, — two very pleasing old ladies,
I thought, evidently from the country, — the very ones
who would be likely to take the wrong road in travelling.　They both wore neat black-straw bonnets, which
had crowns and forepieces, and which were trimmed with
black ribbon bows.　They wore gowns of gray or drab,

or some dull color, not just alike, and loose cotton gloves of some other dull color, very bright black shoes, and very white stockings.

The taller of the two had a black shawl on, and carried a woollen carpet-bag on her arm. The other wore a black cloth cloak, and a long black veil which was thrown back. She was not so straight as the tall one, and seemed to support herself by an umbrella (grandmother's own umbrella, hastily substituted by L. M. for lame Betsy's cane). Their cap-borders particularly pleased me. The tall one wore a quite wide figured collar outside her shawl; the shorter a three-cornered checkered silk cravat, pinned close up under her bonnet-strings.

They took the chairs offered by Lucy Maria. Grandmother seemed quite upset. She put another stick on the fire, remarking that it was a pretty chilly evening.

"You couldn't keep them all night very conveniently, could you, grandmother?" asked L. M. Then to the travellers, "My grandmother isn't very strong; and I suppose she hardly feels equal to entertaining strangers as she would think they ought to be entertained."

"Well," says grandmother, "hem! — well, I'm not much in the way of putting up travellers. Do most of my own work after my fashion. Suppose you would want supper and breakfast. I don't know — if you could put up with such as we've got — why, don't like to turn anybody away."

I spoke up then, and said I should be very happy to harness a horse, and take them to the hotel. There was a good hotel a mile or two distant, I said.

"You'd be a good deal better off there," said grandmother.

"Yes," said Lucy Maria, "a great deal better off."

"But still," added grandmother, unwilling to be inhos-
pitable, — "still, if you are willing to put up with what
we have on hand" —

"Then they can put up here, do you mean?" asked
L. M.

I whispered to the old lady, "No, you don't mean so:
they can just as well go to the hotel;" thinking, of
course, to save her the thousand steps she would feel herself obliged to take.

"Why, yes," said grandmother.   "But no doubt you'd
be made more comfortable at a public-house, where they
make it their business to entertain people."

Just then came a knock at the door.   Grandmother
opened it; and there stood a figure muffled up in a gray
plaid shawl (grandmother's), tall hat (Mr. Carver's), and
carrying a cane (Lame Betsey's).   His hair was brushed
about his eyes; and he held the shawl in a very *hiding*
way.

"Could I get a bed and supper and breakfast here?"
he asked.

Grandmother looked up at him over her glasses, — an
earnest, steady look.

"You young rascal!" I shouted, springing at him.

"Why! why! wh—y!" screamed Georgie.

For he couldn't keep sober under that steady look.
He had to smile; and, the moment he smiled, we both
knew him.   He burst out, dropped shawl, hat, and cane,
and gave the old lady a tremendous hug before she had
time to speak his name.

"And so you don't want to keep them!" he cried, chuckling, and catching his breath, and holding on to his sides. "Oh, what a grandmother! After all you've said about wanting to get acquainted with 'em, and now to be offish about letting 'em stay! Oh, oh, what a stingy grandmother! Turn out the Two Betseys!"

Her face lighted up like an illumination.

"*Be* you the Two Betseys?" she cried, putting both hands on the shoulders, first of one, then the other, and looking them full in the face. Then to Billy, "Oh, you naughty boy!" Then to them. "Do take your things right off!" Then to Billy, "Sober down a little, can't you?" Then to them, "I never was so glad to see anybody! Here's Mr. Fry: you've heard of him, haven't you? he's one of the family. — Billy, you and Lucy Maria — oh, Lucy Maria, you knew! you knew!"

This tumultuous young couple had seized each other by both hands, and were dancing up and down like crazy creatures; that being the readiest way which occurred to them of expressing their delighted state of mind. I, too, danced up to the travellers, and shook hands as hard as I ever did in my life. "I'm delighted!" I cried, — "perfectly, absolutely, and every way delighted! The very thing I wanted! Three" — I was going to say, "Three old ladies in one house," but checked myself. Perhaps they didn't call themselves old yet, or wouldn't like to be called so. Grandmother went on (she was just as excited as any of us): "Oh! what made you play me such a trick? Oh, you Lucy Maria! Oh, you Billy! Draw your chairs closer up. You must be tired, travelling so far. Here, give me your bag. Welcome a hundred times! I'll hang the teakettle right over."

"Oh! they'll be better off at a hotel!" cried L. M.

"'Cause they're more used to entertaining travellers!" shouted Billy.

"Harness up, Mr. Fry! — hadn't you better?" cried L. M. And away they went at it, dancing again.

"Call Phebe!" grandmother exclaimed, beginning to come to her senses.

"Yes," said Lucy Maria: "I'm going over to get mother and the girls. Billy, you hide in the closet. Don't one of you smile, now, when they come in. Georgie, be tending your baby."

Lucy Maria then ran home and told her mother that grandmother wished she would step in there a minute; for two old travelling women had stopped there, and seemed determined to stay all night.

'Twas only a few moments before Aunt Phebe appeared, with Hannah Jane and Matilda. The two Betseys had taken their things off, and sat warming their feet, holding their folded pocket-handkerchiefs, appearing to be made up for a long stay. We kept very sober, as ordered. The girls stared, and looked at their mother. Aunt Phebe stared, seemingly at a loss what to say. I observed that Billy was enjoying the whole scene through the crack of the closet-door.

"Been travelling far?" Aunt Phebe inquired at length.

"Considerable far," they answered both together.

Aunt Phebe seemed decidedly puzzled. I saw very well that she was contriving some way to rid grandmother of the two unwelcome guests, who seemed to feel so very much at home, and, at the same time, not be impolite. Don't know what happy plan she might have hit upon could Billy have stood it a minute longer. But suddenly there came what he once called a "sort of squelching out;" then a "guggle, guggle, guggle;" then Billy himself, tumbling and pitching headforemost into the lounge.

"O Aunt Phebe!" I cried, "how can you be so cold-shouldered to folks that have been so kind to our Billy?"

"And have come all the way from Crooked Pond to see you!" shouted Billy, turning right end up.

"How?" cried Aunt Phebe. "What? Who?"

"The Two Betseys!" we all shouted.

"The Two Betseys! What do you mean? The two Betseys? I can't believe my own eyes! You dear souls! (smack, smack.) You don't say you've come! (smack, smack.) Here are my girls!—here's Hannah Jane (smack), and here's Matilda (smack), and there's Lucy Maria!"

"I'm *very* glad to see you!" said L. M., coming forward demurely: at which Billy, Georgie, and I exploded; and even grandmother laughed so heartily, wiping her eyes with the corner of her apron, that Aunt Phebe, by one glance at that solemn damsel, guessed, and immediately proceeded to give her a good rousing shake. "So this was your famous secret, was it?" she cried. "'Double-header' indeed! But run, call your father! Somebody go and see if father's got home!"

Having charged us all to *look sober*, L. M. ran back and found her father at home, and Uncle Carver, so she told us afterwards, just coming in at the other door, on his way back from the post-office.

Any letters from Billy?" she asked him.

"No," said Mr. Carver, looking quite serious. "I felt almost sure of a letter to-night. Billy hasn't written now for a long time."

Then she begged them both to come to the rescue; for two old women, strangers, who appeared to be wandering about the country, had stopped at grandmother's, and seemed bent on staying all night there.

"I don't want ter stay all 'lone!" Tommy called out from up stairs: "I want ter see them ole stragglers!"

"Come down, then!" cried Uncle Jacob.

L. M. said, that no sooner had Tommy appeared in his night-gown than her father wrapped one of his own long black coats round him, and made ready to carry him in his arms.

"Now I guess we'll scare 'em off!" cried Uncle J.

We were so busy talking, that nobody heard them coming until they stepped into the entry. Billy hadn't time to get to the closet, so dove under the table; and the girls stood about it to hide him.

The others marched in, — Lucy Maria, Mr. Carver. Uncle Jacob, with Tommy in black and white, his "hair all over his head," riding pussy-back.

"Well," said Uncle Jacob, seating himself very composedly, and tipping Tommy off into his lap, "who might you two be dressed up to be?"

He told us afterwards, that, at the first glance, he thought Lucy Maria had been dressing up a couple of girls for tableaux or something, and was trying to cheat him.

I observed that Mr. Carver had a roguish twinkle in his eye, a remarkably roguish twinkle for him, and that he looked slyly about the room, and out into the kitchen,

and even opened the closet-door, keeping all the while a
mysterious smile on his countenance; which smile suddenly widened into a laugh. I followed the direction of
his eye, and saw that it rested on a boot which protruded
from under the table.

"I suppose you girls are standing up to grow," he
remarked at last quite calmly. "Very good plan."

By this time Uncle Jacob had found out that the two
old ladies were real, and was just going to say something; when Mr. Carver stepped up to them, and put out
both hands, smiling, and said, —

"The Two Betseys, I believe. We are glad to see you,
— very glad. We hope you've come to make us a long
visit."

Uncle Jacob took it all in in a moment, and began to
laugh, — not loud, but a steady, shaking, inside laugh.
Couldn't say a word, but just sat and laughed and twin-
kled, and wiped the tears out of his eyes: the man was so
entirely and exquisitely satisfied, he didn't know what to
say. Moved his chair up towards them, Tommy and all.

"I declare, — well, I declare (another hitch of his
chair), — you've come, haven't ye? How did ye happen
to come? I declare! How long shall ye stay? Hem!
Funny, isn't it? Well, you've come, haven't ye?"

Mr. Carver touched him on the shoulder, and pointed
to the *boot*. More silent laughing from Uncle Jacob,
and twinkling, and wiping of eyes. Then he quietly
took the poker, and, hooking it about the ankle of the
boot, began to pull. It slipped. He dropped Tommy,
and caught hold with his hand: whereupon the girls
scattered, and Billy was dragged forth midst uproarious
shouts. Tommy slipped out of his skin, which his

mother immediately shoved him into again, as far as she
could get him in, lest he catch cold; and there he sat in
the big chair, the skirts crossed over his knees, bare feet
sticking out, sleeve-ends flapping, — the only trouble
being that he found great difficulty in eating the pepper-
mints given him by the *travelling women*, because he
couldn't come at his hands.

This is the way Mr. Carver found it out: —

A lady whom he met at the post-office told him that
his son came in the same car with her, and that two old
ladies, one of whom was lame, accompanied him; and
that Lucy Maria met them at the station. Armed with
all this information, he was not only able to escape being
sold, but, with his sober answers, contrived to *sell* the
great head-plotter herself. Or, to use Billy's favorite
figure, Mr. Carver held the blank card, and so euchred
L. M.

The following letter, written during the Two Betseys' visit,
will not, I think, be uninteresting here: —

Mr. Fry to his Sister.

MY DEAR JULIANA, —

Received your letter this noon. I'm sorry to hear
that little Mary has taken cold again. It is, as you say,
a bad time of year to have a cold settle upon the lungs.
The coughing, however, may proceed from a slight irrita-
tion in the throat, — or tickling, to give it a jollier term.
I have recently been troubled with this, and experienced
great relief from the use of colt'sfoot-candy (probably a
glutinous or gelatinous secretion from the feet of colts).

Boneset-candy is also good : but as I used them both, in my haste to get well, cannot advise her which prescription to follow ; so perhaps she had better follow my example·

I have been helping in the farm-work lately,—husking, barrelling up apples, and taking vegetables to market; Mr. Carver and Uncle Jacob being very busy, doing a profitable job of teaming for some Ellerton people.

You may look for me in less than two weeks. My time is up here, and more too ; and I must certainly make you a visit before settling into winter-quarters. My health is steadily improving; and, having — I *won't* say *wasted* so much time here — having taken such a long resting-spell, I feel that business should claim my strict attention. In fact, I don't know why I should say *wasted ;* for staying among these dear Summer-sweeting friends has done my heart good and my soul good; and why is not the good of one's heart and soul as good an object as making money? Still, I have no objection to this last. Quite recently, I had an opportunity of giving away a large sum; that is, a large sum for me. The object was so worthy, and more than worthy, I did long for money so! Just for a question to speculate on, I wonder, if I were rich, if this longing to give would continue as strong. Another question : Which should you rather have, — a wish to give without the means, or the means to give without a wish? There's a conundrum : so get your answer ready, and let it be an honest one.

Neither of the Mr. Carvers thinks much of laying up money for his children. Uncle Jacob says he wouldn't, if he could, leave thousands of dollars to his, so they wouldn't have any thing to try for, and the girls do nothing but sit along in a row, and *"tat, tat, tat"* (what he calls tatting).

"Now, what should you think," says he, "of a farmer going to a young apple-tree, and tying apples all over it? Wouldn't it tend to stop its growth? Or suppose, when your pumpkin-vine had just taken a start, you should go and put a great pumpkin on it: would it ever come to any thing? A tree can't be much of a tree without 'tis made to grow its own fruit; same of vines; same of people."

So, you see, Uncle Jacob thinks 'tis best for apple-trees to work out their own apples, and pumpkin-vines their own pumpkins, and boys and girls their own fortunes. All of which — you being the mother of a family — I submit to your careful consideration. Mind, now, I don't say that giving money to young folks won't make them *rich;* but I do say that it will never bring out the energy that's in them.

The people here have some sensible ideas about laying up money, and about giving. Consider this last as one of their pleasures, and treat themselves to it as they do to any other pleasure; though. of course, they haven't the means of indulging very extensively.

Mrs. Paulina "wonders *at* them Carver folks." She thinks that "folks's chief duty is to look out for their families, and lay up for their children; and ten to one but some o' them Carver gals'll come to the poor-house, for all their book-readin'."

The Carver gals, however, don't seem at all troubled by the prospect. Lucy Maria says there are fine views from the poor-house windows, and a very wavy tree near one of them. — nice place to sit and read or draw: of course, they'd be past labor, — that would be one comfort, — and so have nothing else to do. Or, if worst came to worst, why, write a poem, starting with that wavy tree, and so branching out across the green and grassy meadows to the silent pond, which in such a case would be a lake, or a loch, or a lagoon. Hannah Jane might be bolstered up in a chair, and oversee the cooking, and break up the hens' victuals. "There's a flower-garden there : you'd like that, Matilda; for flowers will be flowers, wherever they grow. And, if you couldn't crawl out doors, you might have some little no-handled mug or porringer, and set something a-sprouting."

And really, Juliana, there might be comfort taken, even in a poor-house; for, as L. M. suggests, flowers will be flowers, and trees will be trees, and green fields will be green fields, and blue sky blue sky, whether seen from a poor-house or a palace. Disgrace? Well, if I get into one by laziness, it will be a disgrace to me, that's a fact; but even then it will not be the place, but the laziness, that disgraces me.

Another thing that puzzles and even vexes Mrs. Paulina is, that the Carver folks buy and take such an unnecessary amount of reading. She says, that, if Mr. Wallace Carver had known how to lay out his money, he might have owned a great deal of land. One day, after she had thrown out something of this kind in my hearing, I asked her a question. Asked it in this way, because Mrs. Paulina rather plumes herself on her piety. I put it thus: "Which is of the greater importance, — worldly possessions, or matters pertaining to that which we call mind, soul, spirit, heart ? "

"O Mr. Fry!" said she, "if you were a Christian, you wouldn't ask such a question as that. The body perisheth like the flowers of the field. Things of this

world pass away, and shall be no more; but the soul liv-
eth eternally."

"The body, then, drops off, and the other part lives
always."

"Certainly!"

"Very well," said I. "Now let's suppose a case, or
two cases. Say a man has fifty or a hundred dollars to
invest. Say he lets it go towards buying a field. Say
the next year he lets his spare cash go towards buying
another field. Say the next year he invests it another;
and so goes on investing the income in more land till he
dies. He has had the satisfaction of owning the land,
paying the taxes, and keeping out the neighbors' cows;
and, at the end, leaves all to his children, who will probably go on in the same way, buying fields, paying taxes,
and keeping out the cows.

Or, on the other hand, suppose he lays out his fifty or
a hundred in books, — books containing the lives of noble
men and women, whose example his children may be led
to follow, — encyclopædias where they can find out almost every thing they want to know, or stories which
shall teach the beauty of high moral principle. Suppose
he invests in this way occasionally, from year to year, all
his life. He dies at last, having given his children a
love of knowledge and of truth, a taste for the best sort
of enjoyment, and a high tone of mind, which they, in
turn, will give to their children; and so on, in an ever-
widening circle. Now, it appears to me," I said to Mrs.
Paulina, "far more desirable to be the centre of this latter kind of circle than of the land circle: this last
father would do more for the everlasting good of his
children than the first."

I don't think she quite took my meaning (it was not remarkably well expressed); for her only reply was, that " books were very well if anybody could only get time to sit down and read."

Time !—time indeed ! And how long did she tell me herself she had stood that very day rolling out pie-crust ? " Now, why," I ask, " should the body have pie-crust, and the mind scarcely get bare bread ? If the Carver girls made pies all day, or ruffled skirts all day, like her Mercy and Ella, Mrs. Paulina would be content; but if they should take an hour or two of daylight for reading, even from the most instructive book, she would say they wasted their time."

" *Time !* wasting *time !* getting *time !* " said I to myself, walking home. " And what is *time* for, I wonder ? and what does make everybody take for granted that the mind must only have such crumbs of it as the body throws away ? "

In talking this over with Mr. Carver, he suggested that I might have used one argument which even she would have understood : and this was, that reading about remarkably enterprising or energetic characters often puts it into the heads of young people to be enterprising and energetic themselves ; and they might, in consequence, be successful, even according to her ideas of success.

Dear Juliana, if I were writing to anybody in the world but you, I should never run on in this way. But what's the use of a brother having a sister, if he can't run on to her in any way he likes ? I haven't run on in the way that I liked. I took my pen in hand to run on about — you know the Two Betseys, don't you ? No, you don't. I wish you did. But, at any rate, you've *heard tell* of them.

Well, they've come, — both, — Lame Betsey and The Other Betsey. Both come. We had such a funny time! You see it was a perfect, unmitigated surprise, planned and carried out by that very *surprising* damsel, Lucy Maria. I will begin at the beginning, and even before the beginning. (Here follows an account of their arrival, the greater part of which has already been given.)

They've been here two days; and you may imagine how much I enjoy their company. They are very lively, talkative old ladies. *Lame* appears to be somewhat superior to *The Other;* and *The Other* rather defers to *Lame,* asking her opinion, and usually agreeing with her. *Lame's* dress is just a trifle smarter than *The Other's.* She wears a better style of cap; also a round black silk cape, with a puckered ruffle round it; and above this cape she wears a worked-muslin collar, and a green bow of ribbon, — dark green, with small black figures or leaves on it. There's something striking or noticeable about this collar; but I can't tell what. *The Other* merely has the edge of her dress turned away, showing a narrow rim of white handkerchief, lace. or muslin. Billy declares that they told him once that they had to dress differently so as to know themselves apart, especially when they were sitting down. They don't look very much alike. The two together amuse me excessively; and it is really quite touching to see how thoughtful *The Other* is of *Lame,* — how quick to run and fetch and carry and pick up for her! *Spry Betsey* she might be called; for she steps round light as a grasshopper. They have a habit of talking both at once. I

16

suppose, that living together so much, in a lonely way, both know the same things; and both, when they do get a chance, are eager to tell them. Still they have such a knack at it, that you can understand them just about as well. The Other Betsy (now, this is quite amusing) she casts little quick glances at *Lame* while talking; thus, as you might say, constantly taking her *cue:* and if she stumbles a little, or gets out of time, she right away comes into step again, repeats, or throws in an additional word, or perhaps runs ahead, and waits for *Lame* to catch up; and so, at last, both come out together like an old *fugue*-tune. Indeed, you might call them first and second treble, if you wanted to. . . .

Will write again during their stay.

With love,   Silas.

Mr. Fry to his Sister.

Dear Juliana, —

I've so many nice little things to tell, where shall I or can I begin? I wonder if there'll never be any better contrivance for getting thoughts on to paper than letting 'em run down your arm and drop off the pen word by word! The Two Betseys still remain to bless, delight, and entertain us. Grandmother does have such a good time! and so do I; and so do we all. Yesterday the girls managed so as to have Mother Delight come to spend the day; and I tell you, Jooley, — didn't that *use* to be your name? — that I never did, through and through, enjoy a day more thoroughly. They supposed I was minding my book, without taking the least in-

terest in their plain, every-day talk; but sitting apart
in a corner, holding in my hand "The Philosophy of
Science," preserving at all times — not without effort —
a serious expression, I kept my ears open, thereby
learning something of the *philosophy of life.* And
such entertaining, such comprehensive conversation!
Starting with Billy, of course, they began and told the
natural history of about all the boys they ever knew,
taking them up one at a time, and carrying them through
whooping-cough, measles, canker-rash, and similar
pleasant experiences, in which old-fashioned medicines
came in with telling effect. By the way, what is pykry,
or pikery? I never took any; did you? Whatever it
is, or was, that came to the surface, along with snake-
root, jalap, sulphur-and-molasses, opodeldoc (I have
a glimmering of opodeldoc), calomel, and also all the
old doctors and ministers, with their jokes and their
saddle-bags. Bless you! I could write a ream, and not
tell the half! And then think of their faces, their attitudes, their exclamations of astonishment, wonder, and
pity! The Two Betseys now going it like a span; now
coming in like a chorus, with their "How you talk!"
"I never!" "Do tell!" and "Did you ever!" Grandmother went on with her house-work through it all,
talking, listening, or standing still now and then, with
pan, poker, or spider in hand, as some story passed its
crisis. Lame Betsey borrowed an apron of grandmother,
and insisted on preparing the vegetables, as that was
sitting-work; and then on darning stockings; and, as
Billy had been some time away, there was no lack of
boggles to *unboggle.* Mother Delight and The Other
Betsey set the table, frisking about like young girls.

Mother Delight takes little, short, pudgy steps. *The Other* gets round in a more striding way. Grandmother told them, that, when Billy was a little boy, he used to say, —

> "My ganmuzzer sets ze tabawl;
> My farzer yeads ze Bibawl!"

Mother Delight wears black caps now. The young people made her a present of a couple. Though not pleased with the change at first, I have come to liking them. They look very tasty, laying their "*tabs*" alongside her fat cheeks, — rosy cheeks, I was going to say; for they do have a flush of color. The girls, knowing it would suit her, put just the merest trifle of a rosebud or two among the *tab's* bows. That "*Tycoon rep*" appeared in all its glory. The old lady considers herself more as *company*, and therefore more bound to dress up, when particularly sent for, than when she merely happens along. The "*Tycoon rep*," and the rosebud cap, and her beaming countenance, taken all together, when the sun is shining on them, are enough to put your eyes out.

Lame Betsey's cap has a decidedly *boughten*, and even boughten-for-the-occasion, aspect. There are layers of what the main structure is made of, flanking her face; and smaller white silk layers, — more than likely what the female sex call "sat'n folds." Strings to hang down, but none to tie. *The Other's* is a more unpretending affair, — a sort of *cappee*, or cappette, set 'way back on her head, just, as she explained to grandmother, "to cover up her little mite of a gray pug." What I took to be caps, that first night, were only ruffles, or something of the ruffled sort, basted inside their bonnets. Guess you'll think I've got cap on the brain; but you see I like to keep the idea from dying out of your mind, and also to present all these different styles for you to select from. Of grandmother's every-day cap I have already spoken. Its narrow, unpretending border, closing in that gentle face, is exactly the thing, though it might not suit all old ladies as well. If your eyes are as blue, and your gray locks as wavy, and your complexion as fair, when you arrive at her age, as hers are, such a cap will be very becoming. Judging from present appearances, your greatest lack, when that far-off time shall arrive, will be a lack of nose. It will not, I fear, be large enough in the right place. Yet I don't know why I should have fears, or why I should not have faith. Nature and time work wonders. Every old person that I ever saw had a tip-top place on the nose for spectacles; and yet they couldn't all have been born so.

Not the least amusing part of the play has been the losing and the mixing of so many pairs of spectacles. They have two pairs apiece, — one for in-doors, and one for looking out the windows; or, according to *Lame*, "one pair to look after the other pair with." Eight pairs: no wonder they got mixed! But Georgie thought a bright thought. She placed the whole collection in a tray; had them identified: then, taking down her German worsted, she proceeded to label the property of each owner with a different color; Billy, meanwhile, trying them on. Nobody gets more fun out of the whole thing — unless it be the present writer — than Billy. He is continually rushing in with, "Grandmother, you don't want them to stay here, do you?—let 'em go to the hotel!" or, " Grandmother, why don't you send 'em where folks are used to putting up company?" or, " Mr. Fry, hadn't you better harness up? 'tisn't convenient to keep 'em here!" Yesterday afternoon, when the sun shone out warm and pleasant, he suddenly appeared at the door with Uncle Jacob's best Sunday carryall, to take the two Betseys, so he said, " somewhere to get put up," but really to take the whole four out riding. And, by coming in this sudden manner, he made every one of them start up and get ready.

Their getting ready and getting in, take it all through, was decidedly entertaining. Billy announced that he was going to put the best-looking ones front; and each declared that she herself was the best-looking. Then he declared that the best-looking must sit back, for fear of making him look too homely. By the way, Billy has a grand face. The freckles, as he said in one of his early letters, " have faded out to the color of my skin." You would like the expression of his countenance, I know, and his whole air and bearing. A frank, whole-souled fellow: bless him! how much he is to us all! It was settled at last, that, as _Lame_ was less used to out-door air, she should sit back; and grandmother, having sympathy for invalids, sat with her.

The others took the front seat; Billy accepting a situation between them, a trifle nearer the horse, on the end of a board, the other end being shoved under the cushion.

We all came out, Aunt Phebe's folks and all, to assist in the starting of the expedition. Uncle Jacob told Billy he should rather prefer his best carryall shouldn't go through very many picket-fences; and Lucy Maria gave the ladies solemn warning that their beau had a habit of taking girls to ride, and making them walk home. Billy was in high glee; but in the midst of the fun he very soberly handed Mother Delight a budget, or large package, with the seemingly innocent request that she should hold it for him. I noticed, however, a twitching round his mouth, and made him own up afterwards that he gave her something with nothing in it to hold, so she might keep her hands off his elbows.

When they came back, we all went into Aunt Phebe's She invited the whole crowd of us there to tea. Tea, indeed! I think Lucy Maria did it on purpose. I think she wanted to make the old ladies lively. Such tea I never saw. The whole teakettle full of water couldn't weaken it. Suppose you will smile when I tell you what we had for centre-piece at supper, and would smile more if you had some. It was a large pudding-dish full of "hard-bread" toast. I have misgivings that this is the wrong name for it, inasmuch as there was no toasting at all in the matter. Hard-bread, or pilot-bread, soaked and put up with milk and drawn butter. There! give it a name, will you? It is eaten with a spoon. Hannah Jane thought this would be the most satisfying food she could provide for them. Give it a real good name, if you give any; for 'tis real good stuff. Hannah Jane said she expected the rest of us to eat bread; but we didn't. Tommy called, " Plimmy (please give me) hard-bread and joosth!" till somebody either trod on his toes, or kicked him under the table. L. M. whispered to Billy, that he needn't go out in the kitchen to look; for the whole of it was taken up. Upon which that youth declared he had graduated from toast, and was a candidate for the next course.

Just imagine us all sitting round there, lively! Imagine Uncle Jacob fairly set agoing, Aunt Phebe with her repartees, the happy old ladies, Billy with his tricks, and the girls helping the fun along! If you only could have been there! The young folks began telling stories about each other when they were little; and, when the Carver family are fairly started on that track, look out for a good time.

"And Matilda's two beaux," said L. M., "came walking along" —

"They weren't my beaux!" cried Matilda.

"Yes, they were!" says Billy. "Go on, L. M. Two beaux from Ellerton. Go on."

"You can't remember," says Matilda.

"Can't remember what?"

"Why, nothing."

"So I can't," says Billy: "I don't call beaux nothing. Go on. L. M. *came walking along.*"

"Feeling so big, dressed up in their best clothes, — Sunday-go-to-meetin'," L. M. continued.

"Poh!" said Matilda: "I wasn't over twelve, if I was that!"

"Didn't mention age or sex," says L. M. "Best clothes, bright buttons, hair parted behind, pure-white collars, and — I'll almost say — bosom-studs."

"Say 'em!" Billy put in.

"Bosom-studs, came walking along," L. M. continued; "kept going by the house, backwards and forwards, looking out the corners of their eyes; and Matilda she sat in the house."

"Looking through a hole in the curtain," says Billy.

"Looking through a hole in the window-curtain," said L. M., "with great cruelty, not letting them get the faintest glimpse, when those very same identical youths, as we found afterwards, left, just inside the gate, two small brown-paper packages of quite good confectionery."

"One sugar-kiss," cried Billy, "and sugar-cockles! I had one."

"Marked in quite plain writing, 'Miss Matilder Carver;' and not get a glimpse!" said L. M.

"The female sex are noted for their cruelty," I remarked, "and the sterner sex for their generosity. Both appear early."

"But this was quite late!" cried Billy; "most dark. Go on, L. M. And grandmother came across."

"And grandmother came across," L. M. went on, "quite troubled, — 'twas in Summer-sweeting time, — and said she wished father would drive off that couple of little boys; for she'd been watching 'em, and she believed they were after her apples!"

"Now, I'll tell about the fat meat!" said Matilda as the merriment subsided. "Once, when Billy was a little bit of a boy, he didn't love fat meat; and one day he had quite a big piece of fat meat — clear fat — on his plate, and couldn't bear to see it, and didn't know what to do with it, and wanted to put it somewhere, and couldn't find anywhere to put it. He didn't want to put it on a clean plate; and didn't dare to tuck it under the rim of his plate, for fear of a grease-spot; and didn't want to get up and carry it out; and the window was shut, so he couldn't toss it out; and called Towser, and he didn't come. So what do you think he did? Did so."

Here Matilda opened her mouth, and went through the motions of taking a pill; upon which the whole company exploded.

"Swallering fat is'nt so bad as having a beau, is it?" asked Georgie, all ready to stand up for her brother

"Not half so bad as having two!" said Billy.

The table was cleared off in Coot-pint fashion, Tommy playing a lively march on his harmonicum. Billy took it for a dancing-tune, and began to *polka* at an alarming rate, putting in his very best and most astonishing dancing-school steps, and seizing, at last, a partner wherever he could catch one, young or old. The girls, to help him along, struck up a polka-tune as they washed the dishes; and I, in helping to carry them away (dishes, not girls), actually stepped out a polka myself!

"Why not have a cotillon?" some one suggested.

"That's the talk!" cried Billy. "One, two, three, four, five, six, seven, eight! Aunt Phebe, come, you dance; won't you, now? 'Course you will."

"Yes!" cried Matilda; "you and father! do now!— and Uncle Carver. Come, you can all hop round. Anybody can just hop round."

"Hop round!" cried Uncle Jacob: "I dance; I don't hop round! Don't you think I can dance? I'll leave it to mother."

Aunt Phebe said she believed he could do something of the stirring kind; but she didn't know as there was any special name to it.

"I've made up my mind," said Lucy Maria at last, "to have every one of you upon the floor, and start a contradance."

And this, by coaxing, commanding, and entreating,

aided also by the tea, she accomplished. In fact, Mother
Delight and The Other Betsey almost danced while helping clear away. *The Other* said music always did set
her feet agoing.

"Come, Mother Delight," says Matilda, "you know
you're as young as any of us, and a great deal better-
looking." Whereupon Mother Delight declared that she
felt as young as ever she did. "When I was a gal,"
said she, "folks thought, being weakly, I should never
live to grow old; *and I never have!*"

"Bully for you! Shall I have the pleasure?" cried
Billy, with his dancing-school bow.

"But I guess my dancing-days are over," added the
old lady, bashful when it came to the pinch.

I immediately seized upon Aunt Phebe, and took the
floor, that there might be the encouragement of a beginning: upon which Uncle Jacob made his bow to *The
Other*, who, seeing Aunt Phebe up, allowed herself to be
led forward.

"Hurry!" cried Billy, pulling his lady along. "We
don't want to be down to the foot!"

And so our contra-dance was rushed together, — Aunt
Phebe standing up with me, *The Other* with Uncle
Jacob, Mother Delight with Billy, grandmother with
Tommy ("to please the child"). As gentlemen ran
short, L. M. put her father's coat and hat on Georgie,
also one of his dickies and one of his checkered neck-
handkerchiefs, called her George Washington Carver,
and stood her opposite Hannah Jane. Matilda having no partner, L. M. seized upon Gus, who, having
just come from an evening meeting, and hearing the
racket, came to see, and stood transfixed in the entry.

As for Lucy Maria herself, she was not only committee of arrangements and floor-manager, but the band of music; she was also the dancing-master, and explained the figure before we began. These several duties were highly conflicting: for she had constantly to drop her in-

strument, — a comb, covered with paper, — and pounce upon the dancers; push one here, another there; calling out, " Balance!" "Right hand!" "Down!" "Now *up* the middle!" "Turn!" "Quick!" " *Turn!* TURN! TURN! Can't you *turn?*" For Uncle Jacob, when once set a *balancing*, bobbed about in one spot until shoved into another; making it up afterwards, however, by turning everybody he could lay his hands on.

The dancers, having caught the tune, sang to their own dancing; and, taking the whole together, — the music and dancing, — Juliana, I don't know how I kept the breath of life in me for laughing! Such bobbings and friskings, and bumpings and jumpings! Such singing! — oh, if you only could have heard the singing! — the whole ending in a general confusion of down the middle, up outside, turning, balancing, all going on at a time. Billy showed off his dancing-school airs, and made bows that Mr. Tornero himself might have envied. Mother Delight took little diddling steps; but *The Other* went up and down like a churn-handle, branching out, in her extensive *balances*, to the right or left. Indeed, when *The Other* began to "take a balance," there was no telling who might not be run down. I saw Tommy at the point of annihilation more than once, dodging among the big ones.

Juliana, don't you remember hearing father tell about dancing "fore-and-after"? I do. 'Tis a sort of old-fashioned jig. Well, after our contra-dance was broken up, Mother Delight and The Two Betseys began talking about "fore-and-after," and of particular *fellers* each had known who used to dance it with a *double-shuffle* till you couldn't see their feet. Uncle Jacob said he had danced it many a time: so I proposed that they should give us some idea of how it was done. It took only two couples, they said. Well, we had the two ladies, but only one gentleman; Mr. Carver declaring solemnly that he never learned it.

"Gus," said one of the girls, "you know how: I know you do!"

"Oh, yes, he knows how!" said Mother Delight. "I've seen him, when he's young, knock his feet together twice before they touched the floor!"

Gus allowed that he " did use to."

"Stand up then instantly," said L. M., "and be the right man in the right place!" Gus has a good-humored, pleasing countenance, and, leaving out his shoulders, is by no means ill-looking.

"Fore-and-after" is arranged in this way: One couple stand facing each other, in the middle of the room. Just behind the lady stands the second lady; and just behind the gentleman, the second gentleman.

The inside couple begin to balance, and balance the tune out, — balance the four lines through, that is, or four measures. None of your walking-round balancing, but step the tune out lively. The best tune for it has about forty quirks to a measure. I'm not speaking professionally now, or artistically, or scientifically. I only want to say that the tune shakes itself all over; and heels and toes have to keep time to it. When the inside couple have balanced the tune out, they *turn* the tune out; by which turning, the other couple are swung inside, and *they* balance; and so on. Not much variety in the figure: the main thing is the balancing, and the steps put into that. Gus said he used to spring up and knock his heels together *three* times before touching the floor !

That fore-and-after was about as entertaining a performance as I ever witnessed. Billy whispered to *The Other* to hold her dress up, and take the balances she showed him once when he began to go to dancing-school. So she held up her dress each side: and away she went, up and down, spry as a grasshopper; and Uncle Jacob kept up with her. I'd no idea he was such a dancer. I tell you, he made his feet fly! — turned them out or in or over, coming down on his toes, heels, flat-foot, or any way. And such dancing-school bows!

Then the other two began. Mother Delight went stub-stub stub, stub-stub stub, her face shining like a transparency. The old lady did the thing handsomely, and looked handsomely too. Gus, owing mainly to his peculiar shape and motions, brought down the house entire, — beams, rafters, and ridge-pole! Throwing his head back, — his way of straightening up, — and placing his arms akimbo, he *put in*. Very likely he did hit his heels together three times before coming down. I can't say; and I guess none of us could say; for we couldn't see out of our eyes for laughing. I saw them wiping their eyes, and stuffing handkerchiefs in their mouths; and Billy, when he couldn't stand it any longer, ran and pitched his head into the rocking-chair cushion.

But I must stop some time or other, or I shall never get through. I won't say another word; for, if I begin on — no, I've said I won't; and I won't, except just to add, that the party left off at nine o'clock, and that Gus very gallantly escorted his lady home, to the smothered delight of the girls.

I hope little Silas will not be away when I come to make that visit. Is there any thing to talk over? If so, pray have it brought forward. My stay must be a short one, and this letter must be left short off.

Affectionately your brother,

S. Y. FRY.

A glance at the number of the page reminds me that this narrative must also leave short off. Indeed, what other leaving-off can there be when thus giving an account of two families whose lives and letters and good times still went on ? I certainly could not stop at a better place than at the close of that delightful evening at Aunt Phebe's. The subject I would not allow myself to begin on in this last epistle to Juliana must have related either to Mother Delight's love-affairs or to the prize flapjacks. Grandmother, I remember, walked home with me, directly behind Gus and Mother Delight, and astonished me with the information that he used to be, in his youth, that lady's beau ! She also explained how the match was broken off, and gave some interesting particulars of their after-life.

I think the flame of Gus's quenched love burned anew that evening; for, instead of bidding good-night to his lady at the door, he went in, and permitted his eyes to feast on her while she prepared something for us to feast on in the morning.

Billy had said so much about the Two Betseys' flapjacks, that grandmother and Hannah Jane declared they should never rest satisfied until they had tasted them. In fact, all the members of both families announced themselves as existing in the same unsatisfied condition.

The Other promised reluctantly that she would try, though she never had so good luck when she tried. It was at Aunt Phebe's merry supper-table the subject came up: and, in speaking of the different methods of preparing the delicacy, Mother Delight told her way; and it was settled that each of them — Mother Delight

and *The Other* — should have, that very night, a spoon
and pan assigned her, with every material aid she asked
for, and be dared to do her best; also that a prize of a
spectacle-case should be awarded to the one who achieved
the greatest success, both families being judges.

As may be imagined, I rose betimes next morning,
not to lose the fun of the great frying-match. I found
the two old ladies up and *stirring*, and was rewarded
for early rising by being elected to the office of "tryer" ·
or "taster" of the little "try-ones."

How gladly would I record the sayings and doings of
that eventful morning! but this my limited time and
space forbid. If they did not forbid, I might be tempted
to allow myself not only this satisfaction, but the satisfaction and delight of describing particularly the remaining part of the Two Betseys' famous and ever-memora-
ble visit. It did not last one quarter long enough; yet
we were so glad of their company, even for a little while!

And the enjoyment was mutual. *The Other* assured
me that they had had a beautiful visit, and that they
thought the folks were beautiful folks.

I became very much interested in these agreeable old
ladies, not merely beause they were old ladies, as might
be inferred from sentiments expressed in some of my
letters, but for other reasons, to which I can but very
briefly allude.

Notwithstanding their cheerfulness, there was something about them which made me feel that they had
known sorrow. Lucy Maria gave it as her opinion,
that, even then, some secret trouble disturbed their
peace of mind. A remark or two which they dropped
in the course of conversation confirmed her in this

17

opinion, which was afterwards found to be correct. Dear old ladies!

But this is not doing what I have just declared must be done. My conscience tells me, however, that it really would not be fair to break short off without stating the fact, just the bare fact, that William Henry did earn the sum required, and did find a place — thanks to the *squirrel-man* — where he could begin at the beginning, with a prospect at least of "keeping going up." The great event of his departure took place early in the spring following my vacation at Summer-sweeting Place. Business-affairs calling me to the city at about the same time, it was decided that he should accompany me, and that I should attend to his eating and sleeping arrangements, thus saving Mr. Carver the trouble of taking the journey. They wished me to come out over-night, and start from there. All right, I said: nothing could suit me better.

When I arrived (this is not breaking short off; but it does come so natural to say a few words about that last evening! it shall be only a very few), — when I arrived at grandmother's, which was soon after dark. I was rather surprised at seeing a light in the front-room; for grandmother's front-room was almost never used in cold weather. The light shone but dimly, however.

I opened the outside-door softly, and stepped into the entry. The front-room-door was open: and in there I saw Lucy Maria bending over a well-filled trunk, into which she was placing a few *last things ;* the tears, meanwhile, streaming down her cheeks.

"How do you do?" I said; "and what are you doing?"

She came forward to shake hands, laughing and crying together.

" Why," said I, " he has been away from home a great
many times ! "

" Yes," she answered : " I know he has.   But this is
different : 'tis for good and all now ! "

She was doing up little surprise-packages for him to
come upon accidentally, — a cooky, say, in a stocking-
toe ; a ginger-snap in a pocket ; a " home-sketch," in-
cluding several family portraits. among some note-paper.

" Just for fun," said L. M., laughing any thing but a
funny laugh.

" Where is he ? " I asked.

" Went to bid some of the neighbors good-by, and
took Georgie with him.   They two have been quite intimate lately.   He takes her to walk and ride with him,
and seems to begin to feel quite proud of her.   Yesterday
he asked grandmother to let her wear her best clothes, —
Sunday hat and all. — and drove off with her in the riding-wagon grand enough.

" It seems quite unlike Billy," I said, " to be particular about dress."

" Oh, but he's so proud of Georgie ! " said L. M., giving her eyes a furious wipe, evidently intended for the
final one.

Grandmother came in just then with several rolls of
linen and a box of salve.   There were no tears in grandmother's eyes : plenty behind them. though. as it seemed
to me.   She looked very pale. very sorrowful ; and the
three little anxious marks between her eyebrows were
unusually distinct that night.

" Just the things. grandmother ! " I exclaimed, springing from my corner, and shaking her left hand: "you couldn't have done better. I've seen the time when a bit of soft linen like that would have been worth its weight in gold to me! Carrot-salve? Excellent! Nice! So soft and healing!"

"I don't know," said Lucy Maria doubtfully, and turning her red eyes from the old lady: "I'm afraid it is really putting temptation in his way. You make cutting his fingers a too pleasant business."

As grandmother hurried out at one door to get my supper, Matilda came in at the other, bringing, among various articles, one of Georgiana's corn-cob babies.

"Why, Matilda!" I exclaimed, after the "How-d'ye-do's" were over, "your face looks as if it had been caught in a shower!"

"So it has," she answered with a most wretched smile: "for I've just been up in Billy's room; and every thing there does have such a good-by look! Oh, how we shall miss him! This place won't seem like the same place when he don't — belong — to it!" she added with a somewhat *shaky* voice.

"You know we've agreed to be cheerful this evening," said Lucy Maria solemnly.

"But he will belong to it," I said.

"Not in the same way," said Matilda: "will he, Lucy Maria?"

"No," answered L. M. thoughtfully: "I don't think he will. 'Tis a breaking-up."

"He will be almost a dead loss," sighed Matilda, as, with a nondescript laugh, she tucked the corn-cob child into a shirt-sleeve.

"How do you do, Mr. Fry? Now I am glad! Just

the one we wanted to see! Going to have beautiful weather: don't you think so?"

It was Aunt Phebe, beaming and radiant, evidently determined to flood us and swamp us with her cheerfulness, — rather too evidently. She brought one more pair of woollen stockings.

"Kept them to *run the heels*," said she. "Boys away from home can't have too many stockings, or too stout, especially when they're hard on 'em. Isn't that so, Mr. Fry?"

I agreed with her entirely.

"Here's Hannah Jane's letter," she went on, — "something new for Hannah Jane to think of doing. But she said she had a few words to say to Billy, and wanted this put towards the bottom of the trunk. And now, girls, don't you be foolish, — you two! Consider 'twould be worse if he couldn't find a place, or if he wasn't fit for any. It has a good many bright sides to it. Come, don't be foolish!"

"Some other folks have been foolish, I guess," said Matilda, "by the looks of their face! I guess somebody's got a red nose!"

"Pshaw!" said Aunt Phebe. "What you want to talk nonsense for? Don't you know we've all got to be lively to-night to keep grandmother up? Come, Lucy Maria, don't you give out! What's the use of having a nonsensical one in the family if they give out when it comes to the pinch? There! your father and Uncle Carver have come. Poor Uncle Carver, he don't feel so altogether calm as he makes for. I know him of old!"

They all went out to see me eat supper. Aunt Phebe told me to make it last as long as possible; which request

I gratified without making a martyr of myself, taking at least four cups, and calling out " Waiter, waiter!" from time to time, the girls answering. Then they made me help clear away, and we had it quite lively.

When sitting-down time came, Aunt Phebe seemed determined that the talk should not lag.

"Here's your knitting-work, grandmother," said she. "Now sit down and knit just as you always do: you know, we want Billy's last night to seem natural and pleasant to him. — Lucy Maria, can't you draw something, or draw us? You always can. Wait till grandmother sits down, and then draw her, and give it to Billy. — Can't find your knitting-sheath, grandmother? Never mind! take a knitting-core: you used to knit with a knitting-core."

Grandmother trotted into the bed-room, looking for her knitting-sheath; and then Matilda told us in a muffled whisper that she saw Billy tuck it into one of his boxes. L. M. said he'd had one of his rummaging-days that day; and she expected they should all miss things.

A substitute for the knitting-sheath was found; and, before Billy and Georgie came back, we were all quietly seated, and all talking, of course, of the great event. Such a capital place! Firm so liberal with their clerks! actually took an interest in them!

" He'll have to see to himself now," said grandmother. " At school, there was somebody to see to him; but he'll be all alone now."

"That," I remarked, " will teach him self-reliance."

Grandmother sat with her hands clasped around her knitting, her eyes seemingly fixed on some distant object, — probably the image of Billy " all alone." I saw that

across her mental vision were flitting ghosts of damp
sheets, thin blankets, unaired linen, with other nameless,
shapeless hobgoblins supposed to haunt cities.

"I expect the city is a dreadful place," she said at last.
"They say there's dreadful snares there! This is a long
going-away. 'Tis a breaking-up. All you are younger;
but I — 'tis different, you know. I sha'n't see very much
more of Billy."

"Oh, yes, you will, grandmother!" said Aunt Phebe.
Billy may be anxious to go; that's natural: but he'll
always be glad to come back. This will be his home,
you know: and folks don't ever drift wholly and totally,
heart and soul, away from home; they can't."

Uncle Jacob, who had been knocking about in the
back-room, appeared just then with a kettle of molasses,
saying 'twas best to have something going on, if nothing
more than a kettle.

"To be sure!" said Matilda. "We'll put up some
'lasses-candy for Billy!"

Some one suggested pouring it, warm, into an old
tin mustard-box; then getting it out would take up his
mind. L. M. thought he'd be more likely to pound the
box off.

"I think," remarked Mr. Carver, "that the city, in
one way, is like the country in another. For instance,
a person coming to the country can walk over the hills,
in the woods and fields, and other pleasant places, or he
can walk in the quagmires. And just so in the city:
there are all kinds of places, and all kinds of people.
A young man won't be obliged to go in the mud."

"True enough!" I cried, — "true enough! Grandmother, you mustn't think the city is wholly vile. Why,

the city is something like your buttery, — all in shelves; and a fellow may stay upon just whichever shelf he chooses. If he wants to use up his leisure in amusements, he can : that's one shelf. If he wants to spend it in low company, he can : that's another shelf. If he wants to become interested in ideas, he can : that's another shelf. There's the scientific shelf, and the musical shelf, and the artist's shelf, and the religious shelf; and so on. There's no end to the privileges of the city! A young fellow can make of himself whatever he chooses. Some don't choose to make any thing at all of themselves; but that is their own fault." Then I went on to tell, with the greatest enthusiasm, of the free reading-rooms, free libraries, free lectures, free evening-classes, free rooms for social intercourse, — especially these last. "Why," said I, winding up and warming up, "the city is no more a bad place than it is a good place! A young man can find and keep as good company as he pleases. No need of Billy feeling lonely very long!"

"No; he'll soon find friends," said Aunt Phebe; "everybody will like Billy."

"And they'll invite him to their houses, likely as not," said Matilda; "and I don't doubt he'll begin to feel quite acquainted."

"But that won't seem like home," said grandmother: "there's no place like home. And the folks won't seem like our folks."

"I don't want they should!" said Lucy Maria. "I want we should seem better to him than anybody!"

"Yes," said I: "that is just what you all wish, — wish him to feel truly that there's no place like home; to look

the world, and the place where
sympathy."
said Aunt Phebe, "always!"
from his friends?" I went on
g away from his friends? He do
part of you goes with him. Th
it being made all body! Home l
as will go with him. He cai
about him, and can't help being
All these young men who seem
really adrift. There are anche
no only you can't see the cables
went on talking, until a familia
us of Billy's arrival. Aunt Phel
in the middle of a sentence.
whispered, holding up a warning
ate click! Now all look natural.
r! Knit away, grandmother!
Billy's been mopy all day!"
hing by and by," added Aunt Pl
ot quick as they get in."
en Matilda muttered. "Th

be all sitting down!" said L. M.
cried Uncle Jacob. "Some of yo
"

ood candy, and they pulled it whi
Brown," and Billy came in on the
ever, that I had heard that Hallelujah
much more uproarious manner.

www.ingramcontent.com/pod-product-compliance
Lightning Source LLC
Chambersburg PA
CBHW020052030726
47498CB00006B/1742